# Toonamint of Champions

## *and*

# Why Golf is so Exciting!

Todd Sentell

*Toonamint of Champions* and *Why Golf is so Exciting!*
The Stairway Press Collected Edition
©2014 Todd Sentell
All Rights Reserved

ISBN 978-0-9897605-7-7

eBook ISBN 978-0-9897605-8-4

The Armchair Adventurer

# STAIRWAY≡PRESS

STAIRWAY PRESS—SEATTLE

Cover Design by Guy Corp www.grafixCORP.com

**www.stairwaypress.com**
1500A East College Way #554
Mount Vernon, WA 98273

# Toonamint of Champions

*How LaJuanita Mumps Got to Join Augusta National Golf Club Real Easy*

A Particularly Allegorical Comedy of Real Bad Manners

*A Novel*

## TODD SENTELL

*to* Errol Sanders

*Who got all this started in 12th grade*

This would be a great club if it weren't for the members.

—*A post-consulting pronouncement by Zoran Geckstein, a distinguished private club management consultant, on a number of notable American golf clubs*

There are psychologists who believe that in playing golf man is in a way reverting to the primitive, that striding over the course, occasionally searching for the ball and then hitting it, reproduces, in mild form, the hunting life and activities of the savage man. How they square this with the hundreds of thousands of women who play golf, I do not understand!

—*from Bobby Locke on Golf, 1954*

I wouldn't go *near* a golf course.

—*Martha Burk, a women's rights agitator*

# PART I

## RELENTLESS OBSESSIONS

# Old Mrs. Willard

*In conclusion, we weren't real surprised to find that every teenage male human on earth concocts frantic sex fantasies for fifty-six seconds out of every waking, sleeping, and comatose minute. Their thoughts during the other four seconds range from the outcome of professional and collegiate sporting events to the condition of their zits to how to get their parents to buy them a BMW.*

*However, we also found that middle-aged male humans concoct frantic sex fantasies, but for only one second of each minute. Their thoughts during the other fifty-nine seconds of each waking, sleeping, and comatose minute, relentlessly obsess about how they might get a tee time at Augusta National Golf Club.*

*And then there's the women.*

—From the March 2014 issue of *Go Figure*, the monthly report of the American Psychological Association

WAYMON POODLE WAS a teller at the TrustTrust bank branch inside the Publix grocery store on Confederate Victory Parkway in Mullet Luv, Georgia and no other human being on earth loves more than he does the Masters, the golf course on which it's played, the wonderful sport of golf in general, and the iniquitous allure of what goes on behind the gates of ootsie-tootsie private golf clubs. No one. Not even Jack Nicklaus.

Waymon constantly dreams of one day, somehow, some way, getting to play Augusta National Golf Club if LaJuanita Mumps, his new fiancé, was okay with him being gone for most of a Saturday or a Sunday or a Monday or whenever the miraculous morning or afternoon or whenever the miraculous moment happened even though she articulated in Waymon's face, a lot, that she thinks the wonderful sport of golf in general and the iniquitous allure of what goes on behind the gates of ootsie-tootsie private golf clubs are for flaming squids, bald fat farts, and mules. "Mules" was the mean and awful word LaJuanita calls women. She knows it's mean and awful, but that's just the way LaJuanita feels since she deals with women and the hair on their head or their upper lips or around their nipples or in their armpits or down there between their fat legs all day for six days a week so she says to everybody she's justified. "Here comes that *mule*," LaJuanita says when she sees her customer and the customers of the other hairdressers get out of their pick-up trucks with cigarettes in their mouths still eating something.

"Iniquitous" was a word Waymon and LaJuanita learned in Sunday school.

Anyway. So Waymon dreams.

Constantly.

No other word comes close to describing Waymon's obsession with his thing: unrelenting, skull-exploding fixation, perhaps, but that's four words.

For example, a very regular customer at Waymon's bank branch, Old Mrs. Willard, wrote Waymon's branch manager, a couple of days ago, a letter. In the letter she said when Waymon serves her lately she's pretty dang sure he's not concentrating on his work and if Waymon didn't seem to care for her business that she would come and get all her money from TrustTrust and go give all her money to them people over at the BB&T, which was actually closer to her vein clinic, her dead husband's grave, the Pontiac dealership where her sister works the cash register in the parts department, and that new Super Wal-Mart where you can buy food, so that tells you something about how much I love Waymon Poodle. Old Mrs. Willard underlined: can buy food, so that tells you how much I love Waymon Poodle.

For instance, Old Mrs. Willard wrote that two weeks ago she gave Waymon a check to cash for $250, given to her by her brother-in-law for something personal, and she was always thankful, by the way, that in all these years Waymon never asked her why her brother-in-law gave her money for something personal. Anyhow, Waymon gave her back $82,000! Old Mrs. Willard underlined $82,000! four times. She wrote that TrustTrust should thank the Lord God Jesus that she was an honest Christian martyr and immediately, without Satan consuming her old tired body and soul, made Waymon aware of his mistake. And even when she made Waymon aware of his mistake she thought she might have gotten a better reaction. Plus, he's been giving me those big fat orange lollipops that taste like my colon polyp medicine. I done told Waymon exactly ninety-two times I don't like those kind of lollipops because they taste like my colon polyp medicine, but he keeps on giving them to me. It's like he's all of a sudden from some outer space planet standing there looking at me with that eye of his. But please don't fire him, she wrote, as I truly think in my heart Waymon's a fine young man and a dang good bank teller. I really do. Old Mrs. Willard underlined fire and eye and dang and fire, one time. Colon polyp two times, in the second reference.

The branch manager, who was also named Waymon, went to Waymon at his teller window with Old Mrs. Willard's letter in his hand and right in front of a valued customer who was supremely enjoying being served by Waymon, waved the letter, limply, back and forth, but with a perceptible level of obnoxia, and then moaned, "So—day *dreeeeea*ming about playing Augusta National Country Club for the one hundredth billionth *time?*"

"Golf club!" Waymon squawked. "*Golf* club!"

It was well known.

3

# Worshipping Satan

WAYMON IMMEDIATELY REMEMBERED what he was thinking about when he accidentally gave Old Mrs. Willard an extra $81,750. And it made him feel good: it was how he would play the par 3 twelfth hole, also named "Golden Bell," if he ever got a chance to play Augusta National Golf Club.

Waymon knew that Jack Nicklaus, who had won six Masters beginning in 1963, said the twelfth hole at Augusta National Golf Club was the hardest par three in the world in championship competition. So if Jack Nicklaus thought this about Golden Bell, then Waymon knew in his heart it was true. Actually, if Jack Nicklaus marched up to Waymon at the bank branch, and instead of initiating a banking transaction asked Waymon to gouge his eyeballs out with an ice pick and worship Satan, Waymon, even though he was a type of Baptist called "Primitive," and could speak in "tongues" when he got all emotionally riled up, would immediately march to aisle seven where the ice picks are sold and gouge his eyeballs out and worship Satan. Just because Jack Nicklaus told him to. Right there in aisle seven.

It was the calm, quiet Monday after the Masters, Waymon had daydreamed as he flipped through the cash drawer for Old Mrs. Willard's money, and all the pin placements he saw on TV the previous day were the same and it was sunny and about seventy-nine degrees, just as the announcers said when the telecast started on Sunday. All the trash and half chewed up pieces of pimento cheese sandwiches people spit onto the grass had been cleaned up and the TV cameras and those awful TV tower things and the concession tents were long gone too.

During the night, all the bunkers on the golf course had been cleaned out and filled with new sand and raked to a consistency like Dixie Crystals. Plus, Fuzzy Zoeller and Tiger Woods were in a twosome ahead of him, just out having a nice time, swapping socially acceptable racial jokes and making birdies and eagles and holes in one and laughing and walking down the fairways of Augusta National Golf Club without all the patrons drinking alcoholic-based beverages and pointing at them. And in a threesome behind Waymon were Arnold Palmer, Gary Player, and Jack Nicklaus doing the same thing: out having a nice time at Augusta National Golf Club, something that happens naturally after you drive through the gate. Actually, earlier on the practice range, Jack Nicklaus had marched up to Waymon and complimented Waymon on his swing. Jack Nicklaus said Waymon's swing was, for a non professional, the greatest swing—technically and aesthetically—in the *world*. This brief interaction with the greatest golfer who has ever lived made Waymon really happy.

Waymon had also been assigned the best and wisest caddie at Augusta National Golf Club and the caddie had been reading Waymon's putts real well for the previous eleven holes. So real well, in fact, that all Waymon did was place his Titleist Scotty Cameron "Newport" putter behind the ball, then would say to the caddie in his most business-like tone, "Tell Waymon what to do." Waymon never argued with the caddie and was planning on giving him a big tip.

The caddie had also been complimenting Waymon on his swing and never once seemed to mind he was asked to take a picture of Waymon holding his golf bag on every tee and by every green and when Waymon insisted he pause in front of a number of landscaped areas and clumps of azalea bushes that were particularly memorable.

When the caddie complimented Waymon on his swing, which was after every swing, the caddie would say, "Good *swing*, Mistah Poodle."

5

Then, because Waymon knew the caddie to be wise, he would look the caddie squarely in the eyes and say, "Yes. I'm nutting it today here at Augusta National Golf Club."

"You surely *is* nuttin' it, sir. *Surely* is," the wise caddie would say to Waymon.

And the wise caddie would also say to Waymon—about a million times—throughout the round, "You surely is rollin' yo *rock* today, too. Rollin' that rock."

"Thank you," Waymon would say in return—softly, reverently, with his eyelids half closed in near exaltation, to the wise caddie. "Thank you very much for noticing."

Hole after hole, Waymon thought: Oh, Lord God Jesus, how incredible it was to be finally walking on the other side of the ropes. Sometimes he would say "Oh, Lord God Jesus" out loud as he gazed at the incredible blue sky watching over Augusta National Golf Club. Oh, Lord God Jesus.

Waymon was six under par as he stood on the twelfth tee. Remember to look at the top of the pine trees behind the green Waymon, of course, remembered. Waymon knew the wise caddie would, by the twelfth hole, instinctively know his game. How by that time the caddie would know exactly what club to give him as he stood there looking at the flag on the historic twelfth green, flapping lazily, with his right arm extended toward the caddie and his ball freshly rubbed with a wet towel and his white tee—one of a handful grabbed out of a wicker basket in the pro shop—shined so brightly in the Augusta sun.

How when he nestled his 6-iron behind the ball something wonderful happened: a little butterfly twittered around the ball, then lighted upon the ball. A butterfly. A little yellow one, innocent, never in harm's way as he sat on the golf ball of Waymon Poodle.

Waymon watched the butterfly open and close its wings as it sat on the ball, Waymon's favorite type of golf ball, a Titleist balata, 90 compression. Waymon loved the way the black Titleist lettering and the red number looked on the ball—so dang professional. He knew at that instant how he would explain the greatest moment of his entire life to his friends he played golf with at the Mullet Luv Golf Center.

He would explain it in rich, somber detail.

He knew he'd probably even tear up.

Using his 6-iron as a support, Waymon leaned down to gently brush the butterfly away so he wouldn't kill it at impact, and reached out with his gloved left hand (FootJoy, white, medium) and took back the enormous wad of money from Old Mrs. Willard and became unnerved by the odd expression on her face and wondered for the millionth time why in the world TrustTrust would put a branch office in a noisy supermarket right by the condom and genital lubricant counter.

# Flop Shot

BUT OLD MRS. Willard was right.

Waymon was a fine young man and was indisputably proven—revealed every year of his employment by the massive TrustTrust customer survey—to be the friendliest and most competent of any teller in any branch in all five states and the District of Columbia in which TrustTrust did business. But for some reason, no one at TrustTrust ever told him.

"How are *you* today?" he'll chirp in a tone of voice, however squawking, that was unequivocally unconditional in its sincerity, no matter if Waymon knew the valued customer to be annoying, stupid, a fornicator, morbidly obese, foreign, gross, fraudulent, or who smelled really bad—or all of those things in one. They were still the valued customer. And he dang loved them.

And when the transaction was complete, no matter how difficult or how long it took, he'd squawk, "My name is *Way*mon and it was a pleasure serving *you!*" Waymon then, on purpose, as the valued customer walked away, would reach over and move his nameplate in the direction of the valued customer so they would remember him. Then he'd quickly turn the nameplate toward the next valued customer as he called out (squawked), "Waymon's here to help our *next* valued TrustTrust customer to-*day!*"

So screeching was Waymon's squawking that valued customers would scrunch up their shoulders and make expressions as if they heard a cell phone go off at a funeral. But Waymon never noticed.

Couple this remarkable customer service with the way

Waymon looked: Waymon looked faintly similar to how aliens are described by those who demand to Larry King on TV that they've been abducted by space aliens and taken to outer space and had their anuses probed with big tubes by the aliens. Big eyes. Big head. Long skinny arms. Long skinny fingers. A scalp of blond fuzz, but when the light hits it a certain way it looks a little orange.

Important to mention, too, that Waymon's eyes are exotropic. In other words, that means the left eye points one way and the right eye points way out the other way. And once a person gets to know him they still have a hard time dealing with it. Plus, one eye was blue and the other one was green. So Waymon was what anthropologists call a one in a million human being.

It should also be mentioned that Waymon's banking career didn't begin at the Publix. It began at the TrustTrust free standing branch, right down the road, also conveniently located on Confederate Victory Parkway where they had him work the drive through window most of the time. After Waymon's first few weeks there were collisions by customers into the support poles and into the two ATMs and into the air shuttle machines in the drive through area and other tie ups as most customers would not immediately drive off after their transaction was complete. When they did drive off they usually weren't paying attention to their driving one bit. A number of loyal customers were finally compelled to say something. Although new business increased. One even took a picture of Waymon from his truck and e-mailed it to a Mullet Luv radio station. Certainly. The citizens of Mullet Luv loved having TrustTrust in their community, but were compelled by Lord God Jesus himself to tell the branch manager and the police who came to handle accident scenes and to break up fights between the drive through window area loiterer-gawkers who were starting to congregate every Monday through Saturday afternoon that it was like watching a freak show—even though it's unchristian and uncouth the way we've been carryin' on— pointin' at it—but you just cain't look away—what with that

9

lizard demon from outer space on the other side of the window, flapping around in there and talking at us through the intercom. So TrustTrust had transferred Waymon to the Publix branch, where he now thrives professionally.

And that's it, really, unless Waymon's intimate psychological, fashion, sportsmanship, automotive, and coital-related particulars are fascinating and unusual and odd and have absolutely anything to do with Waymon ever in his life playing Augusta National Golf Club.

# The Particulars

## THE INTIMATE PSYCHOLOGICAL PARTICULARS

WAYMON WAS SO profoundly afraid of giant cicada killer wasps—not just any kind of wasp, as there are a lot of kinds of hymenoptera—but the giant cicada killer wasp who sports a pulsating yellow and black thorax and a long stinger, that a Christian psychologist he finally consulted on his giant cicada killer wasp situation labeled Waymon "insectophobic," specifically concerning giant cicada killer wasps and told him, under no circumstances whatsoever, to daydream about them. Or, if encountering one, to never reach out with your hand, gloved or otherwise—even if you've got your golf glove on and one gets on your golf ball—and try to flick a giant cicada killer wasp away. Just run off real fast. Six female giant cicada killer wasps got into Waymon's car in 1998. Female giant cicada killer wasps, of the two sexes, are the more aggressive. The windows of Waymon's car were closed and were of the manual type. Waymon drove his car through a McDonald's dining room and into, and around, for five minutes, as his brakes were now not working anymore and the accelerator was stuck, the new car lot of a Porsche/Ferrari/Bentley dealership. When it was all over, the police and the paramedics and the firemen and the general manager and the top salesman and a guy still clinging onto Waymon's windshield wiper who'd been eating an Egg McMuffin and four potential customers of the Porsche/Ferrari/Bentley dealership found Waymon grasping, very tightly, his steering wheel, speaking in tongues. A paramedic had to pry Waymon's fingers off of the steering wheel with a screwdriver as Waymon was experiencing a cadervic spasm even though he was alive.

After further pondering Waymon's situation and discovering there were no giant cicada killer wasp support groups anywhere in the world, the psychologist browsed the Internet and found two web sites completely devoted to giant cicada killer wasps. The psychologist was amazed anyone would care enough about some freaking *bugs* to develop web sites about them. She nonetheless suggested that as part of Waymon's therapy he consult these two web sites as often as he could stand it and to possibly, one day, appreciate giant cicada killer wasps as God's creatures too, as he was one as well. She thought that might appeal to Waymon, her saying "God's creatures." She said it a lot when she talked to him. It didn't appeal. Okay. The Christian psychologist said he could read about, on those web sites, what turns out to be their fascinating pupation habits and safely gaze at giant cicada killer wasps in color photograph form on a computer screen. Think that might help? Pupation habits? Praise Jesus?

Shakily, wearily, and with extreme tension, Waymon said he'd give it a try. But he told her CompuServe always took a long time to come up.

# THE FASHION PARTICULARS

At the bank branch, Waymon wore only white, short sleeved, button down, 100% polyester dress shirts until TrustTrust issued a company-wide memo saying that long sleeved dress shirts, for male employees, were more appropriate in the work place since a number of you people should not bring attention to yourselves. Waymon never knew he was the one who forced the memo. He has long, freakishly skinny, pale white arms that seem to flap everywhere when he talks or when he swings his golf clubs.

The ties Waymon wore when he first started at TrustTrust

were the most anonymous ever sold by Sears in the history of the company as Sears was his favorite place to shop for clothes as many of the male salespeople there reminded him of himself and this made Waymon feel welcome. But, one day, when Waymon ordered through the Masters web site, an Augusta National Golf Club logoed tie, which has a green background covered with little Augusta National Golf Club logos, he began wearing it to work every day and to church every Sunday. It's a tie people notice. But Waymon has to endure from his so-called friends at church and from a large number of valued TrustTrust customers upon noticing the tie, this repulsive question: "Oh, *Way*mon, so you're a member of the Masters?" Waymon, as his patience was constantly tested by this query, has to explain, in his squawking voice, that a person isn't a member of the *Masters*. That that's the *tournament*. A person would be a member of Augusta National *Golf* Club. That the Masters is the tournament they have at Augusta National *Golf* Club each year in April. Waymon will then make sort of a huffing sound, similar to the huffing sounds made by three year olds.

Plus, when valued customers, from time to time, appear at his window with a Masters logoed shirt or sweater or jacket it makes Waymon's heart race. Sometimes a Masters logoed wallet or money clip. One time a valued customer was wearing a gold signet ring with the Masters logo engraved into the ring. When Waymon saw it he about fainted.

# THE SPORTSMANSHIP PARTICULARS

Waymon never cheats at golf, even though his golf buddies at the Mullet Luv Golf Center do, and, unlike these people, Waymon never shoplifts boxes of balls and drivers and shirts and golf bags and umbrellas out of the pro shop when the assistant pro was helping somebody else or playing video poker.

Waymon prays at Waffle Houses before he starts in on his food without feeling embarrassed one bit, even when the waitress was standing right there with more iced tea. Waymon loves iced tea, sweet. With nine lemons.

# THE AUTOMOTIVE PARTICULARS

Waymon changes the oil in his car's engine every two thousand miles, as opposed to every three thousand miles. Waymon's car, the one he bought after his fender bender, was a green (for the Masters) 1978 Chrysler "Diplomat." He would have bought a Volkswagen "Golf"—sure, an obvious choice—but Waymon bought American. Waymon loves America. Waymon believes in wearing a car out before you get another one.

# THE COITAL PARTICULARS

Waymon was proud he met LaJuanita at one of those church watermelon socials where everybody ends up squirting each other with Silly String, and not at a bar or disco or rock concert or adult video/sex toy store, although Waymon would never go to a bar or a disco or a rock concert or an adult video/sex toy store anyway, even though there were four adult video/sex toy stores within easy walking distance right next to the apartment complex where he lives in Mullet Luv.

Although LaJuanita oozes frantic sex fantasies in a caked-on makeup sort of way and when her hair was real huge and fluffy looking and when she has on all of her rings and has all of her earrings inserted, and sometimes when she wears a fake diamond-studded choker, Waymon was proud he has not yet fornicated with her although he was hard at work currently denying the temptation to fornicate with LaJuanita even though LaJuanita said it was all right to fornicate since they were definitely getting married. *Hell*, LaJuanita says, there's somewhere in your *B*ible that says it's okay to fornicate all you *want* if you're officially engaged—but Waymon knew she was lying. He knew the Bible. After they got married, LaJuanita was planning on keeping her last name so she'd stay LaJuanita Mumps as opposed to LaJuanita Poodle.

Anyhow, a lot lately, LaJuanita was attempting to dial up a sex channel available for $12.95 for a six hour "Sex Attack" on

14

Waymon's local cable television provider in hopes that seeing other people for six hours—however attractive or unattractive or sex-mixed—in the act of love making would arouse Waymon to fornicate.

Waymon, of course, wrestles the phone out of LaJuanita's hands before she can successfully place the order. Plus, he's always watching his favorite channel, The Golf Channel, when LaJuanita grabs the channel changer and tries to change the channel to get the 800 number for the Sex Attack because she never can remember—except for the 800 part—the number for the Sex Attack.

So Waymon courageously denies LaJuanita's attempts at fornication as well as sexual acts on a lesser degree than fornication with a biblical strength of will not to be believed, such as when late in the evening three days ago, as Waymon and LaJuanita were the only folks in Waymon's apartment clubhouse hot tub, when LaJuanita, on purpose, let her left titty flop out of her bikini top. LaJuanita's titties are the size of pink grapefruit. LaJuanita was hoping Waymon would scoot over there and gnaw on it. It was glistening with hot tub water, the titty, and she was holding it up with her hand and was winking at Waymon and her nipple was as red and inviting as a cherry. Waymon gazed at LaJuanita's titty and thought of Augusta National Golf Club—and it suddenly occurred to him that he might be the only person— the only *golfer*—in the world who really enjoyed pondering the original names of some of the holes while he was driving to work or sitting in a hot tub with his woman. One hole name Waymon thought was a dang *vine*. Waymon suddenly felt the urge to work through them—right—okay, now—"Pink Dogwood" used to be "Woodbine"—*that's* right—and "Tea Olive" used to be "Cherokee Rose" and Waymon remembered "Pampas" was called "Cedar" and he smiled when he remembered "White Dogwood" used to be called just "Dogwood" and by gosh ol' "Chinese Fir" used to be called "Spanish Dagger" believe it or dang not and then Waymon sort of snickered when he remembered "Three Pines" is now called "Golden Bell." But Waymon was still gazing at that

15

shimmering huge left titty of LaJuanita's. And LaJuanita was still holding it up—and still squeezing it and still winking at him because she was real horny for Waymon. She could just imagine what it would be like. Them two really going at it like they were on drugs—like they were part of some government experiment. Right there in the greasy bubbles of the hot tub—steaming wet sexy Waymon action—especially if another hot, sexy couple like them came walking up and wanted to get in there with them and have a sex orgy.

Waymon unconsciously winked back at LaJuanita—and thought about how he'd play the par 3 fourth hole at Augusta National Golf Club, Waymon knew to be originally called "Palm," now called "Flowering Crab Apple," traditionally one of the hardest holes for a Masters' titty. Invitee.

He'd hit a 4-iron. Smooth.

# The Mantra of Portent

SO SUCH WAS the level of Waymon's particular focus on his thing.

Looking at him, a person new to Waymon would immediately, without an instant of giving him the benefit of the doubt, consider him to be a flaming squid, potentially dangerous, a serious ectomorph. Hard up. Haunted.

Maybe.

But could drop anytime and do one hundred without stopping. Ran a marathon once, just for the fun of it, in tennis shoes and swim shorts. Arm wrestle him and get yours wrenched off at the elbow. Is always sweet to LaJuanita and somehow understood she thought the wonderful sport of golf in general and the iniquitous allure of what goes on behind the gates of ootsie-tootsie private golf clubs are for flaming squids, bald fat farts, and mules. Actually, LaJuanita makes him nervous and Waymon tries real hard not to show it. Waymon would be a perfect Marine, except for all the profanity he'd have to use. Waymon loved the music of the Carter Family, especially any song that included Mother Maybelle Carter. When she sang it made Waymon's skin crawl and his hair stand on end. Her intonations also sent chills up Waymon's spine. Waymon liked an occasional movie, too. Listen to Waymon imitate his favorite movie star, Ernest P. Worrell, and it'll make your skin crawl and send chills up your spine and make your hair stand on end just like Mother Maybelle does him.

But he's not a loser either—or those other things. Focused as a red laser beam Waymon was on his thing. Prepared to lose his woman over golf. Prepared to die in his quest to play Augusta National Golf Club if he has to, gladly. Waymon Poodle, prepared to squawk at Death, "Sir, I've caught up with you on the twelfth tee of heaven on *earth*, which is called Golden Bell at Augusta National *Golf* Club. Let *me*, Waymon Poodle of Mullet Luv, Georgia, play through, and we'll have a Coker-Coler in the men's grill after our round of golf and talk about my appointment with *heaven*."

Death, most likely in a sarcastic tone of voice because Waymon figured he brokered more souls for Satan than Jesus, would snarl at Waymon, "We won't be talking about *Hell, Waymon?* You're *sure*—absolutely *positive*—Waymon Poodle won't be going to mother scratchin'—*Hell?*"

After taking a real deep breath, Waymon would squawk at Death: "*Yes.*"

Waymon Poodle of Mullet Luv, Georgia: suffering from something.

Of course. Waymon had thought many times of how his life would turn out if he never got to play golf at Augusta National Golf Club and this was a horrifying thought.

The thought made his brain squirm.

Made his heart race.

His lungs suck for air.

Waymon's dreams, nearly every night, thoroughly dealt with this topic, in omni-color.

All this made him a little self absorbed, Waymon.

In other words, in Waymon's mind there are two distinctly different types of people in the world: those who have played Augusta National Golf Club and those who have not played Augusta National Golf Club.

In a hazy faraway place, where screams echo, Waymon saw the two groups float around in monstrous hoards, dressed in white robes, naked underneath, but wearing FootJoy golf shoes with Softspikes, and the ones who had played Augusta National Golf Club had satisfied expressions on their face and enjoyed lives that were finally worth living. Now they went forth and prospered and finally cured all the people in the world who had colon polyps.

The ones who had not played Augusta National Golf Club spewed things from out of their mouths that were not nice. These horrifying people drooled and giggled and screamed and reached through the clouds and touched each others' private parts with their fingers and lips and allowed giant cicada killer wasps to crawl around on their hands and up their arms and up their necks and onto their faces without even trying to knock them off—not one bit.

So Waymon prayed, mantra style, for fifty-nine seconds of each minute, that the Lord God Jesus would see fit to place his name on the Augusta National Golf Club tee sheet and on a guest list with the guard in the guard house on Washington Road.

Waymon asked the Lord God Jesus to drive him through the gate after the guard saluted him and told him—Mr. Waymon Poodle of Mullet Luv—how nice it was to have him as a guest today and hopefully many, many times in the future.

Waymon, then, with the Lord God Jesus' assistance, would drive slowly, reverently, desperately trying not to run over all those weird looking magnolia pine cone things on the asphalt of Magnolia Lane, then into the locker room, to lunch in the men's grill, into the pro shop to say hello and to thank them and to buy seventeen logoed shirts, onto the practice range, then onto the first tee of Tea Olive. Amen. Corner.

# *Refrigerator Gone*

WAYMON BELIEVED IN omens. Especially omens that directly related to him getting to play Augusta National Golf Club.

Not that he couldn't think for himself—obviously, he could, in quite imaginative ways—it was just that Waymon needed incessant confirmations his dream to play Augusta National Golf Club was valid and the tremendous mental energy and prayer time he'd been investing all these years would not make him look goofy.

In Waymon's case, his most recent omen's message was truly undeniable. And when the omen was revealed to Waymon, even under the horrible circumstances, Waymon breathed, "Thank you, Jesus. You are the man."

What happened was this: Waymon's apartment was sanitized. Burglarized—as in sanitized. Wiped real clean—as in burglarized by professionals.

The two guys who did it, a Mitch and a Ken, while staking out Waymon's apartment complex a few days before the break in, couldn't help but notice the bug eyed, creepy looking motha scratcher in the beat up Diplomat whose comings and goings were as predictable as they'd ever seen in their combined twenty-two years of robbing people's homes, apartments, businesses, out buildings, lake homes, beach homes, detached garages, attached garages, mountain homes, Dempsey Dumpsters, basements, warehouses, self storage garages, pontoon boats, cars, and sport utility vehicles. They had also once wiped out two coolers of sirloins at an Omaha Steaks in Gourd, Arkansas and ate like restaurant critics for three and half years. So they had seen the business thoroughly.

Anyhow, here's how predictable Waymon Poodle was to Mitch and Ken, the burglars. Wednesday night, since Waymon didn't sing in the choir—but was thinking about auditioning for the tambourine—Mitch and Ken quickly discovered Waymon would come home to his apartment at exactly 7:39 in the evening, always covered in sweat and with his hair all wet and matted. This was his night to hit two large baskets of range balls with his friends at the Mullet Luv Golf Center. And like all places called golf "centers," it consisted of a baked-out, divot infested nine holes you play twice from two different sets of tees, a practice range (lighted) with hard-packed dirt and Astroturf mats, a pro shop that sells the worst stuff and a grill that serves those ubiquitous orange crackers, hot dogs, beer and iced tea, and one brand of cigarettes, Marlboro Lights. So here he comes, Waymon Poodle. And there he goes inside with his golf clubs slung over his shoulder. Saturday morning: out the door with his golf clubs slung over his shoulder at 7:45 a.m. and back at 6:03 p.m. Sundays: church, lunch, etc., etc., etc.

After several days of watching Waymon, Ken said to Mitch it seemed like the motha scratcher was *taunting* them. That the motha scratcher probably *knew* they were casing his motha scratching ass and that he was probably a motha scratching FBI agent or some *other* motha scratching type person. Ken would get madder and madder as he pondered this scenario, while hitting himself on the forehead with the butt of his pistol.

Mitch, the more reasonable of the two, lit yet another cigarette and didn't say a word so he would look cool to Ken and continue to dominate the relationship as the mastermind and whatnot. After a moment, though, and after having been bugged by something for years, Mitch very politely asked Ken if he'd quit saying motha scratcher and instead might he consider saying "motor scooter" as motor scooter was a bit more socially acceptable when a person had to talk like that. Plus, saying motor scooter was sort of funny and really caught people off guard when they thought you were about to say motha scratcher and actually helped you make your point more effectively in an oddly humorous way.

Ken looked at Mitch in disbelief, and then said in an unequivocal tone of voice there was no motha scratching *way* he might consider saying motor scooter instead of motha scratcher. And then he said to Mitch real tough, pointing his pistol at Mitch's eyeball, "And *when*, motha scratcher, did you turn into a wimpy person?"

Ken was going to stick his pointing finger into the end of the barrel like he had seen the James Garner character do in that cowboy movie he loved a lot, but all of a sudden Ken began banging the butt of his pistol onto his forehead again. After about a minute and a half he finally knocked himself unconscious.

So, of course, as is quite common to interpersonal relationships of this nature, Mitch knew one day he'd have to slit Ken's throat and shoot him in the head.

Anyhow, on a Monday morning three weeks ago, forty-five minutes after Waymon left for the bank branch, Mitch and Ken rid Waymon of every possession he owned except the items contained in the second bedroom.

Here's the scene: Mitch and Ken moving everything out of there in a hurry, with sweat pouring off of their faces. Like two movers.

A resident of the complex, a former New York Mafia king pin type, who, after a quick career change decision, had his whole head re-sculpted to look like a retired Clark Gable impersonator, who was in the FBI's witness protection program, who lived near Waymon, who was out walking his Chihuahua with one of those electronic leash devices that include a shock button to make the dog stop running away or leaving a big dookie where it's not supposed to, said to Mitch and Ken to wish Waymon well and he'd miss him.

Cordially, as if they'd been trained by Letitia Baldridge herself, Mitch and Ken said they most certainly would and to have good one.

So Mitch and Ken stole everything, everything. Except the contents of the second bedroom. Which included a brand new computer that could have fetched some serious mother scratching cash. But they didn't steal it.

As Mitch and Ken also believed in omens, especially real bad omens, they immediately knew their motha scratching asses would be cursed if they so much as breathed on any of the swag in that room. It was just the way the whole motha scratching thing was set up. Spooky as motha scratching *shit*.

# The Second Bedroom

WAYMON'S APARTMENT NUMBER was 1931. For a real
big reason.

Everybody who loves golf like Waymon knows that 1931,
the year, was when Bobby Jones, the founder of Augusta National
Golf Club, first set foot upon the land that is now Augusta
National Golf Club.

Of course, folks even more like Waymon know Bobby Jones
really preferred to be called "Bob." Waymon always had to
explain this to people once he got real agitated at them when they
said things to him in conversation such as, "You know, *Way*mon,
ol' *Bobby* was one of the greatest golfers in the *world*," and "You
know, *Way*mon, ol' *Bobby* learned to play golf at East Lake
Country Club while he lived in a *mule* shed or some such," and so
on and so on and so on. Waymon would then make that huffing
sound. At that point more like a two year old, which was worse.

Anyhow, five years ago before Waymon moved out of his
parent's trailer, he called every apartment complex in Mullet Luv,
asking them if they had an apartment numbered 1931 and was it
available and did it have two bedrooms. The first complex he
called said yes they do have an apartment number 1931 and it's
available and it had two bedrooms and the second bedroom even
came with a nice view of a dumpster. Waymon looked at the
phone in his hand: *Dang*, an omen.

Nonetheless, here's what Mitch and Ken saw after they
opened the door to the second bedroom in Waymon Poodle's
apartment number 1931 in the "Sans Souci" apartment complex in

Mullet Luv—who strictly prohibited a resident from painting or wallpapering the walls or the ceiling—on the Monday morning they cleaned him out: Old Bob Jones Spalding golf clubs, with the yellow enamel-coated shafts, were laid across the five blades of the ceiling fan and hanging off every club was a set of old leather, plastic, or nylon head covers. Mitch and Ken discovered this almost instantly because Ken turned the light switch on so the fan started up on "high" and all that motha scratching golf memorabilia got flung everywhere which really, really startled Mitch and Ken and made the whole scene even scarier.

Every golf magazine ever sent to Waymon in his life was stacked against the left wall of the room with the spine facing out so Waymon could easily check the date of an old issue for some obscure golf tip when he got on the bogey train.

The magazines were stacked to the ceiling, and because there were so many magazines in the room, the room had that old, musty odor found in libraries and the homes of shut ins. Waymon subscribed to a lot of golf magazines and because of this he secretly thought that at golf magazine conventions he was talked about by the publishers of these magazines. It was just a thought, but Waymon could not believe anyone else in the world went to the lengths he did to find and to subscribe to golf magazines. Waymon even subscribed to a number of foreign golf magazines such as *Golf Russia*, *Golf & Piss* (Ireland), *Hooking in Cabo Del Sol*, and a Japanese golf magazine, whose title, when translated into English, was *Mashie Niblick Tennis Genitals*, that even included full page pornography. Waymon was amazed, gazing a while, at how little the Japanese people looked without their clothes on while they fornicated, but then he'd rip those pages out of the magazine and throw them away. U.S. Open, PGA Championship, British Open, and U.S. and British Amateur Championship programs were also sent to him.

But Waymon's all time favorite golf magazine came out only once a year and that was the *Masters Journal*, distributed just a few weeks prior to each year's Masters. The fact it was available in the magazine rack at the Publix in which his bank branch was located wasn't a big omen, but it did rate as a pretty good one.

Waymon couldn't wait to get his hands on it each year and had even made an agreement with the produce manager, who was also in charge of receiving magazines, that he be allowed to come back there at the loading dock and be the first one to cut through the plastic adhesive tape on the box and reach in and get the first one. The agreement, however, had to be vigorously explained and renewed each year as the turnover rate among produce managers at the grocery store was extremely high and Waymon also learned most people who are produce managers don't quite understand these type sentiments and tend to forget them the second after Waymon went to the trouble to explain them.

Waymon loved to gaze at the cover photograph of his *Masters Journal* issue as it always showed a hole at Augusta National Golf Club with the sun shining so brightly on the sixteenth—the thirteenth—the whatever—it didn't matter to Waymon if they showed an exploding commode as long as it was an exploding commode at Augusta National Golf Club. Seven dollars for so much pleasure. Each page for Waymon was an oasis of golf and Masters information. He would turn the pages slowly, and each re-reading was just like the first, slow and respectful of all this thing meant to him.

And the heft.

The heft of the magazine was so impressive to Waymon, unlike any of his others, those with thin pages and all those dang ads that showed half naked people.

The *Masters Journal*, read with his eyes wide open. Waymon forgot the world existed, didn't hear the phone ringing, knocks at the door, his stomach grumbling. Up until the final putt of that year's Masters, the magazine would rest on his night stand beside Waymon's bible.

Which they stole.

Mitch and Ken stood there still gripping the door frame, wide-eyed themselves, as if the door had opened to reveal an open elevator shaft.

Mitch kept sucking on that cigarette.

# Clickety-Clack

ON THE FAR wall were two windows. Their drapes: golf hole fabric. Like pajamas.

Under the window was a old office credenza Waymon had bought for $3 at a yard sale and the top was covered with various Masters knick knacks, all logoed—ball repair tools, ball markers, money clips, tumblers, mugs, scarves, scorecards, coasters, the whole motha scratching shooting match—he'd purchased at the only Masters he ever attended, 1988, (the Monday practice round actually; the only ticket he could get) and other golf knick knacks people had given him. Waymon was easy to buy for. People felt sorry for him.

On the wall to the right was Waymon's collection of golf books displayed in shelves Waymon built himself that stretched to the ceiling and ran the length of the wall. Every golf book ever written by Bob Jones and O.B. Keeler and every other person on earth who had ever written a golf book on golf or the Masters or Augusta National Golf Club was on those shelves.

Waymon's golf bag full of Nike irons and woods—just like Tiger plays and some of those other pros—leaned against the shelves. His head covers had Masters' logos on them.

All of a sudden Ken said motha scratcher look at *this* shit and that scared Mitch half to death as for some time the mood of the burglary had been somber and quiet. Ken pointed to the center of the floor. On the floor was Waymon's masterpiece, his unabashed most prized possession in the world other than his love of the Masters, the golf course on which it's played, and the wonderful sport of golf in general. On the floor was Augusta National Golf Club. In miniature. To say how and how long it took Waymon to make the model and how possessed he's become of it was fairly depressing, just to say every acre of Augusta National Golf Club, including the par 3 course, the 18 hole course, the cottages, employee parking, the maintenance center, the garbage dumpster, everything, created in such detail it took Mitch' and Ken's breath away. Ken wanted to say motha scratcher, but couldn't.

A small light placed in the corner of the room by Waymon shown on the clubhouse. Waymon kept it on all day and all night, for he wanted there to always be light on the clubhouse of Augusta National Golf Club.

To their left and right, the walls were covered with framed prints of Augusta National holes. Amen Corner. The clubhouse. Bob Jones. Jack Nicklaus. Coody. Palmer. Hogan. Hord Hardin.

The walls, what you could see of them: Masters' green. Augusta National Golf Club green. Pantone Matching System number 560. Waymon had the solution memorized. Seventy-two point five percent green, seven point five percent of warm red, and then you throw in exactly twenty percent black. Or you could look at it this way, he'd explain to you if you were still listening: you got fourteen and a half parts *green*, one and a half parts warm *red*, and four parts *black*.

Masters' green.

Five. Six. Zero.

Waymon knew in his heart it was the green that was the best.

# *The Future*

BACK TO THE omen.

Waymon had come home at exactly the time he comes home on Monday and inserted the key into the lock and opened the door to apartment number 1931.

Waymon stepped into an empty apartment. He stood there in the living room for a moment, not quite gawking but almost, then stepped back out and looked at the number on the door, you know, just to make absolutely sure. Seeing the number—1931—immediately made Waymon feel good as that was a big year for golf.

He closed the door, took a deep breath, then opened it again and stepped into yet again an empty living room and experienced a feeling of vulnerability. And that's what he felt. Vulnerable. Like a kitten. And Waymon didn't like feeling this way as he secretly thought people shouldn't mess with him. But there he was, and someone had messed with him.

Without moving, he viewed the devastation and wondered what might be revealed to him when the looked into the second bedroom.

Seeing the future, Waymon knew, from watching a certain episode of *Star Trek*, could make you go insane.

# The Conspiracy

THE FIRST THING the Mullet Luv policeman said to Waymon, as he gazed into Waymon's second bedroom, was, "Mr. Poodle, I assume you must be a member of the *Masters*."

At that moment Waymon knew once and for all a conspiracy had been developed and the conspiracy was organized in an effort to mess with him because you aren't a member of the Masters. The Masters is the tournament they have at Augusta National Golf Club. This he explained to the policeman.

*Well*, the policeman articulated. He had never given it that much thought.

Meanwhile, an unfortunate turn for Mitch and Ken, at least from their point of view. Two hundred and fifty miles down the road, the huge U-Haul truck they had rented with a stolen credit card for which they used to rid Waymon of everything he owned, except the contents of the second bedroom, blew up. In addition, it happened to blow up and catch on fire right in front of one of those regional Georgia State Patrol center places as U-Hauls will do whose back ends drag on the asphalt for over one hundred miles at high speeds.

In Georgia, as well as in a lot of other states in America, as state patrolmen are trained to do, they ran out and came to the aid of the motorists in the U-Haul with the engine area engulfed in orange and red flames. Mitch, as he quickly exited the U-Haul, forgot his gun was still stuffed into his pants and most of the gun was still hanging out and it was pretty damn obvious to these well-trained state patrolmen that what was sticking out of Mitch's pants was a gun.

This, of course, didn't go over real well with the state patrolmen and Mitch was quickly notified of his particular situation. Ken, still exhausted from the move, was sleeping, and didn't get to see Mitch have to fling his gun down, which he had actually purchased with his own money, which he had stolen, and get it all scratched on the asphalt, then get enthusiastically gang tackled by seventeen state patrolmen.

Anyhow, Mitch and Ken and the U-Haul were brought back to Mullet Luv where criminal punishment precedent was set. As part of their punishment, because the local authorities just thought it was logical and made sense, Mitch and Ken were uncuffed then forced to haul all of Waymon's crap back into apartment number 1931 to be placed in exactly the same spot where his crap was before. Waymon and Mr. Gable, holding his Chihuahua, watched patiently from the parking lot.

When they were finished, Mitch and Ken got cuffed again and hauled off. Before they were hauled off, the Mullet Luv policeman said tentatively, with an edge to his voice, now that he thought he might be speaking to a lunatic, "Mr. Poodle, good luck with your omen situation." Then he left, fled, quickly.

Waymon thanked Jesus by performing a clogging step he learned in church revival camp. He looked as if a bunch of giant cicada killer wasps were attached—by their claws and stingers— to his ankles and arms.

# Friends Like These

SUCH WAS WAYMON'S confidence in the omen. He couldn't wait to tell his friends on Wednesday at the Mullet Luv Golf Center. He really should have known better by now.

These particular fellows, who found irresistible only one thing about Waymon, his golfing, made great sport of him in nomenclature form. They called Waymon "Waymo" or "Way Off" or "Sideways" or "Wide Angle" or "Squidward." Because of Waymon's alien likeness situation they absolutely delighted in calling him "The Experiment" or "The Unthinkable" or "The Mistake" or "The Unexplained" or "Spock" or "The Chicken" and a real favorite was "The Insect."

"Hat Rack" and "Pool Cue" and "Flag Pole" and "The Javelin" because he was so skinny, and from time to time they referred to him as "The Tendon."

They also called Waymon the "Missing Link" and deeply believed in their hearts he was the world's official Missing Link and they had discovered it right there living and working in Mullet Luv and had befriended it. However, there was a special nickname they called Waymon, which was surprising in its conception by folks considered to be hillbilly-type dumb asses, since it had a cinematic, literary quality to it. In other words, a human being had to be fairly alert to come up with it. Waymon's Mullet Luv Golf Center pals called him, on special occasions, "Nosferatu." Amazing their depth of cruelty, from a literary point of view.

They also made fun of his Bible thumping. The way he talked. But his north Georgia twang was just like theirs.

They told him how he'd never get promoted at his job because he was so much like Barney Fife. Now, how Waymon reasoned his future they especially loved. They hooted and hollered and pointed back at him. Clickety-clack. Clackety-click. But he beat their asses in golf and took their money on the eighteenth green then slipped it back under their windshield wipers.

Breaking 80, and sometimes 70, was real easy.

Waymon hit golf shots—that *hissed*.

But Waymon's mission was his wall. It was brought down between himself and outside forces attempting to dissuade him from believing he would tee it up one day at Augusta National Golf Club. Now he knew he would, but he didn't know when. His friends, after the golf ball whacking, tried to help.

THE SCENE: the snack bar at Mullet Luv Golf Center. Many beers. Iced tea for Waymon, sweet. Cigarette packs lying next to lighters. Smoke everywhere, thick as vanilla yogurt. They're sitting around the big, round table. Its yellow plastic top pock-marked by years of cigarette burns.

THE PLAYERS: Waymon, who was "Nosferatu" this evening, and two rurals—"Snort," who two weeks ago, while worshipping Satan, gouged his left eyeball out with an ice pick, and Billy, an enthusiastic Cane Toad licker, best friends—and a nice guy named Jim who was real educated and had clean fingernails and clothes. Billy and Snort drunk before they got there. Getting drunker. Shirley, the sweet country gal who worked behind the counter. Her hair done up, black and shiny, like Patsy Cline. She loved Waymon and thought how Waymon was just exactly like Jesus when Jesus was Waymon's age. After a couple of vodkas, Shirley thought Waymon might be Jesus. Shirley loved Jesus, very much, but smoked, drank, cussed, and kept a vibrator in her pocketbook. Uses it quite a bit through her tight jeans behind the cash register. Shirley loved a rocking orgasm.

SNORT: "Dumb ass Nosfera-*tooo*, that's the biggest crock of dookie story I ever *heard*. Them Pootie Tangs didn't have any more *room* in the truck fer yer *Mas*ters shit."

NOSFERATU, bony finger, wagging it: "I *seen* in the truck. I done told you—they had *room*."

SHIRLEY, whiskey voice, Southern accent out of Hollywood: "Y'all leave him *alooooone*. And quit calling him that awful *vampire* name, you Satan worshiper assholes! Now I *mean* it!"

BILLY, burped, a piece of something flew out and hit Nosferatu in the corner of his eye.

SNORT, slowly, with malice dripping from every word; strange, rubbery facial expressions: "Aw-right. Here's the *deal*. See, since them *dooods*—didn't take off with yer precious *golf* shit—now you think any second some fart wad *member*—of Auguster National *Country* Club—is gonner prance up to you on the *street*—and say Nosfera-*tooo*, since them Pootie Tangs didn't take any of yer *golf* shit—I just feel like *you*, Nosfera-tooo Poodle, a freak from outer *space*, ought to come on down there with *me*— and make *me* look like a *dumb* ass in front of all my *other* member assholes and suck on a *hot* dawg—and play *golf*? I mean—give me a *break*. *Kill* me—just *kill* me, *maaaaaaan*."

The group, except for Nosferatu, let go a tremendous burst of laughter, as if on cue. Laughing so hard their faces turn red. Devil red. High fives. Low fives. They're pointing at Nosferatu's face. Knew they got him good with that one. Cigarettes sucked in so hard their cheeks collapsed. Another high five. Funny, funny stuff. The way it was delivered by Snort—just awesome. The tempo. The facial expressions. The empty, weeping eyeball socket. The way he leaned into Nosferatu's face and kept screwing his head sideways as if he were looking under a sofa for his roach clip. Awesome. Plus, plus. Not done yet...

SNORT: "And hey, Nosfera-*too*. If you really, really look at that Auguster National low-go—the bottom of that flag don't come out nowhere *near* Auguster—that flag looks like it comes right outta Spartanburg, South Caroliner or some *other* hell hole from out of my *butt*. Boy, you just look at that low-go and tell me I—ain't—*right!*" Snort falls off of his chair and breaks his collarbone—but he keeps laughing because he doesn't feel it.

Awesome. Creeped the heaven and hell out of him.

Shirley started having an orgasm. Then her cell phone went off in her pocket. The extra vibration. Shirley falls on the floor and starts squirming around and has the rest of her orgasm down there.

NOSFERATU: Jaw clenched so hard his cheek muscles popped to a visible point. Jesus on his side. Praying again, mantra style. I'm gonner tee it up at Augusta National. I know I'm gonner tee...

JIM, Didn't know how he got pulled into the group, seeing as he was a big shot regional vice president of IBM, but just always happened to be around on Wednesday afternoons. Loved to hit balls for cheap, and found out pretty quick this was what you got. This scene. People who will definitely mess with you, without permission. But sort of understood the Waymon situation as he had a brother like Waymon whose life mission it was to marry Barry Manilow. The restraining order came last Thursday. But Jim was laughing too. "Nos—I mean *Way*mon, you know, there are some ways to play Augusta National without being invited by a member."

SNORT AND BILLY, as if on cue: "*Bull* shit." A palm-smacking high five, with the broken collarbone. Then a low five. Loud, too. They had it down, but couldn't do it sober.

NOSFERATU: Knew this was what hate felt like.

JIM, waited for total silence: "*Way*mon, look at me—"

SNORT AND BILLY: "*He caint!*"

SHIRLEY: "Y'all leave Jesus alone!"

JIM, holding firm, needed to get this over with: "I know you know the qualifications to get into the tournament, Waymon. I'm sure you've got them memorized."

NOSFERATU: Tapped a finger on the side of his enormous head.

SNORT AND BILLY: Leaning in so they can hear.

JIM: "You don't think you'll be going over there and winning the British Amateur anytime soon, do you? Although

35

you're a great player—don't get me *wrong*."

SNORT, nudging Billy: "Nosferatooo, you *are* a great golf player. You really are! You go over there and win yer-self the goddamn British *Oh*-pen!" Laughing. Laughing like hell at that one. Trying to catch their breath. Holding their throats.

JIM: "Waymon, *you* know what I'm trying to say."

NOSFERATU, wide-eyed, mesmerized. Didn't say a word. He knew.

JIM: "And I bet you saw that article the other day in the *Wall Street Journal* about Bill Gates and how he wants to join Augusta National. Loves golf. Seems like a pleasant enough guy. The richest son of a bitch computer geek booger eater in the universe. The shit he invented has given millions of people around the world opportunity and made whole economies and made our worthless lives easier. You saw the article. He wants the hell in there and he licked their asses *big* time and those boys told Bill Gates the big billionaire to back up slowly down Magnolia Lane and hit the *road*."

NOSFERATU: "Okay, then. I saw it. I *read* it." The profanity, Waymon thought. Does everybody at IBM cuss like that?

JIM: "I knew you'd find it somehow. You're a magnet for that stuff. But, Waymon, if they won't let Bill *Gates* be a member, that just shows you how hard it is for some regular stiff like you to just *play*. Well, I mean you're not regular at *all*, Waymon, you're special."

NOSFERATU: "I've been *told* that." Nosferatu gave Snort a look.

JIM: "All right then, here's the deal. There are exactly four ways regular stiffs can play down there. They let the golf writers play the day after the tournament or you can work there at the club and there's an employee day once a year or you can get a job as a volunteer during the tournament and they let you play on a day near the end of the season. Other than *that*, you have to be invited by a member. No offense Waymon, but I don't get the impression you know a whole bunch of Augusta National

36

members. Bill *Gates* sure as hell ain't one, we know that. And by God those crackers are dug in tight on not letting some ol' big tittied, complainin' *wo*man in there."

SNORT AND BILLY: Gaping mouths. A spooky quiet. Cigarette smoke slowly pouring out of their nostrils like white ropes. They never knew what to say when this Jim cat befriended Waymon like this. At some point every Wednesday night Jim did—had to. This Jim asshole had class. Assholes with class scared Snort and Billy shitless.

JIM, with an exhilarating hopefulness in his voice, a squeeze of Waymon's bony shoulder, and a life-altering wink: "Waymon, *amigo*. Those four ways and you're on the first tee at Augusta National Golf Club looking up the emerald fairway of *Tea* Olive. I'm pretty sure."

# PART II

## WAYMON'S VOID

# Removing a Wart

LAY DOWN YOUR bet if you thought Waymon got any sleep that night. Darkness enveloped him like a casket and he couldn't wait to get rid of it so he could get rolling again.

Waymon didn't sleep. He squirmed.

Waymon's plan was to get a real good job in the accounting department at Augusta National Golf Club as soon as possible.

Although Waymon thought he might be a good waiter at Augusta National Golf Club, since he really enjoyed serving people, but then he knew he'd be serving folks alcoholic beverages, and drinking alcoholic beverages or being the person serving them, was a one-way ticket to You Know Where.

One thing was certain, Waymon Poodle wanted to be an employee at Augusta National Golf Club right now. Nothing else would do. He wanted to work there every day of the year. Wake up in Augusta, Georgia. Live in an apartment there, number 1931. He wanted his business card to say Waymon Poodle, Accountant, Augusta National Golf Club. He could see this clearly in his mind—his Augusta National Golf Club business card, as big as a billboard, hovering there in front of him.

For lunch, Waymon and all the other tellers got thirty minutes. Waymon wanted an extra ten. He was going to hustle back to his apartment and call Augusta National Golf Club from the second bedroom and get a job in the accounting department then hustle back to his old job at the bank branch and resign real quick and start packing. He'd figure out what to do with LaJuanita when he got to Augusta and moved in somewhere.

Requests like this, especially to a guy like Waymon's boss, excited the man to no end. Waymon said slowly, with a canned hesitancy in his voice, "Well—I just don't—*know*. An extra ten minutes. That's a *lot*, you know. Ten minutes could alter the state of the future of TrustTrust Banks Incorporated—*Waymon*"

"If I'm back any later," Waymon said seriously, "you *dock* me."

"Oh, Waymon, I wouldn't *dock* you. But you know I *could*."

"*Dock* me."

Waymon made a sinister smile and tried to put his hand on Waymon's shoulder but Waymon juked his shoulder to the left so Waymon's hand missed. "So *tell* me," Waymon moaned, "what's so imp*ooo*ortant that you need an extra *ten* minutes as opposed to an extra *el*even minutes?"

Waymon looked at him. He barely, barely squinted.

"Well, pardon *me* then—okay—but as a seasoned manager of human beings in the *work*place, I'm always just so *fas*cinated by this moment in the work day. I read *books* about it."

Waymon really squinted at Waymon this time.

Waymon cocked his head, inquisitively. "*Say*—you're not in any sort of *trouble* are you? I could *help*. Or, come to think of it, if you're out looking for another *job*, I'll need to know right this instant so I can *fire* you."

Waymon looked at his watch. "*Per*sonal business."

"Oh. *Per*sonal business."

"*Per*sonal business."

"Oh, oh-*kay*. Well, *Way*mon, did you know that that's a signal to me as a manager of human beings in the workplace that you're *up* to something, you know, cloaking your sneakiness in those famous words"—Waymon made quote signs—"*personal* business. See, if you had an appointment with a *brain* surgeon to have your *head* operated on you'd have written me a memo with all the fascinating *details*. But you *don't* have an appointment with a brain surgeon *do* you—to have your head operated on? Or do you really have an appointment for an afternoon sexy massage, *Way*mon? Know what I'm talking about? Guys like you who have to *paaaay* for pleasure at those ubiquitous Asian *jack* shacks along our most attractive Confederate Victory Parkway? Know what I mean? *Jack* shack? *Spank* shop? *Slap* Shop? *Squirt* bucket? Where anonymous and illegally imported fast talking Asian women lubricate your little troublemaker, then vigorously massage your little troublemaker."

"*No.* I *don't* have an appointment to have my troub—"

"Right. *Suuuuuure.* So *Way*mon—running out for an afternoon lubrication and jack and spank and slap and squirt bucket sexy *massaaaaage?*"

Never, ever, in Waymon's life had he ever encountered such a person as Waymon. Waymon considered witnessing some of the more important Primitive Baptist beliefs to Waymon right then and there in the bank branch but he was in a hurry. Waymon pursed his lips. "*No,* I said. *Per*sonal business." Now Waymon's face was turning red and he was starting to twitch. He said deliberately: " I have got to *go!*"

"So *okaaaaaaay*—like going to the dry cleaners or going out to have a wart *remoooooved?*"

"I clean my *own* garments."

"But *Way*mon, you wouldn't hack off your own wart—*would you?*"

Waymon gave Waymon a hard, hard look. "I would if I *had* to."

41

# Mr. Rafsooliwicki

BELIEVE IT OR not, Waymon walked into an empty apartment.

Believe it.

Again.

Seems that Mitch and Ken had their bitches come up with the bail money, and then Mitch and Ken went right back on over and cleaned out Waymon again. This time they got (stole) a rental truck from Ryder instead of a U-Haul and were now heading for Scottsdale, Arizona with Waymon's stuff. Why they chose Scottsdale, Arizona no one really knows, not even the bitches, who were mad Mitch and Ken didn't invite them to tag along. Scottsdale, Arizona, the bitches had heard, was a real nice place.

Anyhow, when Waymon stepped into his empty apartment he was already in a sort of a frenzy, him being so nervous about calling up Augusta National Golf Club and asking for a job even though the recent omen was a big one. But then he immediately felt better because he knew if Mitch or Ken had been back, or some other guys, and if they left the second bedroom alone again, then this omen business was really, really working in his favor and in just a minute he'd be the new guy in the accounting department at Augusta National Golf Club.

With a shaking hand, Waymon opened the door to the second bedroom.

Omen city.

Except the overhead light that shone on his model of the Augusta National Golf Club clubhouse had been turned off by Ken because he felt sorry for Waymon for having to steal all his stuff again and even though he thought Waymon was a creepy motha scratcher, he didn't want his light bill to get run up.

But this definitely did it.

Waymon now figured he could probably ask to be head pro since the omens were coming in such powerful waves, but he didn't know that much about selling overpriced pro shop golf socks.

Waymon took the portable phone (which they did not steal, another minor omen) off the kitchen wall and took it into the second bedroom and shut the door.

He turned on the little light that shines onto the clubhouse—which made him feel even more wonderful—then held the phone up in the air as if he were displaying a fish he just caught and made one circle in the room showing the contents of the room the phone. Waymon wondered what assignments he might get. Calling up members whose accounts were past due? Helping members with their investments? He thought TrustTrust had some real good ideas he could bring to the job. Balancing their checkbooks or whatnot?

Waymon had the number memorized, of course. Actually, he had it programmed into his phone if he, for any reason, had to call Augusta National Golf Club, then the call could be made with absolute precision and efficiency. He pressed the button and listened to the awesome beeping of the phone number of Augusta National Golf Club. He smiled. Waymon was now as calm as a sleeping infant, and wasn't at all surprised how quickly the phone was answered at Augusta National Golf Club.

Good things happened there.

Yes.

Lives changed for the better.

Of course they did.

Waymon Poodle knew this.

"*Good morning*! Augusta National *Golf* Club! This is Betty *Simp*son. How may I *help* you?" The voice was as sweet and as pleasant as Shirley Temple's. Well, why wouldn't it be? Waymon assumed Augusta National Golf Club hired only the most congenial people in the world.

Waymon, still just as calm as a sleeping infant, just minutes away from getting the job even though he had to bother with the formality of asking for it, said, "Yes. Hello. I'm calling to inquire about working in your accounting department."

"Well isn't that *wonderful!*" Betty said "wonderful" as if she were competing in a contest of who could say the word with the most gut wrenching exhilaration.

Waymon gazed at his golf clubs. He felt more wonderful as each second of his life passed. "Yes, *thank* you."

"No sir, thank *you* for calling Augusta National Golf Club. And *your name?*"

"Yes. This is Waymon *Poo*dle calling."

"Mr. *Poo*dle," she said as if hearing from someone thought to be dead for thirty years, "It's so good to *hear* from you!"

Obviously she was expecting my call, Waymon thought. But so cordial of her to go through these niceties.

"And you'd like to work in our accounting department?"

"Yes ma'am. I would. *Very* much. And as soon as possible."

"Then you just hold the line, Mr. Poodle. It will be my honor to connect you to the head of our accounting department, Mr. Emiglio Rafsooliwicki, who is in complete charge of hiring people for the accounting department and who is not on his phone right now and is sitting at his desk and is not at lunch either. As a matter of *fact*, Mr. Rafsooliwicki told me not *two* seconds ago that if anyone called for him, even if he didn't know the person or even if the person was a *sales*man, or even if he was about to lick a taco or take a bite of a clam sandwich or even if he was in a *mee*ting or on the commode, to connect that person to him immediately and without hesitation."

"Thank you so much."

"May I connect you now, Mr. Poodle?"

"Yes, *please. Thank* you."

"My *plea*sure Mr. Poodle. I will connect you now to Mr. Emiglio Rafsooliwicki, the head of our accounting department.

And thank *you* again for calling Augusta National *Golf* Club!"

*Click.*

"You're welcome," Waymon said to the hold music, which was the finest hold music he'd ever heard in his life, which he got to listen to for approximately sixteen minutes. No problem. No problem at all. The music was airy, uplifting, easy to listen to. Of course. It was the hold music of Augusta National Golf Club. I'll listen as long as you folks feel I need to, thought Waymon Poodle. Take me into your arms.

"WHAAAAAA!"

Waymon jumped.

"Emeeeglio Rafsoooliwicki on the phone here! Can I *hep* you now please—*yes?*"

Waymon instinctively felt he needed to raise his voice since he was all of a sudden talking to a foreign person. "Yes, this is Waymon Poodle calling to inquire about working in your accounting department?"

"Whaaa! Don't talk to me so loud Mr. Waymon Poodle!"

"Sorry."

"You want to work in accounting department did you say to me?"

"Yessir. I have a feeling there might be an immediate opening?" Waymon was pretty darn sure. Mitch and Ken. Two times.

"*Why* you want to work in accounting department Waymon Poodle when I have way too many crazy men-stroooo-ay-teeng lunatics in my accounting department already!"

Waymon wasn't expecting that one. "Well, sir—"

"What do you do *now* Mr. Waymon Poodle calling to work in my accounting department?"

"I'm a *bank* teller."

"Whaaa! A *bank* teller! A bank teller isn't an accountant I don't think!"

"But I believe," Waymon said with a rising tone of panic, "that the *skills* of a bank teller are certainly, in this case, transfera—"

45

Just then someone screamed so loudly Waymon could hear it in the background. Some horrible, screaming woman: "This Mr. Farnsworth wants a two dollar and fifty cent credit for a soda! He's the fourth richest man in the world!"

"You stop that screaming right now about that Mr. Farnsworth! I'll fix *him*!"

Still screaming: "You got his number!?"

"Memorized!"

Waymon thought it sounded like a mental hospital, although he'd never been in a mental hospital. He'd only seen some on TV. "Uh, Mr. Rafsooliwicki?" Waymon said meekly.

"Yes, this is Emeeeglio Rafsoooliwicki! Who is this please talking to me? And did you know I was about to eat a clam sandwich!"

"Waymon *Poo*dle. We were just discussing—"

"About how you want to work in my accounting department while I'm about to take a bite of my clam sandwich and call a member to tell him he can stick the two dollar and fifty cent credit for a can of soda up his hairy—?"

"Have I called at a bad time?"

"*No*, Mr. Waymon Poodle. Not at all. It's been a pleasure speaking with you today. Now I bite my clam sandwich."

*Click.*

# Inhuman Resources

BETTY, HER REAL name was Betty, Betty Simpson, punched the inter-office number of Frank Johnson, otherwise known as Emiglio Rafsooliwicki, head of the accounting department at Augusta National Golf Club. As Frank Johnson was not about to bite a clam sandwich, he picked up his phone. "Yeah?"

"Whatcha think?"

"*Strange.*"

"How long you *do* him?"

"Sixteen minutes. He was still on the line when I picked up, humming along with the hold music. Stravinsky. Who in the hell knows Stra*vin*sky music?"

"Damn."

"I know."

"Hey, *Frank*. Employees can't say 'fuck' in the clubhouse. You didn't get the memo?"

"I didn't get the memo. But *they* say 'fuck' all the time—the damn *members*."

Betty gazed at the oil portrait of Jimmy Carter for a moment. She forgot to give Frank the memo. "Well, anyway, you give him that crazy men-strooo-ay-teeng lunatics bit?"

"Yeah. *Nothing*. Didn't seem fazed at all."

"Did you do the thing about the members stealing range balls?"

"That's gotten old, actually. We did the Farnsworth soda credit shtick. I had my new girl scream it."

"*Wow*. This guy wants it bad."

"No kidding. You got him pulled up yet?"

"I will by the time you get up here."

"Coffee? Cold Red Bull?"

"Coffee. You know how I like it."

"Sure do—you nasty thang."

Computer whirring now. All Betty typed in was "Waymon Poodle" into a special Interpol-Scotland Yard-Royal Canadian Mounted Police-CIA-FBI-Justice Department program. That was it.

Frank put the mug of coffee down by her mouse. "Seems to be taking a little longer than usual."

"I know. There can't be many Waymon *Poo*dles in the world."

"Betty, you've been doing this for *way* too long to think his name is actually—"

"Shut the hell up, Frank. Here he is."

"Wow," Frank mumbled. "His name really *is* Waymon Poodle and he really *is* a bank teller at a grocery store. Mullet Luv? Where the hell is Mullet Luv?"

"Northeast Georgia somewhere. I'll bet he's inbred."

"Well—pull up some pictures. That'll tell you right there."

Two simple keystrokes. Waymon's past and current driver's license pictures popped onto the screen along with three satellite pictures taken of him just last Tuesday loading groceries into his Chrysler Diplomat. "*Wow*. Looka *this* guy."

"Damn. Remind me never to spend the night in goddamn Mullet Luv."

"Frank, watch your *mouth*. Some dip wad member might walk in. I'm sure we can't say 'goddamn' either." Betty glanced through the window at the driveway in front of the clubhouse, then back at the screen.

Frank said, "Do voice evaluation."

"Yeah. Good idea." Betty called up the entire Poodle-Simpson-Rafsooliwicki conversation which had been recorded by the computer and evaluated by a software program designed by a number of eminent psychologists, psychiatrists, astrologers, and sociologists, as well as the CIA, the FBI, and some seasoned criminals. Betty hit the "Report" button, and then they leaned toward the screen. Betty said, "Well now. Says here he's extremely regional, honest, intelligent, loves the Masters, the golf course on which it's played, the wonderful sport of golf in general, and the iniquitous allure of what goes on behind the gates of ootsie-tootsie private golf clubs. Says he loves collecting golf memorabilia and golf magazines, lacks a few of the more sophisticated social skills but can still communicate with other human beings in his own particular way, and he's a hard and loyal worker. Oh, looka here. Guess what freaks him out?"

"His reflection?"

"*Funny*, Frank. Says here he's afraid of giant cicada killer wasps, as opposed to just *regular* wasps. Says regular wasps don't scare him one bit. Now ain't *that* strange."

"This creep's *all* strange, Betty."

"Now, on his dangerous side, just one characteristic— obsessive—but he's the type of person who will channel it for something he thinks is vital to life it*self*. That's it. The whole report. Damn*n*ation. This is one focused *cat*."

"The *hell* with this guy, Betty. He's pulling one on us so bad it's historic. I just feel it. Pull up the bio. Birth to today. This is the new software version, *right*?"

"Yeah. That smelly, butt crack geek from the CIA installed it for me yesterday. God, I had to spray the room after he left. His hair had wasp nests in it."

"This is the one that includes bank accounts, physician records, credit card use, web site time, and magazine subscriptions? All that other stuff?"

"Yeah. Oh—*look*."

Betty and Frank leaned toward the monitor again, as if their heads were connected. Usually, birth-to-today bios on every person who calls, writes, plays as a guest, digs a hole under one of the fences and urinates on a green or goes skinny dipping in one of the ponds or pulls up a chunk of something, or is on the ticket list, every vendor, every other whacko or scum bag who drifts into the air space of the radar of Augusta National Golf Club is ten to twenty pages long.

Waymon's was half a page. Real boring stuff. Said he spent an hour an evening going back and forth through the Masters tournament web site. Never once—not once—pulled up a porn site. He'd never even checked a stock because he didn't own one. There was even a question on the screen, "Does the subject occasionally speak in Tongues?"—followed by a box the system checked or left blank. The box was checked.

"In all my years," Betty said with a sigh, easing back in her chair, "I ain't *never* seen a cat like this. Says he's a virgin, too. That wouldn't be the case with you, Frank—now *would* it?" Betty lit a cigarette.

"Baby, I ain't been a virgin for a long, long time. Like since I was *nine*. Go back to his pictures."

Betty pulled up Waymon's pictures again.

Frank pointed at the screen. "Look. He's wearing the same tie in every shot. Kind of nerdy, don't you think?"

"Of course, Frank—you dumb ass. It's nerdy as all *get* out. I mean, who other than the *mem*bers wear ties with the club logo every single day. *Jeee*-sus."

"I swear, Betty. We need to have this dude checked out. Let's send Dick up there to Mullet Luv and check his ass out."

"Waste of time. Where's Dick been for so long anyway?"

"Cincinnati. Went to make sure that old McFarley guy was really dead."

"So, take his dried-up ass off the ticket list after sixty-two years?"

"Oh, yeah. I forgot to tell you. Got Dick's e-mail this morning. McFarley is as dead as *hell*. Dick decided to have him exhumed and have his DNA tested—you know—to be sure it was McFarley. So honey, pull up McFarley of Cincinnati on the computer and hit de-*lete*." Frank smiled an evil smile. "Never used his tickets anyway. Never scalped, never gave them to a friend or relative. Just sat on them. Sixty-two damn *years*. What a piece of shit. Who do these patrons think they *are?*"

Betty pulled up the McFarley file. Hit delete. Took one millionth of a millionth of a second. *Blip!*

"So why not? Dick's perfect for the Poodle case."

"I'll tell you why not." Betty spun around in her chair and gave Frank a sexy look, then eased her hand between his legs and began rubbing, then squeezing, fairly hard, his scrotum. "Because I think this Poodle is actually a normal person. I got a good gut feel on this one. I mean, we don't spend seventy-eight million a year on all this software and investigative time and new satellite acquisitions on the invasion of the privacy and the strict adherence to Masters' ticket policies of sixteen billion people for fun. *Right?*"

"*Yeah*, baby. Squeeze like you *mean* it."

"Frank, pay attention—the system ain't lied *yet*." Betty tapped the screen with one of her sharp red fingernails. "Says right *here*."

"Tonight I'm gonna spank you so bad your pink booty's gonna turn a purplish ma*roon* color."

"Oh—that's *reeeeal* sexy talk, Frank, *dumb* ass. Anyhow, my gut tells me this flaming squid's running down the usual list and the phone's going to ring in just a minute and it's going to be Waymon Poodle of Mullet Luv, Georgia calling now to see if he can become a volunteer for the tournament. Perfectly normal. He really was nice when you think about it. A corn cob butt rubbing hick from Mullet Luv—but *nice*."

Frank was boning up pretty good. He said in a voice he was sure was sexy this time, but still sounded pretty clunky, "Baby, you a-*maaaaze* me with your uninhibited and spontaneous acts of foxy, physical love."

Betty appraised Frank for a long moment. "Well, *Frank*— you're getting more amazing by the *inch*, you greasy halitosis *sleaze* bag." Betty took a big drag from her cigarette and blew smoke in Frank's face.

Frank began to lean down anyway, with his tongue already poking two inches out of his mouth, to French kiss Betty, who was seventy-nine years old. Frank, forty-two. Just then the front door blew open and four hundred and thirty-two pound Herman Warthawg, a member for fifty years of Augusta National Golf Club and the third richest human being in the world (self-made chicken parts rendering magnate from Cow, Texas) who just so happened to be the newly elected chairman of the Radar and Air Space Committee of the club and the long-time Tournament Volunteer Discipline Committee Chairman, rumbled toward the reception desk. Mr. Warthawg had never once in his life been told he bellowed when he spoke even though people always cringed and sort of leaned back when he spoke/bellowed at them.

Betty stopped squeezing Frank's scrotum and tossed her cigarette into Frank's coffee mug. "Mr. Warthawg! Good to see you again! How was your submarine trip to the polar ice cap?"

"OVERRATED!"

"Well I'm so sorry to hear that!"

"BETTY! CUT ALL PLEASANTRIES. HOW'S IT LOOKING OUT THERE TODAY? MY FELLOW MEMBERS CROWDING UP THE COURSE AS USUAL?"

Seven and a half hour rounds today. Waiting on every shot. Betty lied, "You'll have it all to your-self!"

"STIMP?"

"Seventeen!"

"TOO SLOW! WHO DO YOU HAVE TO FIRE AROUND HERE TO GET THEIR ATTENTION? HAVE THEM SPEED UP THE GREENS BEFORE I GET OUT THERE!"

"Yes, Mr. Warthawg! I'll find someone for you to fire."

Mr. Warthawg caught a glance at Betty's computer screen, then openly gawked. "HOLY LORD IN HEAVEN HAVE MERCY SWEET PRECIOUS JESUS!" WHAT'S WRONG WITH THAT PERSON?"

Betty said as if she were describing someone who just died, "Mr. Warthawg, this is the latest catch. A Waymon Poodle of Mullet Luv, Georgia—who just called."

"TRYING TO GET ON, HUH?"

"Afraid so. Yes."

Mr. Warthawg wagged his big fat pointing finger—which

also had a bellowing quality to it—at Betty then at Frank who sort of snapped to attention so quickly he jerked coffee all over his club logoed tie. His purple wang doodle was already at attention.

"IF I EVER SEE THIS SPACE ALIEN LOOKING PERSON AT AUGUSTA NATIONAL GOLF CLUB SO MUCH AS ROTO-ROOTERING AN EXPLODING COMMODE—"

"Yes, Mr. Warthawg," Betty said.

"Yes, Mr. Warthawg," Frank said.

"THEN YOU TWO WILL BE IMMEDIATELY AND WITHOUT HESITATION RELIEVED OF YOUR—"

"Yes, Mr. Warthawg?"

"Yes, Mr. Warthawg?"

Mr. Warthawg lowered his voice just a little: "DO I NEED TO CONTINUE?"

"No, Mr. Warthawg."

"Yes, Mr. Warthawg."

"WHAT!?"

Frank croaked, "I mean—*no* Mr. Warthawg."

"THAT'S WHAT I THOUGHT. NOW ALERT MY CADDIE!" Mr. Warthawg started for the secret locker room door, bumping the one hundred and ninety-eight pound solid gold bust of Dwight Eisenhower off of a side table and onto the floor. Fat finger pointing at the bust as it rocked back and forth: "SOMEBODY PICK THAT HEAD UP!" Then he disappeared through the door.

Betty gripped Frank's scrotum again.

Frank flicked his tongue at her.

Then they both said in unison: "What an irksome individual," and began rubbing their hands all over each other's bodies while they French kissed enthusiastically.

And the phone rang again at Augusta National Golf Club.

# Volunteerism

"GOOD MORNING! AUGUSTA National *Golf* Club! This is Betty *Simp*son. How may I *help* you?" Her voice was yet again as sweet and as pleasant as Shirley Temple's.

"Yes. This is Waymon Poodle calling again?"

"Mr. *Poo*dle," she said as if hearing from someone thought to be dead for thirty years, "it's so good to *hear* from you again!" Then Betty breathed into the phone with a hand cupped to the side of her mouth as if discussing something confidential, "How did it go with Mr. Rafsooliwicki?"

"He seemed to be about to bite a clam sandwich."

"Well, Mr. Poodle, he is a busy *man*. Busy, busy, *busy*. Always about to bite a clam sandwich. Did you get the job?"

"I'm not sure."

"Would you like to speak with him again?"

"I'm not sure."

"Well, he's probably about to bite another clam sandwich anyway. Or sometimes he's about to lick a taco. You know, if the man's near a snapper, fresh or spoiled, he goes nuts for that, too, that Emiglio. Well—*any*how—is there something *else* I can do for you Mr. Poodle?" Betty said as she flipped open the safety cover of a bright red button on her desk, then poised her finger over the button of a device that could, depending on how she felt that day, mildly or severely electrocute the head of the person on the other end of the line.

"Well, yes, there *might* be."

"And what is that? How may I *help* you?"

Waymon swallowed hard. "I'd like to inquire—"

"*Yes*, Mr. Poodle?"

"—about how to be a volunteer for the tournament. You know, the—"

"The Masters?"

"Yes. The—*Masters*." Waymon took a huge breath.

"Well isn't that *wonderful!*" Betty said "wonderful" as if she were competing in a contest of who could say the word with the most gut wrenching exhilaration. "Well, Mr. Poodle, you've certainly called at the right time and to the right place. This *is* the home of the Masters and I am extremely pleased to announce that I have an *immediate* volunteer opening, even though the tournament is just one week away and even though we have such a huge and loyal volunteer corps that we haven't even *needed* a waiting list in the last twenty-eight years. It's truly unbe*leee*vable that we can accommodate your request at such incredibly short notice, but we're more than happy to. *More* than happy." Betty fired up another cigarette. That chicken lip rendering piece of— threaten *me* with my job? After sitting my butt in this chair with no armrests for over half my life listening to you scream and complain for fifty years? Yes indeedie—I think I'm gonna stick a Poodle four feet up your rear end, Warthawg. Betty took a suck of that cigarette as if it was the last suck she'd ever get.

Waymon's heart began to race even harder. He tried to speak, to say thank you one thousand times Mrs. Simpson, but nothing would come out.

"Mr. Poodle? Are you *there*?"

Nothing.

"Are you *there*, Mr. Poodle?"

Finally, faintly: "Yes. Don't you need—uh—a resume or anything? References? A personal meeting with the board of directors? Do you need to talk to the assistant pro at the Mullet Luv Golf Center about me?"

"Not at *all* Mr. Poodle. We actually know all we need to know," Betty said as she squinted at a satellite photo of Waymon talking to man who, *damn*, looked exactly like Rhett Butler. "And we are absolutely honored you've picked Augusta National Golf Club and its rich and historic major tournament heritage and whatnot in which to lend your time and skills as opposed to some hideous Australasian golf event in Fiji or something."

"I think I'm about to *faint*, Mrs. Simpson."

"Then you just go right ahead and faint, Mr. Poodle. And when you wake up you can look forward to to*morrow* morning, the earliest and most ex*pen*sive delivery, where one of those nice Federal Express truck drivers, hopefully wearing those tight little blue shorts, will deliver to you at the TrustTrust Bank branch in the Publix grocery store on Confederate Victory Parkway in Mullet Luv a package from me with *all* the details on how to be a Masters volunteer and how to get signed up for the volunteer outing in May where you'll get to play the Augusta National Golf Club course as well as our par *three* course. Actually, you'll have an entire *day* to play as much golf on the two Augusta National Golf Club courses as you can possibly pack in before the sun goes down. And it's all *free*. And now that you're in the volunteer corps, you're a volunteer for the rest of your *life* and can play golf at Augusta National Golf Club every single year for the rest of your life on volunteer day, you know, if it doesn't get rained *out*, but volunteer day hasn't been rained out in thirty-nine *years*. Just remember to bring your own golf balls and clubs. We don't have rentals, so we have to turn away a lot of Japanese guests. So how does *that* sound, Mr. Poodle?"

Nothing.

"Mr. Poodle?"

# *A Docking*

THE WOUND IN the center of Waymon's forehead—obtained by fainting, and then falling like a chopped tree upon the cupola of the clubhouse model of Augusta National Golf Club in the second bedroom of apartment 1931—was hideous.

It was a wound that looked as if someone held Waymon down and reared back and clocked him one good time with a ball-peen hammer. The wound, bloody in the center, with a swollen purple and yellow ring around it, seemed to visibly throb, as if it had its own heartbeat. If Waymon ever looked like an individual who popped in from outer space, then he did now.

Waymon, the branch manager Waymon, was actually tapping his wristwatch when Waymon walked, or sort of stumbled, into the employee break room of the branch office. "This has *certainly* been a new and fascinating interpretation of an extra ten minutes, Mr. Poodle."

"Like I said, *dock* me."

"Oh I most certainly *will*—because since I'm the boss I *can!*" Waymon caught a look at the wound as Waymon brushed past him. "My *God!* What sort of personal business were you *up* to?

"The personal kind. Now I need to go serve my valued customers. Excuse me."

"*My* customers? It's *our* customers! They're not all *yours!* And not with that creepy bloody *mess* on your pumpkin head!" Waymon shouted at Waymon's back.

But Waymon was already at his window—squawking with unconditional professional affection for the next valued customer to come and be served.

# Let's Get It On

A FEDEX DELIVERY guy, the next morning, in tight little blue shorts, rushed through the two sets of sliding doors at the Publix on Confederate Victory Parkway, took a left and approached Waymon as he sat at his window waiting for a valued customer.

But not a valued customer because it was Waymon Boner sitting there and not Waymon Poodle. Waymon Boner, even though he was a branch manager secretly thought customers were a horrible nuisance and did not particularly value them. He was also upset he had to work a window today because Katrina, a large woman teller who couldn't hear well and absolutely refused to shave her mustache and had a tattoo on her neck and who had just gotten off the boat from Latvia, had to leave for the day as she'd broken both her arms and legs that morning on aisle eight. She had slipped on a shrimp. A shrimp she had started to "sample," but had spit out on the floor. Then slipped on it. Waymon was also upset this Latvian person who had only been working at the branch for four days, would probably "own" Publix after a couple of legal proceedings. So there he sat, Waymon, all upset.

"Waymon?" the FedEx guy said, holding a letter-sized package.

"Yes?"

"Sign here. Thanks."

Waymon looked at the address block on the FedEx package. From Augusta National Golf Club. A Betty Simpson. Nice handwriting. To a Mr. Waymon R. Poodle. "*Ohhhh,*" he moaned, looking over at Waymon next to him, serving Old Mrs. Willard again. "This is for Waymon *Pooooo*dle." Waymon motioned with a thumb over toward Waymon.

The FedEx guy hated it when he got held up by being sucked into some weird internal office joke or people who obviously hated each other or some funked-up attitude. Plus, these Waymon guys looked real strange. The FedEx guy and Waymon Poodle did the signing tango and the FedEx guy rushed back out. Waymon, upon reading the address blocks, felt his forehead wound begin to pound again, his throat squeeze shut, and without thinking he handed Old Mrs. Willard, instead of her money, a yellow Post-It pad and a stapler.

Waymon Boner, mouth open, watched Waymon slink toward the break room without asking permission. Immediately, on instinct, without hesitation, and even before Waymon got to the break room door, Waymon mashed a little buzzer button that buzzed in the break room. When the break room buzzer buzzed, it meant help was immediately needed up front even if an employee of the branch were having a heart attack or eating a burrito. Waymon mashed the buzzer twice: *buzz—buzz*.

Waymon sat at the break room table, with hands trembling with excitement, and opened the package. He pulled out its contents. Reverently, his mantra excited his mouth. "I'm gonner tee it up at Augusta National. They didn't touch the stuff in the second bedroom. Mitch and Ken didn't touch the stuff in the second bedroom...

*Buzz—buzz.*

On Augusta National Golf Club stationery, in memo form, written to Waymon from Betty Simpson, in crisp, boring, old school, conservative, twelve point New Times Roman, were the following words:

THE MEMO: Augusta National Golf Club is honored to have you as a volunteer for the Masters golf tournament. I personally know your involvement will alter the future of Augusta National Golf Club.

WAYMON: "Dang."

60

*Buzz—buzz.*

THE MEMO: And your volunteer number will be 1931.

WAYMON: "Dang—*dang*."

*Buzz—buzz.*

THE MEMO: This Sunday morning you are to meet at exactly 9 o' clock the Augusta National Golf Club Radar and Air Space and Tournament Volunteer Discipline Committee Chairman, Mr. Herman Warthawg, in the amphitheater of the media center to be briefed on your duties as Manager of the Rope at the Practice Facility Invitee Entrance and Exit and to pick up your volunteer credential and yellow helmet. Please be prompt. You will be the only volunteer to be briefed as you are the only new volunteer to be accepted into the group in twenty-eight years so Mr. Warthawg is excited he has something to do.

WAYMON: "I get a *hel*met."

*Buzz—buzz.*

THE MEMO: When Mr. Warthawg enters the room, please immediately stand up like you've been shocked by electricity and face Mr. Warthawg directly and when he asks your name, please tell him your whole name slowly to make sure he understands your whole name one hundred percent and extend your right hand to see if he wants to shake it. If Mr. Warthawg seems stunned and doesn't say anything for a moment and/or begins blubbering and huffing and puffing his cheeks or looking around the media amphitheater like he's trying to find somebody playing a joke on him, say your whole name again, a little more loudly the second time, and tell him you're the guy from Mullet Luv, Georgia. Waymon Poodle from Mullet Luv, Georgia. More than likely, he'll immediately exit the media center real fast and your meeting with Mr. Warthawg will be concluded at that point. Just make sure you grab your volunteer credential and yellow helmet and appear at your post promptly at 8 o' clock Monday morning in real boring khaki pants, a real boring white golf shirt and clean sneakers. You get a smock from us.

*Buzz—buzz—buzz.*

WAYMON: "Okay then."

THE MEMO: Directions to Augusta National Golf Club and its media center are enclosed. (They were enclosed.)

THE MEMO: Once again, we are pleased to have you as a volunteer. Your presence at this year's Masters will be, because of this feeling I have, not ordinary. Now please read the next correspondence. Thank you very much.

*Buzz, buzz.*

The next correspondence was a hand written letter on heavily perfumed, pink stationery from Betty Simpson to Waymon. The next correspondence also included a helpful photograph at which Waymon was very focusly gazing.

WAYMON, very focusly gazing at the helpful photograph: "Oh, my *Lord.*"

*Buzz—buzz—buzz—buzz.*

THE NEXT CORRESPONDENCE: Dear Waymon, On a personal note—you need a place to stay. I called all the motels and they're booked, as usual. North to Raleigh. South to Orlando. West to Phenix City. And East to Myrtle Beach. So I've got a wonderful proposal—why don't you stay with me? I've got a one bedroom apartment and you certainly won't sleep on the kitchen floor or in the bathtub so you'll just sleep in my bed on top of me. Okay? Don't worry. I'll be happy to cook and take great care of a void in your life. I know you have a void. Know what I mean? Your particular void? Really, where else were you going to stay? In the trunk of your car?

*Buzz—buzz—buzz.*

So, come see me in the clubhouse after your meeting with Mr. Warthawg Sunday morning and I'll go over the exciting details. Let's Get It On, Betty.

THE HELPFUL PHOTOGRAPH: Betty was sitting by a swimming pool with a cigarette in one hand and a can of Miller Lite in the other. Dark sunglasses. Dark tan. Big smile. Sharp yellow teeth. And a teeny weenie leopard-skin bikini.

*Buzzzzzzzzzzzzzz.*

# Give a Damn

THAT AFTERNOON AFTER work, Waymon was in the parking lot of Sans Souci fiddling with his trunk lid.

Closing it, but not hard enough for it to catch. Then pushing the lid back up again and poking his head in the trunk—looking around in there—then he'd pull his big head back out again then poke his big head back in again.

Mr. Gable was out walking his Chihuahua with one of those electronic leashes with the shock button and watched this odd scene for a moment from behind a pick-up truck. Then, on purpose, because Mr. Gable was fairly bored, he and the Chihuahua snuck up behind Waymon and Mr. Gable hit the shock button and the Chihuahua barked real loud and it scared the hell out of Waymon. Plus, Waymon thought Chihuahuas were, of all the dogs in the dog world, messengers of some kind. He thought that for no good reason, really, that they were messengers of some kind, Chihuahuas, but had no proof. That's just what Waymon thought and God forbid Waymon Poodle change course on something.

Mr. Gable got a good chuckle seeing Waymon bump the back of his head against the sharp tab of the lock.

But of course Waymon had that irritating, Christian, unconditional, and immediate power of forgiveness, and even as he was in horrible pain and rubbing the back of his head and gazing at that Chihuahua, Waymon asked Mr. Gable how he was doing today.

"If I was any bettah," Mr. Gable said in his horrible New

York infected, forced Charleston, South Carolina accent as he went to town on a piece of gum, "then I'd have to be locked *up*." Mr. Gable gave Waymon a strange look. "You know what I mean there Waymon?"

"I'm not really sure what you mean, Mr. Gable. But I'd certainly hate to see you locked *up*."

"Well, what would you want to see me—you know—*do?*"

Waymon turned and poked his head back into the trunk. "To have a nice day."

"Hey, I can live wid dat."

The reason for all this innuendo—imbedded in every single conversation every single time Mr. Gable encountered Waymon in the years they'd lived at Sans Souci together—was that Mr. Gable secretly thought Waymon might be a hit man from any number of very, very upset New York, New Jersey, Detroit, Las Vegas, Los Angeles, Philadelphia, Miami, Chicago, Boston, Kansas City, Biloxi, Reno, Atlantic City, New Orleans, Toronto, London, Tokyo, Tunica, Hong Kong, and Moscow crime families. Mr. Gable asked, "Mind if I ask watcha doin' there, Waymon, lookin' around in ya trunk, there?"

Waymon was so focused on what he was doing he didn't say anything, so Mr. Gable shocked the Chihuahua again so he'd bark. The Chihuahua barked.

"Hey!"

"I asked whatcha *doin'* there."

"I'm trying to see if a person could fit in the *trunk* space."

"Like *who* are you thinking might need to fit in the trunk space there, God forbid?"

"Me."

"*You*, Waymon? And why would you need to fit into the trunk space there?" Mr. Gable, at this moment, was as sincere as he could be, as he was an expert at putting whole bodies and bodies that had been altered in order to fit into trunks of cars, and he sincerely felt he could, after all these years, really connect with Waymon and assist him with something useful, even if the body was still alive and squirming when it was placed into said trunk.

"I'm gonner need a place to stay while I'm on a special vacation next week."

"You tawkin about stayin' in da *trunk?*"

"Yessir."

"Sleepin'—in da *trunk?*"

"Yessir." Waymon turned and gazed into the trunk of his Chrysler Diplomat and smiled. He spread his arms. "Yessir. Right here."

"Lemmeassyouaquession."

That Chihuahua barked again.

"Where would youse be goin' where you gotta stay in a stinkin' *trunk?* Unless ya *dead.*"

Waymon reached out and patted the Chihuahua's head. "Augusta."

# PART III

## A BERMUDA GRASS MASTERS

# As for Mr. Warthawg

HERMAN WARTHAWG WAS not having a good Masters week not one bit.

His particular anxieties began Sunday morning—the tournament week hadn't officially started yet—and there he was having to huff and puff his cheeks out and look around the media amphitheater like he was trying to find somebody playing a joke on him. Well, not having to. To him it came naturally, the huffing and puffing part, sure, but it took a lot of energy to do it at that rate.

Folks just didn't understand. It also took a lot of energy to be the third richest human being on earth and the newly elected chairman of the Augusta National Golf Club Radar and Air Space Committee and the long-time Tournament Volunteer Discipline Committee Chairman and to deal with the hurricane force of this Waymon Poodle of Mullet Luv situation. Plus, he was already overwhelmed with the volume of mail being sent by some crazy woman to Masters invitee Chi Chi Rodriguez which in the former role he had to collect, read, and then go off somewhere and figure out what to do. And this wasn't the usual amount sent to the Puerto Rican professional in advance of the tournament, one letter and a post card or a fax. But this year, whoever this woman was, had sent Mr. Rodriguez eight hundred and forty-eight hand-written letters on stinky pink stationery. So Warthawg had opened the first one, then another, and all the others. Sometime during the Masters, she was planning to show Chi Chi her OH, MY GOD because she couldn't get as worked up when she thought about showing her OH, MY GOD to Hale Irwin or Loren Roberts.

My God, Warthawg thought upon each reading of a letter. Written by hand, no less, the obscene word. Fine, you sex freak woman, but why not show it to Mr. Rodriguez at an event in Palm Springs or Las Vegas? This is the Masters, ma'am. The— *Ma*sters.

So see you at the Masters, each note warned at the end.

Warthawg had never seen such depravity in his life. Why would some woman want to show Chi Chi her OH, MY GOD?

Plus—plus—this was the first time in his life someone had not done what Herman Warthawg told them to do. The source of his additional and extreme displeasure was right there in front of him, not ten inches away. Said slowly, his whole name, as instructed by Betty Simpson, Waymon Poodle of Mullet Luv, Georgia. Who was supposed to have been not allowed onto the property. Not even to fix an exploding commode. Of which Waymon would have been happy to fix.

And now he was one of my volunteers?

Warthawg was blubbering and huffing and puffing. Nothing understandable was coming out.

Waymon was sort of reaching for his yellow helmet and credential held by Warthawg's personal Pinkerton who seemed nervous too.

And then Warthawg, as Betty Simpson predicted, immediately left the media center real fast.

Waymon stood at attention for another ten minutes or so just to make sure. To make sure of what he didn't really know.

Mr. Warthawg, on the other hand, charged up to the clubhouse and banged through the front door to find Betty Simpson with a finger poised over the "Enter" key of her keyboard. Kind of in a hook-like position.

"BETTY!"

"Hi *Herm*. What's shakin'?"

68

"I JUST THOUGHT YOU'D LIKE TO KNOW THAT
WAYMON POODLE IS ON THE PREMISES."

"You're not *pleased?*"

Warthawg suddenly sensed something, as he was a sensitive
person. He squinted at her computer monitor, then at her
crooked finger over an important key, then back at the photo of
him fornicating with President Clinton on a nice blue and white
striped Martha Stewart lounge chair on the sun deck of a nice
yacht by a nice side table with two uneaten shrimp cocktails. But
not the two of them fornicating with other people as couples who
may or may not be swinging. Simply, Herman Warthawg
fornicating with the President. "IS THAT ME THERE, WITH A
MARIJUANA CIGARETTE BETWEEN MY LIPS, ON TOP OF
THE PRESIDENT OF THE UNITED STATES, FORNI—?"

Betty leaned toward the screen for a closer look. She tapped
the screen with a sharp fingernail. "That's you—*yes*—right there,
making monkey love to Hillary—a *lot.*" She moved the monitor so
he could see the picture better. "See, I've got this great new
software program where I can cut and paste photographs together
and extort folks such as yourself. Well, not a bunch of folks—just
*you.* Of course, I have some recent satellite shots of you and your
downstairs maid doing the afternoon delight on your diving board
back at the ranch. Those shots are real, although I can't tell who's
flinging around the riding crop. I love your expression. Like to
see those, too?"

Warthawg grabbed his chest, then his neck, and then his
chest again. "QUESTION!"

"Yes?"

"AND WHY DO YOU HAVE YOUR FINGER POISED
OVER THAT KEY THERE?"

"Well, *Herm.* If I happened to press this key *here*"—Betty
barely touched it with the tip of her sharp looking fingernail—
"then this photograph and its brief paragraph of descriptive
information I wrote myself describing who the two people are in
this photograph having flagrante de-lec-*ta*-to and smoking and
inhaling the smoke from a marijuana cigarette would be sent by an

e-mail blast to your board of directors, your shareholders, and your fellow members. And, oh, to all the golf writers in the world who would be extremely interested in knowing more. And there are a lot of golf writers. You're a *right* wing Republican, right?"

Warthawg grabbed his chest, then his neck, then his chest again, then leaned toward Betty, then cleared his throat, and dramatically adjusted his tone. "What would, Betty dear, say, keep you from, say, not pushing, Betty dear, that button there."

"Well, first, two million dollars."

"I'll write you a check immediately. Pocket change. *Glad* to do it. Certainly."

"Second..."

"Second?"

Second, and finally, since all this computer programming has about worn me slap out, why don't we allow our friend Waymon Poodle to have a wonderful Masters volunteer experience. And let's just make sure he's first on the list to play on volunteer day next month. I think it'll make his *life*. Sound okay?"

Warthawg grabbed his chest, then his neck, then his chest, and then his checkbook and wrote Betty Simpson a check for two million dollars.

"I forgot. And one other thing. *Sorry*."

Warthawg gave her a pretty mean look.

Betty pushed her finger in the direction of the key that would change the rest of Herman Warthawg's life schedule.

Warthawg made a pleasant expression. "And what would the *other* thing be? How may I assist you?"

"During the tournament, Waymon will need someone to bring him his lunch every day and an afternoon snack with an iced tea. Waymon loves iced tea, sweet, with, pay attention: nine freakin' lemons. Not *seven* lemons or *ten* lemons. *Nine*. I also performed some additional research on our boy and believe it or not, he actually loves our pimento cheese sandwiches and a new computer program I just bought from the CIA and the Culinary Institute of America predicts he's going to eat, in four point six seconds for each consumption, between two to three hundred of the things this week without breaking a world record for mammalian diarrhea production. So Herm, *honey*—have a waiter in *mind?*"

So Herm was not yet having a good Masters week not one bit.

# *Nakajima Sez*

AS FOR WAYMON, Masters week was going real super great.

For Waymon, in a word—intoxicating. He kept repeating it to himself, this lilting word, just under his breath, with his chin up. The Masters and the golf course on which it is played is—in*tox*icating. Thank you Jesus for this intox—i—*cation* because now I stand here on the hallowed grounds of where men golf. And thank you Jesus for this view of the clubhouse and behind me the sounds of eager patrons sitting in the Augusta sunshine in these green bleachers. Their conversations on golf, their favorite invitee. Thank you for that. Thank you for allowing me to overhear an informed, sophisticated, cerebral, attentive patron saying to his friend, "See, Edmond, the way the back of Jose Maria Olazabal's left hand is perpendicular to the target line at the moment of impact? *See?*"

And the man's friend had said, and Waymon had been intoxicated by hearing his incredible and observant and awe-inspiring response, "*Yes*, Samuel. I *did* see that our Spanish friend and two-time Masters champion's left hand *is* perpendicular to the target line at the moment of impact—and even right *after* impact for a moment. Yes, I *saw* it! That's such an important thing to *do* in golf."

"*But*," Samuel said, "I've *also* read, Edmund, where you don't want your left hand to be perpendicular after impact for *too* long—as it's urged by some of the finer teaching professionals that a golfer turn his hands over soon *after* impact."

"Samuel, you *certainly* must realize, my fellow lover of golf, that so *much* of what we're told and so *much* of what we read about the mechanics of the golf swing *is*, well, to be *frank*— contradictory."

Tiger Woods and Fuzzy Zoeller and Tommy Aaron and Roberto DeVicenzo and their caddies all backed up at the rope there, wondering when this dumb ass inbred, wall-eyed hick is gonna open his eyes and lift up the damn rope and let us through so we can go warm the hell up.

"Contradictory, *sure*. But *per*haps, Edmond, that's what makes the game of golf so incredibly wonderful, mysterious, and forever challenging on a supremely personal basis."

Waymon, nearly weeping. Floating toward heaven.

"Samuel?"

"Yes, Edmond?"

"Praise Jesus for *golf*."

"Edmond?"

"Yes, Samuel?"

"Jesus *made* golf."

Oh, thank *you* Jesus, Waymon pondered with his eyes clenched shut. Praise you for golf, for bringing golf into our lives, for saving our *lives* with golf. And thank *you* for this incredible yellow helmet which fits perfectly and I think I can keep.

Intoxicating.

And why not?

As Manager of the Rope at the Practice Facility Invitee Entrance and Exit, Waymon Poodle stood in an action spot—a spot where important action took place. A spot made for the most decisive and poised volunteer. Here comes Seve Ballesteros out of the clubhouse. Seve Ballesteros coming this way with a wad of autograph seekers tripping over themselves, agitating him. Shoving things at him. A couple of Pinkertons. His caddie, with the heavy golf bag on his shoulder, muscling forward. Keeping it moving. So when to pull the rope aside for such great men and their caddies? Sometimes the great man and his caddie and his swing coach? Sometimes the great man and his caddie and his

73

swing coach and his agent and his golf psychologist and his nutritionist? When they're ten feet away? Five feet? Twenty feet and risk some kid squirting onto the practice range to grab something and run off and hawk it out there on Washington Road?

Certainly not. Most certainly not.

Waymon Poodle of Mullet Luv, Georgia determined that the pulling aside of the rope—begun with a confident pulling up of the end of the rope which had been tied into a loop—from the end of a beautiful green metal rod thrust into the ground by some obvious expert, some expert who had went around the entire grounds of Augusta National Golf Club thrusting beautiful green metal rods into this sacred soil at the most exact and logical places, that the decision to pull the rope up and off the rod and to move aside with the rope in one hand and to gently, but with a certain amount of authority, sweep back these beloved patrons with the other hand, was made on a case by case basis. And Waymon Poodle was in charge of making that case by case basis decision from 8 o' clock each morning until the final invitee left the practice range. Charles Coody, six feet. Funk, nine. Goosen, Hjertstedt, Struver, and Gogol. Hennie Otto, Bruce Fleisher, just depended. And so on.

And so on they came. Still wearing metal spikes most of the these great men, their clicking on the asphalt, a warning. Here I come. I'm serious about this. Move outta the way folks. I appreciate your affection for me and that you want me to sign something and smile at you and touch your kid on the top of the head or give you a golf ball or my lucky Krugerrand but I'm comin' through. Got to warm up, find my swing for today. I wanna win the Masters real bad, a butt wad load more than those *other* three major championships of the year and I'm not going to the British Open this year because I hate the weird, unpredictable weather—well, you can predict it: it sucks out my greasy butt every day—and I hate the courses they choose and the gross food and those drunk little dried up caddies they got over there that they force on you, so I got only one of three major championship chances this year. I do, folks. Really wanna win the Masters. Look at the expression on my face. Looking serious. Real serious and focused on hitting it close to the pin and making a butt wad load of putts, especially saving the big ones for TV on Sunday. Came all the way from Sweden, came all the way from South Africa, came all the way from Arkansas, came all the way from England, came all the way from the toilet in the men's locker room to win the Masters, so get the hell outta my way and I'll pat your kid on the head later and give him my golf ball after I walk off eighteen after shooting something real nice in the low sixties. Thank you so much. Now let me go win the Masters.

Tommy Nakajima, on Monday, spikes clicking, had said something to Waymon in Japanese as the rope was lifted by Waymon—"Look at this guy who might be from outer space limits"—and Waymon knew it was a compliment. Surely it was. The great Japanese professional. Yes, say it slowly. *Nahhh— kahhh—jeeeeee—maaaahhhh.*

Waymon bows to him now, every morning, upon his coming and going.

Sluman, Palmer, Jack Nicklaus. Mize, Parnevik, Eichelberger. Their paths crossed each day in this holy place. Waymon Poodle, wide eyed. Rich Beem. Esteban Toledo. Sergio Garcia's dad.

Kids wanted Waymon's autograph, too. But I'm not an invitee, Waymon protested. But felt flattered. *You* again. Didn't I give you my autograph yesterday? Waymon chuckling, but still signing the visor, the cap, the hat, the occasional sweaty bicep. Now I told you yesterday I'm not an invitee—I'm not *anybody.* I'm just Waymon Poodle, Manager of the Rope at the Practice Facility Invitee Entrance and Exit. I'm just—so—so—*happy* about all this. I—just—can't wait—to play Augusta National Golf Club next month, all day until the sun goes down, and for the rest of my life on each and every volunteer day, including the par three course. No, kid, I'm not crying—well, I can't *lie* to you—I guess it's all this—this—intoxicating, beautiful pollen.

# Q&A With Huge Pecker

MOST PROMPTLY, AT noon on Wednesday of Masters week, Leonard "Huge Pecker" Leboeuf, chairman of Augusta National Golf Club and the Masters, strode into the media center amphitheater with his green jacketed mob of one hundred or so committee chairmen waddling behind him for the annual golf writer welcome and briefing.

Noon was real early in the morning for golf writers.

The only other time in their lives they're awake and doing something at that ungodly time of day, was if they're teeing off at some real nice private club, or exceptionally real nice public club, or exceptionally real nice resort, after goofing the head pro or the general manager or vice president of marketing for a free round of golf. Otherwise, there they are, golf writers, sitting in the Augusta National Golf Club media center at noon on the Wednesday of Masters week for the annual golf writer welcome and briefing from the chairman, really wanting to be drinking coffee and smoking a cigarette in their hotel room in their underwear wondering why there aren't any real good titty clubs in Augusta they can go enjoy after a hard day of golf journalism.

The real and unspoken incentive for a golf writer to be sitting on his or her ass and acting real quiet at noon in the amphitheater of the Augusta National Golf Club media center on Wednesday of Masters' week was that if you didn't show up for this thing your chances of being chosen out of the golf writer's lottery to play Augusta National Golf Club all you want the Monday after the final round of the tournament for free was swirled down the toilet.

The golf writers who were awake, since nothing else real big was going on in the world of golf at that moment, were wondering why the new chairman of the club, a man of such stature in the world of industry and commerce and golf, went by the nickname of "Huge Pecker." Seemed like "Large Pecker" would have done the job. Plus, they were still recovering from the last chairman's nickname: "Felix." And the chairman before Felix insisted he be called by the world of golf, "Hootie," whose real name was Butch or something like that. So there they were, golf writers from all over the world, wondering about these important things in all their different languages.

Huge Pecker, seated behind the podium, clearing his throat a lot, waited for all the committee chairmen to get settled in along the walls of the media center. This took a little while as some committee chairmen were over one hundred and ten years old and were facing the wrong way or were muttering something about being up at such an ungodly hour and wondering why there still weren't any real good titty clubs in Augusta. Twenty-eight committee chairmen had nurses trying to hold them up.

The media center was finally real quiet as all the golf writers were afraid to breath or make their chairs squeak or have their cell phone go off or their laptop computer batteries go dead and make that beeping noise as this would also, they were pretty sure, be a mark against them in that lottery business.

"Boys," Huge Pecker said real smooth into the microphone in a Cajun-type drawl. He was an oil tycoon from Louisiana. Twenty-four handicap. Big slicer. Former L.S.U. fullback. Was dating Zsa Zsa Gabor and was afraid he might have gotten her real pregnant last week. "We welcome you to Augusta National Golf Club and wish you good golf typing. Each year at this time I read a wildly informative, prepared statement to you boys and then look forward to your questions. As you *know*, I am happy to answer any questions specifically pertaining to the toonamint and the golf course. Even questions about the *driving* range are okay with me. Go crazy. But questions concerning anything about the club and *us* guys are strictly forbidden, and if you *ask* me one then that'll be a mark against you concerning the media day *lott*ery business. We keep a big list of shit around here, as you *know*. So if any of you boys ask me one about the club or us guys, then sometime this week I'll sneak up behind you while you're typing something— even if some of you women are *men*—and mess you *up*."

All the golf writers shifted uncomfortably in their seats and looked around at each other. One golf writer's seat squeaked a little bit and he almost passed out.

"*So*—the first order of business is to tell you we have the first new volunteer in twenty-eight years. His name is Waymon Poodle and he's from Mullet Luv, Georgia and also resides in Mullet Luv and he'll be efficiently lifting up the rope to the invitee entrance and exit at the practice facility and then efficiently putting the rope back down on the metal rod all week, you know, when an invitee wants to go warm up or whatever. I also hear this gentleman is real funky looking. Anybody give a shit about this Waymon Poodle?"

In unison, one hundred or so golf writers murmured, "No, sir, Huge Pecker!" And one hundred or so shrugged their shoulders. Snaps. Pops. One guy thought he had broken his spine, but he bit his right pointing finger, almost in two, to keep from screaming.

"Fine, *fine*," Huge Pecker said. "Furthermore, Augusta National Golf Club wants to acknowledge that we know *you* know some *crazy* women has been sending the club letters about how she is planning to show Masters' invitee Chi Chi Rodreeeguez of Pota Reeco a certain part of her *person* during this year's Masters. *How* you have obtained this information is most amazing to me as we really try to keep this sort of thing real quiet around here and Herman Warthawg behind me, Chairman of the Augusta National Golf Club Radar and Air Space Committee and Toonamint Volunteer Discipline Committee Chairman, is quite at a loss as well, as he told me he locked up all the crazy woman's letters in his locker and hid a few behind some socks in the *pro* shop. Why *any*body would buy overpriced pro shop golf socks is a mystery to me when there's a nice Dillard's right out there on Washington *Road*. Nonetheless, we know some of these letters have been obtained by you folks and you've been reading them in your underwear and passing them back and forth to each other in the bars in your hotels and giggling. We know *you* know in this crazy women's correspondence that she has used the ob-*scene* word regarding the particular part of her body she plans to reveal to Mr. Rod*reee*guez. Certainly, boys, you must do *your* job, but we must do *ours*. In your reporting, Augusta National Golf Club asks you, instead of using the ob-*scene* word, to use the following words..." Huge Pecker paused for a moment whereas hundreds of golf writer breaths could be heard sucking in, in anticipation.

A lady golf writer from Tennessee thought the words might be, "Her Priscilla Presley."

A golf writer from England thought the words might be, "Her Naughty Bit." Then he thought about it a moment longer, and then changed his mind to, "Her Very Quivering and Mysterious Naughty Bit."

A golf writer for a newspaper in Alaska thought the words might be, "Eskimo Fever," as he was intensely fantasizing, at that very moment, about some Eskimos who lived in the apartment above him back home.

A golf writer from North Carolina thought the words might be, "Her Quail Hollow."

Sitting in the front row, a lady golf writer for *USA Today*, who was pretty darn sure it was Huge Pecker who had some goons sneak into her office and change around her typewriter keys after she wrote that column that exposed to the world Augusta National Golf Club didn't have any members who didn't have peckers, didn't care one bit about what words he wanted them to use. She lit a long fireplace-style match, leaned over onto her left butt cheek, lifted her right knee way up then moved it way over to the right, put the end of the lit match very close to her anus, grit her teeth, groaned, growled, turned red, then turned purple, and cut an astonishing fart she'd been saving for three and a half weeks—since the tournament at Doral. The blue fart flame was eight feet long.

Huge Pecker ducked behind the podium, into which she carved her initials with the tip of the flame, which was hissing. Huge Pecker thought about getting one of his Pinkertons to haul her out by her hair, but then he figured if she had the ability to produce a blue fart flame, especially an eight foot long blue fart flame, then he didn't want to tangle with this kitty. He had a golf tournament to run. So Huge Pecker decided to have some flowers, golf socks, and a case of pimento cheese sandwiches sent over to her hotel room. Huge Pecker popped back up real quick and raised a finger in an important looking way.

The golf writers quit thinking about what the words might be and crushed out their cigarettes and cigars and dumped the contents of the bowls of their pipes on the floor and gave Huge Pecker their absolute and supreme attention. Even that lady golf writer made her fart flame stop. When the flame flew back into her anus it made a backfire—*pop!*

Huge Pecker said, "...'Bermuda grass,' *boys*, if you please, in the place of the ob-*scene* word. These precious words, 'Bermuda grass,' which are well known to those who love and respect the game of golf, were chosen by me and the men you see standing behind me in a big super special meeting late last night over highballs and crudités. The words are spelled capital b-e-r-m—"

All the golf writers sucked in a real deep breath and started scribbling, spastically, on their note pads or typing, spastically, on their laptop computers as if they were being told in advance the numbers for the Super Lotto.

"—u-d-a g-r-a-s-s. Bermuda grass should be capitalized, say, if the usage is in a headline such as, 'Bermuda Grass Watch Continues at Augusta National Golf Club,' you know, it being the first word in the sentence, but you probably know that kind of thing by now." Huge Pecker cleared his throat as he looked around the amphitheater to see if any golf writer looked offended. They were all smiling brightly at him. "Okay. Furthermore, Bermuda grass should be used as a noun in most cases. If you use Bermuda grass as a *verb*, as in 'Mr. Rodriguez got Bermuda grassed

80

over by a pine cone on Flowering Crab Apple during the second round,' then that would be, well, correct, I *guess*. Anyhow, Bermuda grass, boys. Thus endeth my prepared remarks. Welcome once again, by God, to Augusta National Golf Club and the goddamn *Masters*. Let's get her done."

Since playing in the media day outing was so important to the quality of their lives, and the two percent discount they got in the Masters merchandise mart, the golf writers stood and gave Huge Pecker a rousing applause that might have lasted for four or five years until Huge Pecker raised a finger again and they all shut up and sat down real quick.

"Thank you. I will now entertain your questions concerning this year's toonamint."

An arm raised: the hand at the end of the arm wiggling and flapping and twisting and squirming and thrashing around as if the hand were competing in a goodbye waving contest. Front row. Gary McCord of CBS in a lime green polyester jacket and an Augusta National Golf Club logoed tie and a white starched buttoned down shirt and gray pants with a fabric belt with Augusta National Golf Club logos all around it and shiny oxblood Weejuns with Augusta National Golf Club logoed ball markers in each one where pennies would go and his hair absolutely perfect and some cologne, but not too much. His eyes weren't puffy and it smelled like he'd brushed his teeth and finally shaved the greasy handlebar mustache off and everything. Actually, he had the mustache in a plastic bag in his pocket for good luck.

"*Please*," Huge Pecker said in a real sophisticated way.

Gary stood up and asked in perfect vocal modulations, "Huge Pecker, how much does it cost to get in?"

As if on cue, everybody laughed and laughed and slapped each other on the back and laughed and chuckled and pointed at Gary. This question he asked every year for the last seventeen years was sort of meant to be an ice breaker, but Gary deep down really, really, really wanted to be a member of Augusta National Golf Club and he thought it was a good way to secretly but openly learn as he was, like a lot of folks who join expensive golf clubs, thinking about cashing in his poorly performing golf equipment company stocks to cover the initiation and the first few months of dues and pro shop purchases.

But, oh no.

Huge Pecker was chuckling too, but in a Cajun accent-type way. "Well, now, *Gary*. You know I can't answer *that* question. How are the chill-ren?"

"Doing *great* Huge Pecker. Hey, you know the best part about kids, Huge Pecker?"

"What's that, Gary?"

"*Makin'* 'em."

Huge Pecker laughed so hard he gagged. "And how's Mrs. McCord doing? She's a pretty *gal*."

"I'll tell her so. I surely will tell her, Huge Pecker. Sure will."

"Fine, *fine*," Huge Pecker said, then turned around to see if any of his committee chairmen were paying attention.

One was. The chairman of the Tee Marker Placement Committee.

"Gary, it's always good to have you with us"—Huge Pecker waggled a finger at him—"but you talk good on the TV this weekend, okay?"

"Oh, I *will* Huge Pecker. I'll mention the fine job you're doing—a *lot*."

"Fine, Gary. *Fine*. How are you hittin' it lately?"

"I shot a seventy-*six* the other day. I did. With a darn *quad*."

"Super, Gary. Just super—a seventy-six. *Other* questions, Gary?"

"Speaking of *gals*, Huge Pecker—"

"Yes—*gals*..."

"Do you think you and your ubiquitous bucket hat wearin', red nosed, pot bellied, palsied, cirrhotic, corporate C-E-O, hush mouthed, Irish, good ol' boy, smug as hell, hog jowled, over par, bald head *members* will ever let some ol' saddle bag butt, slow playin', quadruple bogey makin', vodka slurpin', constantly complainin', cigarette suckin', mustache wearin', corporate C-E-

82

O, over par, *fat* woman be a member in this incredibly wonderful golf club?"

"Fine question, Gary. *Fine.* Only under a most com-*pelling* circumstance."

"Huge Pecker, please *give* us"——Gary waved his arms four or five times in dramatic, circular motions as if he were showing someone the Atlantic Ocean—"an example."

"Well, Gary, all I can say at this point is—I'll *know* it when I *see* it."

"The compelling circumstance?"

Huge Pecker raised an eyebrow. "Yes, most certainly. I'll *know* it when I *see* it. Just like I just *said*." Then he rolled his eyes and made a face.

"Okay then," Gary said. "Would this be the compelling circumstance, you huge question avoider?" Gary made a gesture with his hands as if he were measuring the size of a woman's breasts. Then he made another gesture as if he were holding the breasts up and weighing them, then another gesture, specifically with his fingers, as if he were squeezing the breasts, then twisting the nipples with the tips of his thumb and pointing finger.

Huge Pecker tilted his head appraisingly, and then rubbed his chin.

Then, Gary stuck his tongue out as far as it would go, then flipped his tongue up and back in his mouth and then did the whole tongue thing sequence about three or four more times.

Huge Pecker raised his other eyebrow. Then lit another cigarette.

Gary then put both hands behind his head, interlocked his fingers, and pumped his hips as if he were fornicating. He was also making a loud snarling sound. Gary sat down and winked at Huge Pecker two good times. Gary scribbled a note to that lady golf writer for *USA Today* which asked, "Can you teach me how to do that—while I eat a can of beans?"

Huge Pecker winked back, just once. "Now, Gary," he said, "don't lecture to *me!*" then laughed so loudly the microphone shorted out and blew up, then was replaced less than half of a second later by an Augusta National Golf Club audio-visual expert escorted by a Pinkerton. Huge Pecker said, "Other incredible questions from our golf writers?"

A hand raised. Sort of in the middle right. Glare off the diamond pinky ring was real bright.

"*Please.*"

Rod Suntan of the Las Vegas *Lost Wages*, who, in a secret ballot by all the golf writers in America, was voted to be the horniest golf writer on planet earth and was acclaimed for always having some humid sexual angle in every golf story he wrote, even stories about Craig Stadler or an agate score. "Rod *Sun*tan, babe, of the Las Vegas *Lost Wages*?"

"Please. What is your question?"

He was smacking gum. Really going to town on it.

"What is your *question?*"

"Say, Huge Pecker babe, where and *when* do you think this ol' gal will show Cheech her Bermuda grass?" Smack, smack. Pen ready.

"Rod, we don't exactly know. As is our policy, we'll let you folks know as soon as *we* do so you fellas can be right there on the spot to observe the Augusta National Golf Club Bermuda grass situation and type a word or two about it for your various publications."

"Hey thanks." Gum smacking. Gave Huge Pecker a wink and pointed at him. "Nice jackets."

"*Thank* you."

Hand raised. Sort of in the middle left.

"Domo," Huge Pecker said.

Domo? What the *hell*—isn't that Japanese? The golf writers turned to look. Huge Pecker knows Japanese? Oh yeah, that crazy little guy every year.

It was that smiling Hajime "Jimmy" Yamazaki of some hard to pronounce, much less read, newspaper over there, so they never voted him anything. They could have voted him friendly, though. He was real friendly, and he smiled all the time like the dickens. And they could have voted him to have the distinction, without embarrassment, of wearing the same polyester plaid jacket with a striped shirt every day to the tournament. Like the dickens. They could have done that.

Jimmy bowed. "Ah, Huge *Pecker*-san. Bermuda grass o mite, shigoto ni ikitai *desu*." Jimmy bowed again.

Huge Pecker pointed at him and smiled. "Hey, *Jim*bo. Tetsudatte kudasaimasen *ka?*" Huge Pecker asked, then laughed in Japanese.

Jimmy started laughing too. Just bent over laughing in Japanese.

All the golf writers looked at each other, then at Jimmy, then at Huge Pecker, and sort of shrugged their shoulders. Damn. What the hell was *that?*

Hand raised. Sort of in the upper middle.

"Domo—I mean please," Huge Pecker said, still sort of chuckling in Japanese.

Milt Limp of the New Jersey *Oppressor*, who, in a secret ballot by all the golf writers in America, was voted to be the nerdiest golf writer on planet earth and who hadn't, they were absolutely sure, clipped his nose hairs or ear hairs or toe nails or changed his hairstyle or his glasses or his one golf shirt or his old brown leather belt with the double holes all the way around it or his horrid nasal voice since he began coming to the Masters in 1971. And he had body odor and showed around pictures of his kids who were weird looking. Although he'd won six Pulitzer Prizes for investigative golf journalism, so that was something. "Milt Limp, sir, of the New Jersey *Oppressor?*"

"Fine, *fine.*"

"Huge Pecker, *sir?* That little maple tree way up in the woods on the eighth hole of the par three course?"

"*Yes*, Milt."

"I went out there early this morning and masturba—I mean, measured it with my hand held global positioning system device for the third year in a row to see if you guys moved it during the summer? Three inches?"

"*No*, Milt. We moved it exactly, as matter of fact, three

85

inches and a quarter."

"Oh." Milt spastically scribbled something on his note pad then shook his little global positioning system device by his ear. "Huge Pecker, sir?"

"Yes, *please*."

"Why have you guys changed the pH level in the water in the pond at the sixteenth green? I went out there this morning and measured the pH level in the pond and compared it to my findings from the last twenty-four years? Does that effect the ball flight over the water? The pH level? Are you guys trying to effect the ball flight of the invitees over the water by adjusting the pH level of the water in the pond at sixteen?"

"*No*, Milt. Thirty-two Canada geese and a local mallard duck we know pretty well dropped in there the other day and conducted some fairly rude business. A new fellow on our maintenance staff named Toby is taking care of that today. Oh, and the pH level of the water of the pond at the sixteenth green *does* effect the ball flight by the way, so a real good observation there." Huge Pecker winked and pointed at him. "By the way, Milt, if you don't mind every day this summer when you fly around in that helicopter and take pictures of our course maintenance and construction activities—try not to fly so *low*. The rotors chewed up quite a few of our dogwood trees and some of our extremely rare azaleas last year. Okay? We did get the nice check from your newspaper, however."

"Well, Huge Pecker, what about a hot *air* balloon? Can I use a hot air balloon to see what you guys are up to?"

"Well, *Milt*, I can't *stop* you until we buy the air space above the course, which is a project for next year. Okay then, other ques—"

"Uh, one more question? Huge Pecker, sir?"

"Fine, fine, Milt. *Fine*."

"Uh, Huge Pecker, how much does it cost to get in?"

In this case you spell dead awful silence with a capital "D-A-S."

## Squished Cheese

A FUNNY THING happened at the Masters.

Not "funny" as in "Haw! Haw!" funny, but funny as in unexpected: Herman Warthawg fell in love with Waymon Poodle. But not "fell in love" as in Warthawg and Waymon all of a sudden fell into dreamy homosexual male love during the first men's major professional golf tournament of the year, but "fell in love" as in Warthawg gained a real affection for the new volunteer from Mullet Luv. It just took him a while.

Warthawg, audibly grumbling on Monday as he had made his way down toward Waymon at his post, held the pimento cheese sandwich a little firmly—deliberately—before he gave it to his volunteer. Warthawg had never brought a volunteer his or her lunch before. He'd never brought anybody their lunch before so there he was, audibly grumbling. He shoved it at Waymon. "Here's your *food*," he said huffily, then started to turn around.

But before he could storm off, Waymon said with extreme sincerity but with a tentative hand on the big man's green jacketed elbow, "Mr. Warthawg, I wanted you to know that it's an honor to be one of your volunteers. I deeply appreciate this opportunity to serve you, the Masters, and the invitees. Have a wonderful week."

Warthawg stopped, turned, gave Waymon an odd look, and then clomped off. But then thought about it. Exactly what he would have said if he were Waymon Poodle at that moment. And sort of what he had said to his fellow members when he got elected to his chairmanships. An honor. To serve. I deeply appreciate it. But Waymon Poodle—an honor? What's so honorable about standing in the hot sun all day for seven days in a row with a yellow helmet on your head and doing it for free and gulping down those god forsaken pimiento cheese sandwiches? We'll see if he feels honorable by Sunday afternoon. Warthawg forced a fairly nice smile at Betty as he passed by her in front of the clubhouse.

And here she came, Betty Simpson, every afternoon, taking a cigarette break and making sure Waymon's lunch got delivered, but more so to see if she could cajole Waymon into coming over to her place that night. Virgin men were so rare, such a unique opportunity she couldn't make herself sit still. Days in a row of it. The squirming. Frantic bedroom fantasies of her and Waymon getting it on like wild monkeys or bush hogs. Him bringing her coffee in the morning and lighting her cigarettes in his mouth and giving her one. His giant, country sausage accidentally flopping out of the purple satin bathrobe she bought him. Her grabbing it and pulling him toward her and then having hog sex. Or when Waymon wasn't looking, her just lightly sticking the end of her cigarette on the tip of it. Or her grabbing it and dipping the tip of it into her hot coffee. She had to have relief. She eased up to him. "Sunday, you know, I waited all morning for you to come by," she said out of the side of her mouth. "I skipped church just fer you. Hurts to be rejected day after day, especially when there's love in yer heart. I bought a whole bunch of groceries, too, and a sexy purple satin bathrobe—for me *and* you. Matching."

Waymon really didn't know what to say, except: Well, thank you ma'am, uh, Miss Simpson, but he had a place. He was staying in the Diplomat.

The Diplomat? Ain't heard of that one. *New?*

Waymon sort of ignored Betty until she finally walked off. The type of heebie-jeebies she was giving Waymon every day gave him erections. And for Waymon it felt downright sacrilegious to have an erection at the Masters.

# A Bermuda Grass Masters

EVERY MORNING AFTER Waymon climbed out of his trunk in the parking lot of the Washington Road Waffle House—after he had shaved with an electric razor in the gasoline-smelling darkness and wiped off his nude body with a couple of baby wipes (aloe)—he bought the local Augusta newspaper and read it with his breakfast.

"BERMUDA GRASS WATCH BEGINS AT AUGUSTA NATIONAL," the Thursday headline had blared. Waymon read the story, wide-eyed. He read every Bermuda grass story every morning, wide-eyed.

On Friday morning, wide-eyed, and no sign of the Bermuda grass yet, thus the headline read: "BERMUDA GRASS WATCH CALMLY CONTINUES AT AUGUSTA NATIONAL."

Waffle House waitresses are an astute bunch, customer keen, newspaper readers too. Pouring coffee, Waymon's waitress, the one he'd had all week, asked him what he'd do if that woman showed her Bermuda grass to him instead of Chi Chi Rodriguez. She had Waymon pegged as the kind of fellow who'd definitely grab some Bermuda grass.

"In my position of authority I'd immediately alert a Pinkerton and have the pre-verted woman removed from the premises," Waymon said to her, matter of factly.

She made a face. "You *would*, huh?"

"That's what *I'd* do. Alert a Pinkerton. Have her remo—"

"*Bull* shit. You wouldn't lean over and look at it—or grab the thang with your hand and let out a rebel *yell*?"

Waymon shoved a strip of bacon in his mouth. "Nope. Not *me*. You must be thinking of someone else. Some *fornicator*."

"*Huh*. So how are the hash browns? You gotta be *sick* of them by now."

"They're absolutely delicious."

So the delicious routine continued for Waymon Poodle— and for Herman Warthawg. Waymon had a natural knack for getting attention. He finally got Warthawg's, totally. Waymon knew more about the Masters than he did. He knew more about golf than he did, but the lunch time talk was not provided to impress. Just to make a friend. A golf friend. It took a few days of Waymon's weird charm, and finally Warthawg knew he'd been wrong to judge this book by its cover. But the wrapper was just so strange. On Saturday, he confided to Waymon, just inches from his ear. "*Way*mon, this Bermuda grass, Chi Chi Rodriguez state of affairs situation, comes under my jurisdiction as Chairman of the Augusta National Golf Club Radar and Air Space Committee—"

Waymon lifted the rope for Tommy Nakajima and his caddie again. "Yessir."

" —so I've gone to every volunteer on the whole damn golf course (he lost twenty-one pounds doing it) and I've promised them a little two hundred thousand dollar gratuity if they can in any way spot the Bermuda grass situation before it happens and help us and the rest of the world avoid having to see this woman's Bermuda grass here at our beloved Augusta National Golf Club."

"Yessir." Rope up for Lee Trevino.

"All the magazines and newspapers in the free world and a large number of Communist nations are sending extra photographers, although this has become an extra ten-billion dollar benefit to Augusta and the metro area. But I could lose my membership over this, Waymon, especially if this woman's Bermuda grass is particularly hideo—"

Waymon held up a hand. "Yessir."

"So it looks like I can *count* on you, Waymon? You're my best man. I know that now, by the expert and efficient way you take that rope hook off the metal rod and put it back on there.

Just incredible."

"I'll be on alert, sir. I'll do what*ever* is necessary."

Warthawg looked at the way Waymon's eyes pointed in different directions and knew he had an advantage over everyone else. He whacked Waymon's sweaty back and hustled off.

As for Chi Chi, why a woman wanted to show him her Bermuda grass at the Masters wasn't a problem one bit, he told Warthawg and his member deputies in his Puerto Rican accent. Chi Chi was slurping up a bowl of grits.

They had asked him to attempt to feel as comfortable as possible this week as it wasn't like somebody was trying to shoot him like they were Hubert Green a while back in the U.S. Open or whatever. It was just some Bermuda grass a woman wanted to show him.

"*Well*, gentlemen," Chi Chi said in his Puerto Rican accent again, "I've been shot at. Theees is better. Seeing her naked beauty will help me *win*."

Warthawg and his deputies stepped back for a moment and huddled. Have we ever had a Puerto Rican champion before?

No, by God, we don't think so.

What if he starts chattering in Puerto Rican at the awards ceremony and nobody understands him?

What kind of crazy spicy slop will he serve at the Champions Dinner next year? What if everybody gets the *squirts*? We don't want another Vijay Singh eyeball dish!

They had to worry: Chi Chi became the oldest invitee to ever make the cut in the Masters.

The Sunday morning headline: "CHI CHI SAYS IN HIS PUERTO RICAN ACCENT TO BRING ON THE BERMUDA GRASS. SHOOTS THIRD ROUND LOVE NUMBER AND DEDICATES LOVE NUMBER TO THE MYSTERY WOMAN."

He was in the last twosome on Sunday with Tommy Nakajima.

The Sunday morning sub headline: "NAKAJIMA SAYS SHOW IT TO HIM INSTEAD. SHOOTS 69 TOO."

This was not the Masters they wanted.

91

And neither did Waymon. On Sunday, ever the traditionalist, and the supreme optimist, Waymon wanted to lift the rope for the final twosome he hoped would consist of Jack Nicklaus and Arnold Palmer—that the woman might have the decency to show Mr. Rodriguez her Bermuda grass over at the par three course by a stump or something.

Betty Simpson worked her way through the sweating wad of photographers and golf writers staked out at the invitee entrance and exit to the practice facility on Sunday. She was wearing a dress for the first time that week. "Warthawg bring you your pimento cheese today?"

"Yes, Betty," Waymon said distantly. He was watching in two directions, naturally. He made the mistake of calling LaJuanita about the two hundred thousand dollar Bermuda grass reward. He knew LaJuanita would go out and spend it.

It was hot. So very hot. And no breeze.

The Sunday sub, sub headline: " 'IT'S GOTTA BE TODAY, DARLIN,' CHI CHI SAYS."

Waymon, so sad the experience was nearly over. The week so wonderful. The Wednesday night Bible study with forty-eight Masters invitees at the Holiday Inn Buccaneer Room. That, too. Incredible. Amazing they allowed him in. Allowed him to speak in tongues for a couple of minutes.

Warthawg there now. Using his bulk and the power of his enormous green jacket to bump patrons out of the way to get beside Waymon who was still scanning the universe for the Bermuda grass. Warthawg giving Betty a sour look. Hope she'll enjoy that nice two million.

She was. She was going to go spend a large chunk of it right after she showed Chi Chi her Bermuda grass, as passionately promised Augusta National Golf Club in some recent correspondence—her Bermuda grass—hers—hers for you to see, Chi Chi—in slow motion—and there he was—the victim—the Puerto Rican golf professional—coming at them through an open swath of patrons—Pinkertons holding them back with fat and skinny arms—the tournament leader doing his saber thing with

92

his driver even before he hit his first warm up shot—he was that fired up about this thing—Bermuda grass—winning the Masters—his hair as black as the bottom of Mariana's Trench—skin so brown and shiny—the metal spikes of his golf shoes three inches long, glistening so brightly—even through the building clamor you could hear them crunching on the boiling asphalt—Nakajima right behind him, looking over Chi Chi's shoulder through those thick, goofy glasses from the seventies, or has anyone told the Japs to look at a few of our fashion magazines to see they're way behind in the eye wear department—Nakajima—knew if he got in the Bermuda grass photograph something like this could mean big yen—Betty lifting up the flowered dress with her bird-like claws to show Chi Chi Rodriguez her Bermuda grass on Masters Sunday—A Lillian Vernon dress—very nice on her as she was one of those genetically thin people—no one between her and Chi Chi so Chi Chi was going to get the full benefit—Chi Chi three strokes ahead of Nakajima on a Masters Sunday—a lot of yelling and pointing now the Bermuda grass was being revealed, the clicking buzz of one thousand Nikons and Canons and a whole bunch of Revco and Eckerd and CVS and K-Mart and Wal-Mart and Walgreen's disposables a million patrons snuck in with them—a few thousand people with their cell phone cameras held up, scanning for it—the Bermuda grass in the sun now—tan lines dramatic—the cigarette still in her mouth—she loved Chi Chi Rodriguez—why does everyone need to know why she wants to show him her Bermuda grass?—it's *how* that's the most interesting—it's how that gets shown on TV—Betty Simpson, sure, had completely lost it and was smiling anyway or was smiling because she had lost it—anyway—really hard to say at this point which one came first in this most public of psychosexual scenarios at a major golf event for men—but seemed to have happened a long time ago, the losing of it—she had the fingernail on the button of Technology—an employee with too much free time and power—a thousand reasons why this sort of crazy thing happens at nice golf clubs like Augusta National but no one with the time to explore the reasons now, not now, no, not now of

93

course—hey, safe to say at this point Betty Simpson really was the most powerful person in golf and *not* ol' Huge Pecker—anyway, it's Masters Sunday—no time to explore and debate that now—nope—a golf fan in Nebraska watching this scene unfold but also thinking, Why not just play the back nine only on Sundays at the ol' Masters and get it over with so it wouldn't bump into "60 Minutes"?—but knew it was unlikely they'd ever do it, you know, those hard headed rich members of that place, you know, just playing the back nine holes for the final round and that's it—a big golf fan in Nebraska thinking that—Omaha, Nebraska—Betty had adjusted the satellite to burn rolls and rolls of film over this thing—well, of course she knew it was computer chip space really, not "rolls" as in the typical rolls of film like you get at Walgreens—called the satellite over from monitoring some multi-billionaire fat cat vacationing at that moment in Cabo Del Sol who was wolfing down a platter of fish heads and watching the Masters, who had last Tuesday shoplifted nine pairs of socks from the pro shop when he was a guest and now had it pointed at herself—Betty did—pointed at herself—and the CBS camera right there, right on it, too—herself—Betty Simpson and her exquisite and feral Bermuda grass—sexy, sexy grandmaw type she was—gave responsible, middle-aged men and paw paw types, too, and Methodist bishops who normally used good sexual judgment—well, she made these men conjure up frantic sex fantasies about her, Betty did—on CBS, long timer Verne Lundquist with the call but decided not to say anything at first—you goof this one up and all of a sudden you're Jim Nantz—banished—banished from the Monday after the Masters media day golf outing for being so articulate and precise and appropriately sentimental at just the right moments on TV during the Masters so he got the heave-ho from Huge Pecker and his posse—he can't play for free, in other words, like we can, Lundquist was snickering—but the CBS director was screaming real loud at Lundquist in his ear plug to say something—this kind of thing was in your contract, you know, and you're obligated to make an intelligent comment when a woman shows everybody her

Bermuda grass on worldwide TV during the freakin' Masters, *Ver-no baby*—just remember, in calling historical moments in sports, less is more, less is more, so cough something up like that simple and spectacular contraction you barked in nineteen eighty-six when Jack baby rolled in the big birdie on seventeen—the big Yess-*sir!*—I mean, *hell*, no one's going to hear you anyway, the director says—so Verne Lundquist, he's thinking: What the hell, here's one for golf and television and psychosocial and psychosexual history on the Columbia Broadcasting System, and then he says real loud into his microphone: "Folks, what the whole world's been waiting for. There it is—you're looking *right at it*, the Bermuda grass. Yes *maaaa'am!*"—and perhaps planet earth shook for a moment as several, several hundred million viewers in all nations of the world went nuts all at once—seemed like planet earth did shake for a moment, or vibrate, really, as Verne Lundquist finally made the story of some woman who was determined to show Chi Chi Rodriguez her Bermuda grass at the Masters official, him being an important representative of CBS, and CBS being the long-time television network of the Masters and all—Waymon's hand over the Bermuda grass first—dress pulled up to her neck now so you could even see her bra—a fairly typical black one but no one in the entire world was looking at the bra—they were staring at the Bermuda grass—Waymon now cupping the Bermuda grass with his right hand—warm, of course—good and hairy, of course, like a Brillo Pad the Bermuda grass was, and moist—hot in Augusta, Georgia in April sometimes so Bermuda grasses get moist but it's also been cool during a number of past Masters but it was hot during this one, particularly today, the final round, so the Bermuda grass was moist—only natural it gets that way when it's hot at the Masters, moist—the middle finger of Waymon's hand all of a sudden sort of sinking through the Bermuda grass and into the other part—my God!—Oh, my God!—OH, MY GOD!—that's what Waymon was thinking when his finger did that, sinking through the Bermuda grass and into the other part—and now Waymon's also worried his yellow helmet might fall off then he would be out of uniform and Waymon believed in the rules—then Warthawg's hand over Waymon's—Warthawg's expression one of utter seriousness even with all the sweat burning his eyeballs and the hot sun in his eyes and the flashes of the million cameras—of course his expression was one of utter seriousness—he was a serious man—he had to be in this broken, undisciplined world—Waymon's expression, on the other hand, as if he saw a ghost, but looking right into the camera of the photographer of *Golf*, his favorite magazine behind the *Masters Journal*—but all of Waymon's golf magazine shooters were burning rolls, getting the money shot—the big cover shot—historic—absolutely golden portfolio material—hey, they could use twenty pages and show the Bermuda grass presentation in sequence form beginning when she was just an anonymous face in the crowd smoking a cigarette, like a swing sequence of Lee Trevino or Nancy Lopez—Betty's expression now like a boozed up sorority party girl, still clenching that cigarette between her yellow teeth—sort of a snarling expression—well, not sort of at all—it was a snarling expression, no doubt about it one bit—circus sounds—lots of them—circus sounds back up in Mullet Luv at the hair place where LaJuanita works—open on Sundays from noon to nine at night and LaJuanita and her hair dresser colleagues screaming, then gawking, then screaming, then gawking at the television up there in the corner and pointing at the television with their brushes in their hands, combs, scissors, blow dryers, jugs of gel—these gals and their customers knew nothing about golf, knew nothing about how golf was a multi-billion dollar industry and how imperative the Masters tournament held at Augusta National Golf Club was to the world of golf—knew nothing about how reverent and respectful things were supposed to be down there at the Masters, but knew for damn sure that was LaJuanita's fiancé there on television, Waymon, the bank teller, the "sex monk" LaJuanita told her friends she had nicknamed him, with his hand on that old woman's Bermuda grass in his yellow helmet—and LaJuanita had already told her colleagues that Waymon's performance there at that golf tournament helping people or something like that as a volunteer helper or something helping people, well, girlfriends, they were gonner give Waymon two hundred thousand dollars as some sort of performance bonus which Waymon said she could have so she boogied on down to Atlanta last night with Karl, y'all know my old fiancé Karl, and bought a whole bunch of nice crap at the Rooms to Go for her and Waymon's trailer for when they got married and her and Karl stayed over at the Ritz-Carlton—her and Karl—she had the filet mignon and Karl had the chicken and then they ordered up one of them sex movies in their room—well, *three* sex movies for twenty-five dollars each—so thanks for everybody understanding why she got in a little late today and was limping a little—Chi Chi saying in his Puerto Rican accent while he whipped a sixty-eight inch long driver around like a sword or saber or something like that while staring a hole in that Bermuda grass and then he pointed the grip of the driver right at it—and said in that accent of his, real loudly, "Hey, *doll*! Loo-keen *good*!"—so with that pronouncement, it's like starting a pit bull fight or cock fight or bar fight or WWF Friday night SmackDown thing as Chi Chi pretty much acknowledged the Bermuda grass situation was now in full force and he'd had his look at it and now the rest of the world could have at it while he went and warmed the hell up because here he all of a sudden had a chance to win the biggest cracker golf tournament there ever was and ever will be—him being a shiny Puerto Rican, too—yeah, boycott *this* boys—and old Warthawg—Warthawg liked it when things were in control—and now he finally knew he should have been more cordial to Betty—never in fifty years a kind word said to her now that he thought about it—even when she told everybody who'd listen at the club about how her Chihuahua got in her dryer and she didn't know it when she pushed the "On" button and it sort of dried up pretty thoroughly after forty-five minutes—she thought it was her cross training sneakers in there thumping around as she sipped her coffee and enjoyed a cigarette at the kitchen table while she read her *People* magazine—she moped and moaned about it for days hoping the members might understand that lonely old single women like Chihuahuas as pets—the Chihuahua's name was

"Prissy"—the help, Warthawg thinking—deeply pondering them at this point, but quickly pondering them deeply since he was busy—the little people—pondering them—they can do big bad things—don't give them time to think—and had also heard and read about super sex freaks have shrieking orgasms doing this sort of thing: in public, no less—HOLY LORD IN HEAVEN HAVE MERCY SWEET PRECIOUS JESUS! he bellowed like a moose when Betty finally cut loose on one—her pelvis was really, really juking around—and now Warthawg knew with absolute certainty super sex freaks have shrieking orgasms doing this sort of super sex freak thing on a boiling hot Masters Sunday on CBS.

And so did Waymon, the moist.

# Rain Delay

*We were intrigued by a recent study of the sex fantasy concoction activities of young and middle-aged male humans, which produced unexpected findings relating to golf. A decision was made to further pursue the psychological effects of golf as it relates to rational thinking, as this might be thrilling.*

*We discovered that no matter how hard it is raining, and even lightning, onto the premises of a public, private, semi-private, or resort golf course, and no matter if the Doppler weather radar clearly shows it will continue to rain heavily—even in deluge amounts—for the next several days, non-stop, like in the Bible that time, that golfers, as they gaze at the rain and the clouds and the deadly lightning and even point at it, truly believe in their hearts it will stop raining at any moment. And they can go golf.*

—From the April 2014 issue of *Go Figure*, the monthly report of the American Psychological Association

NEAR SILOAM, EVEN though he remained, a month and a half later, one of the most famous or infamous people in the world, depending on your personal psychosocial or psychosexual predilections and understanding of what happened and why it happened during the final day of the Masters right there at the invitee entrance and exit to the practice facility at Augusta

National Golf Club, Waymon hydroplaned and spun his Diplomat in wild circles from the far right lane of the eastbound direction of Georgia Interstate 20. Then Waymon flew past the "STAY OFF MEDIAN" sign and onto the flooded median for a few wild circles then back into the eastbound direction of Georgia Interstate 20 without stopping, like in a movie. So there he was, Waymon, just spinning down the highway, but moving toward Augusta nonetheless. It's finally volunteer day at Augusta National Golf Club and Waymon was extremely excited.

He wasn't surprised he was spinning his car down the highway as the weather reports he was following on his crusty a.m. radio reported that the band of heavy showers moving down I-20 was the biggest band of heavy showers to hit the area since weather history was recorded. But boy, the announcer was saying, it sure is nice to finally get some rain. Sure is, after all that dry weather we've had lately—well, all last *year* when you really *think* about it—those poor *crops....*

The spinning of his car reminded Waymon, as he tried to man-handle the spinning steering wheel with his skinny arms, of the time those six giant cicada killer wasps all of a sudden appeared in his rear view mirror, then floated over the front seat and onto his face. Of course, Waymon knew if he had left them alone and stopped the car and rolled down his window they might have flown out but he had felt the need to swat at them and that was what really started the whole mess. Dang, he thought, and the one that kept clinging to the back of his hand with that pulsating yellow and black thorax. His Christian psychologist had urged him not to daydream about giant cicada killer wasps. She had urged him, with a hug, but there Waymon was, daydreaming about them as he passed through Siloam—Camak—into Augusta—onto Washington Road—still raining so hard, so violently pelting his Diplomat, that Waymon took an early, incorrect, right turn off of Washington Road and was immediately shocked to find the Augusta National Golf Club guard house had been taken away and all those magnolia trees had been dug up and Magnolia Lane had been widened and a horrible double-yellow stripe had been painted down the middle of the street. And now there was a barber shop on the right? They'd put homes on the practice range—with boats and motorcycles parked in the driveways—rotting Big Wheels in the uncut grass—barking dogs—rusting grills?

He was on Berckmans Road and didn't know it.

Raining that hard.

"Dang," Waymon muttered as he clutched the steering wheel with both hands. "*Dang.*" He could see police lights flashing up ahead—then two police cars pulled up to a monstrous thirty foot high mound of mud, caked dirt, and green grass on top of it all—white pipes poked from the huge pile at odd, broken angles—the whole mess was blocking the entire road. To his right, a sign blasted by shotgun fire, read "Rae's Creek." Waymon lurched forward and through the rain could see, like a single candle on top of a cake, a yellow flag. A golf flag.

It was the twelfth green of Augusta National Golf Club.

A policeman walked over to Waymon's window.

Waymon rolled the window down. "Wow, it's really raining hard, huh?"

"Sir, yes it *is* raining hard. Would you mind turning around? The road's blocked."

"Yessir. But is that a—?"

"A green. A *golf* green."

"A green from—?"

"Yep. Every year the son of a bitch gets washed down Rae's Creek. We report it. They come get it."

"Wow."

The policemen looked Waymon over and glanced into the back seat at Waymon's golf clubs. "Say, pal—you were planning to play Augusta National today?" The policeman laughed so hard he started choking.

Waymon, not yet crying, but still hopeful, pulled back onto Washington Road and saw a sign directing him to one of the gravel parking lots. "Volunteer Parking." Waymon entered the lot slowly, reverently, and discovered it was empty. Of course then he thought when it quits raining he might have the whole course to himself, and even if he had to skip the twelfth hole then he'd just figure up what he thought he might have shot on it—probably a birdie—and that would be okay. Waymon pulled up to the far fence. Still raining so hard—the sheets of rain so white—knew that yards away was Tea Olive—the green would be right up there to the right—he was squinting—looking through the passenger window to try and see it—but was jolted by a sharp knock on his window. Someone in a heavy yellow rain slicker with the hood pulled down. Spinning his flashlight around, signaling Waymon to roll down his window. Waymon rolled it down.

"You gotta be freakin' kidding!"

"Kidding about *what?*"

"You a volunteer?" the guy asked.

"Yeah. What do you think? Passing over pretty soon?" Waymon shoved his head out of the window and gawked up at the sky. Hard rain pellets hit him in the eyes.

"Passing over?" The guy cut loose a stream of tobacco juice across the top of the car. "Lemme show you something. Looka here." He pulled from inside his yellow slicker a device the size of a laptop computer. It had a screen. The logo on the top of it said "NASA."

Waymon looked at the screen. It was a portable Augusta National Golf Club maintenance staff issue weather radar device worth one hundred and forty-eight thousand dollars. Every maintenance employee had one. There were a lot of maintenance employees.

"You see this big ol' blob of red and purple?"

"Yeah?"

"And you know that blobs of red and purple is the *worst* kind of rain you can have? As opposed to blobs of *green?* And green sometimes ain't even hittin' the *ground*. But you know stupid rednecks will sit there and look at that green color on the radar screen on the local news then run out of their trailers and

102

look up at the sky and point and go, 'Well that don't make *any* sense, honey. The radar on the TV says it's raining on our house but it ain't raining on our house one *bit*. Not one damn *bit*.' "

Attempting to be cordial, Waymon said, "Those crazy people."

The radar was spinning around real fast.

"*So*," the guy said, "You know what's underneath that big ol' blob of red and purple?"

"Augusta National Golf Club?"

"Augusta National *Golf* Club." The guy shoved the radar device back into his slicker and spit on the tire. He looked at Waymon without saying anything.

Waymon started to feel a little uncomfortable. It was a look Snort and Billy gave him right before they said something real mean. "So I don't guess we're—"

"Hey, boy! You're that crazy volunteer what grabbed Betty Simpson's Bermuda grass!"

"I'm afraid so."

"You know, I *thought* it was you—hoooo-*weee*! That musta been *hi*deous!"

Waymon huffed like a three year old, then yanked it into reverse and drove back down to the twelfth green on Berckmans Road and lurched out of his car, knowing this was what robbing a TrustTrust branch feels like. From the other side of the window. Once you get the urge to do it it's just real hard to stop. All that adrenaline and free money. All the voices in your head telling you this was okay—the teller probably won't mind if you don't point a gun at them and if the letter was well written.

Waymon marched right by the policeman who was trying to light a cigarette in the downpour—"Hey, you!"—and with both hands, viscously digging in with his fingernails and hands and skinny arms, scooped out a massive chunk of the green of Golden Bell. As Waymon knew a little bit about turf agronomy from some of his magazines, he made sure to get a lot of the putting surface and a lot of the roots.

He sped back to Mullet Luv from there, two hundred and forty-eight miles, to the Mullet Luv Home Depot and bought a plant light and went directly to the second bedroom—and shut the door behind him.

# e-Pulsation

THAT NIGHT, LATE, dark and quiet, and because Waymon felt guilty about stealing some of Augusta National Golf Club, he felt he should punish himself some more even though he felt, at that moment, he was already living in an apartment 1931 waking nightmare.

Waymon crept into the second bedroom, turned his computer on, pulled up the Internet, and typed in that certain address given to him by his Christian psychologist, then hit Search.

Shakily, wearily, and with extreme tension, Waymon was hoping to ease his giant cicada killer wasp fears once and for all and thought that visiting this web site would make him feel better.

**PROFESSOR JEEVPIL BISWAPATI'S ULTIMATE! AND EXCLUSIVE! GIANT CICADA KILLER WASP WEB SITE**

http://www.georgiainstituteoftechnology.edu/Entomology/~bi swapati/KILLER.html

May 2014

I am a calm and reasonable man. You know me as calm and reasonable. Because I am. I am calm and reasonable. But I must confess my excitement about the recent and painful death of my giant cicada killer wasp nemesis, Professor Lamar Feckle of the University of Georgia.

You, as loyal devotees of my lifelong work and research of giant cicada killer wasps, know how Feckle constantly disputed my findings and made fun of me on entomology talk radio shows. So I wear this thing on my head. It's called a particular kind of hat, by the way, not a towel. Fine. I am a Hindu and speak Hindi. So I have a long beard which is braided and comes to a sharp point. And some fairly long fingernails—that come to sharp points also.

Fine. I think I'm a pretty freaking hip dude.

He makes fun of me no more, that dead Feckle. I poke the carcass with a sharp stick. Now I have the only web site devoted to my beloved giant cicada killer wasps. Thus, Ultimate! and Exclusive! I use marketing type words now. I am not a circus barker. I am Jeevpil Biswapati, entomologist. This is what Feckle has done to me.

But even though he was my nemesis and I was his nemesis I was still asked to observe the "crime" scene, if you will because I am known as a smart dude. Crime? Yes. As I had long suspected, that dumb redneck was not satisfied that giant cicada killer wasps were big enough. Upon viewing his laboratory (I had to step over his dried up carcass; his eyes were wide open and they seemed to follow me around the laboratory like Mona Lisa), I discovered Feckle had perverted Nature and had produced a gob of monstrous giant cicada killer wasps. Monstrous? Yes. Seven inches long my devotees, with some nasty "tude." Think of a common blackbird with a pulsating yellow and black thorax. Some he already had floating in formaldehyde just like in "Aliens" (see photo below courtesy of Warner Bros). In his journal Feckle had named these beasts "super whopper" (*superus whopperus hideous*). Thus, super whopper giant cicada killer wasps. Clunky, with a capital "K." Sort of redundant, I know. Perhaps that's why they turned on him. I don't know. Now he looks like a stunned cicada, if you know what I mean. And you better know what I mean because you learn what a stunned, dried up cicada looks like in my giant cicada killer wasp 101 class you took from me your sophomore year.

And more fascinating news. For some unknown reason, even to me, an expert on giant cicada killer wasps, Feckle's gob of super whoppers traveled southeast to Augusta, and have caused quite a "buzz" there. Just one of the super whoppers, I have been told, cleared out the Wal-Mart.

Therefore, I have been hired by the Augusta Chamber of Commerce to investigate why they chose Augusta—instead of more deserving towns like Siloam or Hephzibah—and what might be done to rid this innocent town of Feckle's beasts. Please consult my Ultimate! and Exclusive! giant cicada killer wasp web site for frequent updates.

Devotees, all I can say at this point is this: humans and cicadas of Augusta, Georgia, watch out. Be very watch out.

# Waymon's Reaction to Professor Biswapati's Latest News

VISITING THE WEB site did not make Waymon feel better. Not one bit. He did not add "PROFESSOR JEEVPIL BISWAPATI'S ULTIMATE! AND EXCLUSIVE! GIANT CICADA KILLER WASP WEB SITE" to his "Favorites."

Waymon moaned to his computer screen in the eerie quiet of apartment 1931, "Professor Biswapati, sweet *Jeee*-sus, you got to get rid of those dang super whopper thangs by next year's volunteer day—*please*."

# PART IV

## WAYMON: A CURIOUS REVIEW

## Garlic Pow-Pow-Power

WHEN BARTWICK DILWORTH IV was finally made Executive Vice President of Customer Service of TrustTrust Banks, he planned not to brush his teeth, shave, clean or clip his fingernails, toenails, use deodorant, or cleanse his butt crack for four days.

At the dinner table, the evening of his promotion, as a friendly, deeply loving warning, but with a distinct enthusiasm in his voice, Dilworth announced these intentions to his wife and son.

Xing La La, his wife, thought he had temporarily lost his mind. You don't consciously *not* cleanse your butt crack for four days. You don't consciously *not* cleanse your butt crack for two seconds, actually. You rub on it, from time to time, a mixture of liquefied Chinese herbs with a gauze pad, then meditate.

Dilworth's fourteen year old son thought his father's current freaking out situation was totally cool—and finally and totally time for it as he was always such a serious suit dad who worked at some big bank downtown, and eagerly offered a suggestion that in order to get totally skanky he should also eat, at least, two peeled cloves of garlic before bed, every night, as this would, throughout the next day, make him "crank like a mule."

At this juncture, Dilworth's wife, who was an extremely Americanized, opinionated, and educated big city woman, who lived in a three and half million dollar mansion with her husband

and son, left the table and decided to flee down to Sea Island to their one million and a half dollar beach house and her Pilates instructor, with whom she had been experimenting with lesbianism. Xing La La knew what the word "crank" meant and hated that civilization allowed hyperactive, odd looking, pimpled children—not proper people—to get to add new words to dictionaries.

Wow. Okay then. Bye, Mom.

Anyhow, the kid didn't miss a beat. *Four* cloves, the father was told, in an extremely confidential and business-like tone of voice over his plate of food, would make a person crank like a MARTA bus. *Six* cloves, a 747 jet airplane—or a Howitzer cannon, say. Plus, it was explained by the son, that the cranks would also *smell* like garlic and any doofus who walked into your "smoke trail" would get "knocked *out*." Plus, *plus*—at this level of exploitation your body will begin to *ooze* garlic crank through your skin and you would also win international awards for your bad breath.

Dilworth was mesmerized by this fascinating information, proven by the fact he sat there with his mouth open, gazing at his son as if a broiler chicken was crawling out of the child's ear. Dilworth's son was also named Bartwick, and Bartwick V learned of the garlic eating crank thing from his best friend Ralph Jenkins VIII, who was a huge proponent of a nightly, personal "six clove." Bartwick and Ralph are eighth graders at Atlanta's oldest, most expensive, most exclusive, and most prestigious private college preparatory school where they're co-presidents of the Human Physiology Club.

Anyhow, during his promotion that day, Dilworth was told by the president of TrustTrust that since he was now the new executive vice president of customer service as opposed to his former role as senior vice president of customer service that it was time to really, really come up with some good ideas.

Dilworth said he finally had one that would lead TrustTrust into the customer service future.

The president asked what it was in particular.

Dilworth said he was going to once and for all go check out a Waymon Poodle cat up in Mullet Luv and "bottle" Waymon Poodle and feed it to every employee in all five states and the District of Columbia who had anything to do with customers, as customers and their money, a recent TrustTrust survey revealed, were important.

The president of TrustTrust, who read a huge number of golf magazines in the TrustTrust presidential toilet in addition to his banking magazines said wasn't this the Waymon Poodle who was on every cover of every golf magazine—the energetic chap down at the recent Masters who grabbed a woman's Bermuda grass? Dilworth, we don't grab women's Bermuda grasses at TrustTrust, even the Bermuda grass of our wealth management clients—even if they *ask* us to.

Dilworth delicately reminded his chief that Waymon Poodle was an employee of TrustTrust Banks and was also the finest teller in the history of TrustTrust, revealed every year of his employment by the massive TrustTrust customer survey, to be the friendliest and most competent of any teller in any branch in all five states and the District of Columbia in which we did business.

The president of TrustTrust sort of said, "Oh."

"And now that he's famous for grabbing that old women's Bermuda grass at the Masters," Dilworth chirped, "the Mullet Luv Publix branch is number one in the company. They're lined up to Chattanooga to engage in, and en*joy*, personal *inter*course with *Poo*dle!"

"*Dil*worth, watch your language!"

"Chief, Waymon Poodle is bigger than Phil *Mick*elson."

The president of TrustTrust said, "No shit?"

# Curious Monkey

IT WAS TRUE, Dilworth thought. True. People judge you by
the way you look and that wasn't nice at *all*.

He had stepped out of his new "Phoenix Red" three hundred
and seventy horsepower, eighty-two thousand dollar Jaguar XKR
coupe in the Publix parking lot and immediately the old man in
the Camry next to told him to get a job. Yeah, his old wife said it
too, Get a job. To the tune of that Bruce Hornsby song, no less.
Hey, Bartwick's thinking, this was what very special secret
corporate responsibility looks like, you know, from time to time.
How dare them? If they only knew. I'm Bartwick Dilworth,
Executive Vice President of Customer Service of TrustTrust
Banks. That's who I am. He snarled back at them. The old man
shot him a bird. Dilworth pressed a finger against his left nostril
and blew snot out of the right one. But he accidentally blew snot
on his Jaguar and not the Camry.

Anyhow.

Of course. Four days of bed hair. The skanky, uneven beard.
Bags under his eyes. Butt crack, uncleansed. He was special.

On the walkway now in front of the grocery store. Dilworth
wearing only one shoe, an old snakeskin cowboy boot. Walking
this way made him limp like Quasimodo. Tattered, greasy jeans,
with both knees cut open. The top of his underwear showing.
Three watches on one arm, eccentric style. One of Xing La La's
clip-on earrings hanging off a lobe. The mother snapping up her
daughter as he walked by, clutching her child, her back to
Dilworth. Frozen. Like she didn't know what to do. Dilworth

stopped and gazed at them like a curious monkey until she ran away. *Ran*. Dilworth lit a cigarette. Hadn't smoked in years and remembered how it made him pause and think, and then get a headache. He thought about Waymon Poodle, as he sucked in the smoke, watching a teenage girl at the outdoor ATM, punching buttons. As if on instinct she turned, looked him up and down. Get a *job*, she said with a sneer, you gross skank.

Thank you, dear.

Dilworth could smell his own breath. Knew when you could smell it yourself it was really bad. And the garlic oozing from his skin, too. You could smell it. Gross as absolute hell but he'd achieved what he wanted, Bartwick Dilworth, really thinking outside the old paw paw patch on this one. Way off to Jupiter on this one. Sure, I could come on in here in Saturday morning, rich guy smart casual, clean shaven, no socks, four hundred dollar loafers, and prance up to this cat at his window and inflict the same pain. Customers do it every day. Because they like it, these customer people.

Through the sliding doors now and by the carts, then through the next set of sliding doors.

A Mullet Luv policeman with a package of frozen chicken wings (mild) checking out in lane five looking up at him. Hold everything. The cashier trying to hand the policeman his change but he's glued on this whacko limping into the store. Not bank robber profile, but the kind who cause extensive trouble, especially in the produce section. Just grabbing and eating and they bark at you. Haul them out kicking and screaming about their rights and then they scratch your eyes out and try to spit into your mouth, and then they sue you. Hadn't seen this particular guy around. Just watch him. Don't even let him get started. I could nail him on the cigarette, but...

Dilworth burped at the policeman, then flicked the cigarette into the air. It landed on a plastic grocery bag being filled with groceries and melted through the plastic and fell onto, an into, a three pack of white corn.

Dilworth kept moving. Marlboro Light garlic smoke

surrounding his head. Seven cloves last night of the ancient remedy. Used for centuries for ailments, garlic.

Now for opportunity.

And there he was—Waymon Poodle. *Jeee*sus. Just serving up a storm. Facial action and voice like a cartoon. The guy was genetically wired for this stuff. One on one. Can do. I'm going to make you happy. And the famous right hand, the one that cupped the Masters Bermuda grass. Unbelievable. Customers waiting in line, fourteen of them, all probably waiting for Poodle. And there's that other Waymon dude, the branch manager, snooping around back there behind the tellers, like he's looking for dirty fingernails.

Sensing something strange back there behind them, these valued customers. So they turn, just a little, some over their left shoulder where Dilworth could be discreetly glanced at, some over their right shoulder, but not seeing what it was, whatever it was. Just a sense of something, and it wasn't good. Then a glance over their left shoulder and there this thing was. Sort of hanging there. A look on his face like an animal, looking for trouble, mouth hung open, breathing through it.

Then the smell hits them and all fourteen go in different directions.

Now the space between Dilworth and Waymon was about twenty feet. Dilworth hanging there. His weight more on his left side. Now looking right at Waymon.

Wanting him. Going to mess him up good.

See what he's made of—this Bermuda grass grabber, the future of TrustTrust Banks Incorporated.

Waymon squawked, "Here to help our *next* valued TrustTrust customer to-*day!*"

# Exsqueeze Me?

TWENTY FEET.

That's all the distance and time Waymon Poodle needed to say a prayer.

That's right. As this valued customer approached his window, limping, Waymon Poodle asked the Lord God Jesus—even though TrustTrust didn't require its employees to pray for their valued customers; it was totally optional—to bestow on this valued customer the good common sense to take a bath and brush his teeth as it would just really make him feel like a better person. It was actually a prayer Waymon prayed a lot. It wasn't the fear of being held up or having to deal with check fraud every ten minutes of every day. Not at all. Bank tellers around the world had to, in such quiet, professional surroundings, even in a branch in a dang grocery store, deal with untold numbers of valued customers with body odor. Noxious, palpable, warm body odor that wafted in from behind them, then over the counter and into the teller's face and up their nose or onto the tongue of tellers who breathed through their mouth. God love these people, Waymon thought, but they're still the valued customer. And I value them. Even the valued construction workers who are the worst smellers when they come flooding in here on Fridays around three-thirty. And the valued old, retired people who love to engage in teller transactions but who forget to wash for weeks. And the valued people who work in bars. Valued customers with medical-attention quality halitosis. And especially those valued, fitness-conscious customers who've just come from the fitness center without having a post-workout bath, carrying their valued toddler who has a really bad diaper and more than likely they'll set the toddler up on the counter while they fiddle around in their belly packs and if the toddler doesn't have a really bad diaper and you can even hear the poo-poo squeeze around in there and ooze out the sides and then they'll spew vomit on the teller counter and on the nameplates of tellers. You have to unconditionally love this job. And I do. I am Waymon Poodle and I do.

The valued beast was two feet away, breathing. Breathing hard on purpose. Shooting the odor directly at his target. Decided to save a crank when it really needed to test Poodle's will to live. He was Bartwick Dilworth IV, after all. You don't crank in public, or even private, unless it's medically required. The executive vice president, pushing the hot air out of his mouth as if he were whistling, but no one was hearing a pretty tune.

Waymon Boner was behind Waymon, fiddling with some papers, pretending not to notice, but it was obvious. His head was leaning that way. Starting to catch some of it. Now squinting. Face puckering.

"Good morning! And welcome to TrustTrust!" Waymon nearly screamed. "How are *you* today?"

Let the games begin.

"Yeah, gimme a double cheese with *rings*."

"A double cheese with rings?"

"A double cheese with *rings*! You don't hear so good, *do* you." Dilworth bumped Waymon's nameplate with a knuckle. "Huh? Waymon Pooooooud-sucker."

Contact.

Waymon's face contorting for a millisecond. Steady, the incredible teller was telling himself. Trust Jesus on this one. This was still a valuable customer—who needs to brush his teeth and his tongue for an hour. "*Sir*, actually, I think you might want the deli section of the store, which is located all the way down to your left."

Two seconds of this and Waymon Boner had already had enough. What a scum bag. He nudged up against Waymon's back.

"Sir, the deli is *that* way." He pointed that way. "Thank you and have a roast beef day."

"Awright. Forget the cheeseburger, fellas. I'm just gonna reach back there and pinch your *weenies*."

Waymon Boner: "Oh, my *God*."

Waymon Poodle, giggling. What else was there to do? The valued customer isn't always right, or polite, but by gosh they're still the valued customer even if he says he's going to pinch your weenie. "Sir, this is a bank branch, not one of those—"

"Asian jack shacks?"

"Yessir, one of those. Now, can I perhaps assist you in a transaction?"

Unbelievable. Unflappable. I just asked if I could pinch his weenie. And what eye do you look at?

Dilworth put a rumpled, dirty, half wet check onto the counter and pushed it forward. The dirty fingernails. The three watches on his arm.

Waymon Boner, riveted, rose over Waymon's shoulder on tip-toes to have a look.

"*Well*, now. Thank you sir," Waymon said as he looked over the check like a machine, but still smiling, still poised like a soldier. Red flags everywhere. Every item was written in a different hand. Made out to "Cashh." The amount: $3.28. Waymon's hand on the teller machine keypad entering the account number. Not even looking at the keypad. Those long famous fingers going a million miles an hour, commenting to this vile, vulgar, valued customer about the weather, how the Braves were playing lately—while the valued customer silently whistled, real hard.

Waymon Boner observing like a trainee, staring at the teller machine screen for the signature verification to come up, then to Waymon's fingers, then back to the screen. The mock account set up by Dilworth days ago with one of those suspicious geeks in operations. Only five dollars in the account belonging to this guy, Willie Wonka. It checked out. Both Waymons let out a sigh of relief. Waymon Boner's sigh of relief through his gaping mouth more obvious than Waymon Poodle's who let it out through his nose. He though it was more polite to do it that way in front of a valued customer, let out sighs through your nose. And his hands still going a million miles an hour, flicking through the cash drawer now: bills, coins, then the little envelope, stuffing the contents into the envelope with a neat flick of the hand then handing the envelope directly to the valued customer's hand. Never placing the envelope on the counter and pushing it at them as if you think the valued customer was unwashed. Never distancing himself from the valued customer. He'd reach across the counter and pat them on the back if they'd let him.

Mr. Wonka, on purpose, poured the money onto the counter and took his time counting it.

Now a semi-circle of valued customers, Waymon Poodle fans, had re-assembled, watching. Some on tip-toes, too, some smiling. Some touching their lips with anticipation, some whispering to each other. The Mullet Luv policeman at the magazine rack now and had a good line of sight, right hand near his pistol; a Maxim in the other. It was the Lady Gaga, 1,456 sex positions, and fantastic buns in seconds issue.

"What a *plea*sure it is serving you today, Mr. Wonka," Waymon purred as he waited for Mr. Wonka to finish, thinking that's exactly the name of the guy who owned that chocolate factory in that movie and who ended up giving it to that little boy or the purple girl or whoever. "Yessir. It certainly is good to *see* you." Waymon, instinctively, turned his nameplate a little bit more toward Mr. Wonka. Waymon took a deep, cleansing breath.

Mr. Wonka was really taking his time.

"Everything seem to be in order, Mr. Wonka?"

"Fuck. I need one more penny."

Waymon Boner: "No, *sir*, you chocolate maker. Now you take your three dollars and twenty-eight cents and go to the deli section and pinch those guy's weenies down *there*."

"It's quite all right, gentlemen," Waymon said with a cordial lilt. "I certainly could have miscounted. It's quite possible." He

119

didn't. Instead of recounting the money himself, Waymon reached into the cash drawer and pulled out a penny and handed it to Mr. Wonka. "*Here* you go."

Mr. Wonka took the penny from Waymon, swallowed it, and then burped.

A burp like the breath of a petting zoo llama.

Meaty, with heat and force behind it.

It smelled of nothing of this earth.

Waymon Boner, running toward the break room: "I'm going to totally *puke*."

Waymon Poodle, breathing it all in. No reaction, just a smile. "Mr. Wonka, what *else* can I do for you to-day?"

Dumb question. Mr. Wonka was just getting warmed up.

# Iceberg. Beware

CARMALITA WAS FILING Dilworth's toenails.

He was smoking a big cigar and watching her brown little Venezuelan hand *zip—zip—zip* with a silver nail file on the end of his big toe's big thick, cream yellow toenail. Dilworth and Carmalita were in the sun room, on a lazy Saturday afternoon: Carmalita, their long-time manicurist who made house calls, and thick white cigar smoke hanging around them.

It was the smoke from a victory cigar.

Dilworth pointed at the portable phone by her arm. "Baby doll, would you hand me the phone?"

She didn't speak English. She kissed his big toe. Then bit it and winked.

"No, no, sugar." He made a hand gesture by his ear, then pointed at it again. "The *tele*—phone."

"*Ah.*" She handed it to him then went back to town on the toe. She had already done his fingernails and shaved him and clipped his hair. Dilworth loved women from international countries.

It was a swanky scene.

Dilworth dialed the bank branch he had molested that morning. Fourteen rings. Not good.

"Thank you for calling TrustTrust Bank, conveniently located in the Publix grocery store in Mullet Luv, Georgia. How may I *help* you?"

"Waymon Boner, please."

"Oh, it's pronounced Bo-*nay*, actually. And how may I *help* you?"

"Bo-nay? *French?*"

An audible huff. "Pretty sure. French. And *your name?*"

"Bartwick *Dil*worth. American."

Waymon's eyes widened. Oh *shit.* One of the suits. Calling on a Saturday? "Oh, yes, indeeed, Mr. Dilworth. So how's everything at the old—*head*quarters?"

"*Not* good."

"Not good?"

"*Not* good. I got an upset Mr. Wonka here."

Waymon's heart dropped. "I'd like to explain exactly what happened. He was a horrible and total stink—"

"But a valued *cus*tomer—nonetheless." Dilworth giggled under his breath.

"Well, if I can be forthright about the situation—the man was a horrible and total stinky freak out."

"A horrible and total stinky *freak out?*"

"Yes, he *was.* Very much a horrible and total stinky *freak* out." Waymon was already sweating by this point. Big drops. He couldn't catch his breath

"But Mr. Wonka is a valued customer, Waymon. A valued customer."

"But Mr. Dilworth, he *breathed* on me."

"He was your valued customer?"

"Well, not exactly. I ob*serrr*ved the entire freak out."

"The teller's name is Waymon, too, I think—according to Mr. Wonka, who's very upset." Dilworth winked at Carmalita.

Waymon leaned over and looked through his glass office door at Waymon at his window. Now they were getting somewhere. "*Right.* That's the Waymon. Does he need to work for me any longer Mr. Dilworth, sir—if you know what I *mean?*"

"Actually, I can't decide what to do with him. Give him a promotion or the employee of the year award or *both.*"

"Excuse me?"

"You saw how he handled Mr. Wonka. You were standing right there."

Waymon squinted. "How do you know *that?*"

"I was Mr. Wonka. *Sort* of."

Waymon dropped the phone.

It was loud. Dilworth scrunched his face up.

Carmalita bit his big toe again.

"So very sorry, sir. You really were Mister Wo—"

"Just tell me something about Poodle."

"Yessir. *Really* sorry. But you really were Mister Wo—"

"Shut up a second."

"Yessir." A big drop of sweat dropped into the sour cream on Waymon's burrito.

"What's the one big thing Poodle wants out of his career? His performance was incredible."

"*Well*, Mr. Dilworth. Believe it or not, he really is content to be a teller. He really does like customers."

Dilworth rolled his eyes.

"See"—Waymon sighed for about six seconds—"his whole big life *goal* thing is to play golf at Augusta Country Club."

"Augusta *Country* Club? Good *God. Why?*"

"You know, where they play the U.S. Open or whatever."

"Oh, Augusta *National*. The *Masters*."

"Like I said. What-*everrrr*."

"You're kidding me."

"I swear to *God*. That's all he *lives* for. Except who knows if it'll ever come true *now*—*you* know—since on TV he grabbed that woman's—*Oh*, and I guess you know his big volunteer day was totally wiped out by the wrath of God—his words. So he's still squirming to play Augusta National Country Club. Just squirming, squirming, *squirming*—Waymon *Poodle*."

"*Squirming*, huh?"

"Listen, Mr. Dilworth, you could promote Waymon Poodle to executive vice president—"

"Watch it now."

"…but if he could play that golf course nothing in the world would make him happier. I mean, really. You saw that hideous tie he was wearing."

"*Yeah*."

"Well, sir, he's wears it every—single—*day*."

"No kidding."

"Be very afraid, Mr. Dilworth, that's just the *tip* of his iceberg."

# Kidding Aside

IT WAS 5:30 in the morning on Monday and Bartwick Dilworth was peeking into the office of the president of TrustTrust Banks with a big smile on his face.

The president was sitting back in his chair with a big smile on his face.

The reason they're doing all this smiling at each other at 5:30 in the morning, as opposed to any other time of the day, was that the TrustTrust public relations guy suggested that if all the bank big shots were to get to work at 5:30 in the morning, and if they could get some articles published in the newspaper and some magazines and maybe have a local television station do a story about how the "bank's leaders" arrived at 5:30 every morning because "they cared about you" as opposed to getting there at the crack of dawn because they wanted to beat traffic, then this would increase business and create a feeling of goodwill in the community. Bank big shots being seen and reported in the newspaper to have run in marathons was also suggested. On the day the article appeared in the newspaper about how they cared about you, three million people created new accounts at TrustTrust. So everybody was real happy.

But Dilworth and the president really weren't smiling because of that. They hated to have to get to work everyday at 5:30. They're smiling because word had already gotten around the home office and on the TrustTrust intranet chat rooms about what some downtown muckety-muck did at the Mullet Luv, Georgia/Publix branch on Saturday and the teller dweeb, everyone agreed, whose basic civil rights were violated—and how wild it got and how well the teller fended off the scum bag with great service and a smile. It was concluded by the employees who spent an inordinate amount of time typing up chat room letters to each other as opposed to performing their duties, that the teller won: Waymon Poodle of the Mullet Luv, Georgia Publix branch. He was the winner.

A banner crawled across the bottom of every computer screen of every TrustTrust employee in all five states and the District of Columbia with this announcement: Way to go Waymon!

No one knew that at 5:30 every morning the president of TrustTrust Banks read the chat room comments for kicks. "Ah," the president said with a satisfied tone, "Mr. *Won*ka. Come right in."

Dilworth walked in and sat down. It was a large office so it took him a while to get there. "*Big* news, chief."

"Give me the nutshell, Dilworth. I'm a busy man."

"It's five-thirty in the morning. How in the hell are you busy?"

"Hey, I finally decided to try to make the coffee as a gesture of goodwill to other people who work here. I've never made office coffee in my *life*. Dilworth, you want some advice now you're up here with the big shots?"

"Fuck. I *guess*."

"Just press the goddamn coffee machine start button *once*."

"*Yes*, chief."

"So, did you smell really bad?"

"Like a six pound poo-poo diaper. Remember those?"

"Outstanding, Dilworth. But you know ol' Wonkka down in public relations is upset you used his name."

"He's got an extra 'k' in his name, right? W-o-n-k-*k*-a?"

"Hell, I *think* so. It's not like I sit up here on the tenth floor all day counting the letters in emplo—"

"Well, I *don't* have an extra 'k'. W-o-n-k-*a*."

"Brilliant stroke, Dilworth. Goddamn brilliant. How long

did the transaction take?"

"Two and half hours."

"Jesus! You're kidding me."

"I'm not kidding. I'm pretty darn sure it's a company record. I got my mortgage refinanced. He reconciled my checkbook. And he showed me how to pay my bills online. The most incredible thing I've ever seen in my life—while I was emitting gross flatulence from my butthole the entire time and licking his nameplate with my tongue."

"Brilliant stroke, Dilworth. Brilliant. So he's our *man*, huh? And you've bottled him?"

"I'm typing up a big memo this morning—or one of my secretaries is. We're going to completely change the way we conduct business at the windows just because of this guy Waymon Poodle. We're going to be nice as shit to *every*body."

"All this in the budget?"

"No."

"Oh."

"But *chief*, there's one thing we've got to do for him, but I don't know if we can pull it off. It's a little weird."

"What's weird?"

"I called the branch manager and asked him what Poodle really wanted out of life and it has nothing to do with pecking up the ol' TrustTrust ladder. He's content to stay a teller."

"That's terrible."

"Here's all he wants out of life—this cat's life goal is to play Augusta."

The president made a face. "Augusta? Augusta *Country Club*?"

"God, no. Augusta *National*."

"You're kidding me."

"Hey! We've got some customers who are members, don't we?"

The president of TrustTrust looked to his left, then to his right as if he were looking to see if anyone else was in his office, then mouthed, "*I'm* a member."

"What? Speak up." Dilworth leaned toward him.

He mouthed it again—"*I'm* a member"—then fluffed his tie. An Augusta National Golf Club tie, just like the one Waymon wears to work every day. And to church.

"You're kidding me."

"No, I'm not."

"How come you never *told* me?"

"Look around my office, Dilworth."

Dilworth looked around the president's office. The walls were covered with prints of Augusta National Golf Club holes. Framed flags with invitee signatures. Hole-in-one balls under niche lights. "Chief, every booger eatin' Masters nerd in the *world* has this fake shit."

"Well, *see*, that's how guys like us—you know, *members*—keep it a secret. We all act like wannabees. But I'll tell you something, Dilworth, they don't want you to tell anybody you're a member."

"They? They *who?*"

"They. You know—*they*."

"*Oh.*"

"I swear to God. After you get in they have this super secret real big special meeting with you late at night about not telling people you're a member. And now, because I told you, I gotta to put a *cap* in yo ass."

They both laughed it up. Really laughed it up.

Dilworth secretly wanted to play too, so he kept pressing. "So let's do it then. Hey, all these consultants are saying we give employees movie tickets and carpal tunnel massages and crap like that even though they're doing their job anyway. Augusta National. Now that's a real reward."

"Well, sure, Dilworth, you *dumb* ass. But this Poodle is real strange looking. Plus I don't think I want to show up on the first tee in front of all my other members with the guy who grabbed our club receptionist's Bermuda grass. Hell, he's probably already played in the thing they have for all those volunteers so we're off the hook. So get back to work."

"Volunteer day got rained *out*."

"Well it's not *my* fault. Members of Augusta National Golf Club don't have any control over—the *wea*ther." The president winked.

"Chief, that's the day the hallowed back nine floated away. I heard the twelfth green got washed to Siloam."

"*What!*"

"You're a member and you didn't *know?*"

"Well I'm sure our fine golf course maintenance staff will *fix* it. My *God*. Close your eyes, Dilworth."

"Close my eyes for *what?*"

"So you won't see where I keep my member newsletter. I swear to God. After you get in they have this super secret real big special meeting with you late at night about not letting people see where you keep your member newsletter."

"You're kidding me."

"Shut up. Now close your eyes."

Dilworth barely closed his eyes.

The president kept his newsletter under his toupee. "All right. Yep. Says right here they fixed it the other day. The twelfth green is as good as new except—*huh*..."

"What?"

"Says here we're still missing a chunk of the green and the microchip in the chunk says it's somewhere—good *God*—in *Mull*et Luv. Get a load of *that*—somewhere in goddamn Mullet Luv. Now that's really a hopping place. I've got to get *up* there sometime. Hey Dilworth!"

"Sir!"

"*Cap* in yo ass. That was a *good* one."

Dilworth chuckled then made a strange expression.

"What, *now*? Quit chuckling and then making strange expressions. Get outta here."

"Chief, we gotta *do* something for this guy. We can play when the club reopens in the fall, *right?*"

"*We?*"

"Yeah, *we*. You, me, and *Poodle*—and whoever *else* you pick."

"Listen, just promote him to branch manager or something. Go give him a carpal tunnel massage."

"All he wants is to play Augusta Country Club—Jeeesus! Augusta National. And so do I."

"Fine. *God.* You can play. You're acting like a little kid, Dilworth."

"Well, this is what this thing *does* to people."

"Then call him up. Get him down here. We'll tell him he can play Augusta National and see if he shits."

Dilworth looked at his watch. "It's five forty-two in the *morning!*"

"If he's the bank's savior then he's probably sitting there waiting on the first valued customer to arrive—in the *dark!* And get up off your knees."

"But one more thing, chief."

"I'm *sure* I told you to get outta here."

In the presidential office suite of the president of TrustTrust Banks, Bartwick Dilworth rose from his Augusta National Golf Club begging position, turned around, and after pushing an Augusta National Golf Club paper weight to the side, hiked his rear end upon the enormous Brazilian cherry desk of the president of TrustTrust Banks then pulled the back of his jacket up.

"*Dil*worth," the president barked, "what the hell are you *doing?*"

"Chief, I saved the *big* one for you—from Saturday."

"*Saved* one. Saved *what* big one in God's name? *Dil*worth!"

"It's *Wonka,* chief. Garlic clove abuser—and it's harvest time."

# Air Waymon

THE PRESIDENT OF TrustTrust was right. Sort of.

Publix are open twenty-four hours a day so if he was at his teller window right then he wouldn't have been—technically—in the dark.

But Waymon was in the dark at that moment, the dark of apartment 1931. But the keypad of his green phone was brightly lit.

Beginning at 6:00 each morning Waymon began checking the branch's voice mails as he lay in bed. This was his idea.

It didn't take long for Waymon, who was, obnoxiously, the first to arrive every morning, to discover that valued customers often left voice mails in the middle of the night. Most of them were profanity-laced complaints concerning other banks, but every now and then, a valued customer might leave a reasonable question or a great idea the bank could use without the insistence of compensation. So Waymon decided to check the voice mails beginning at the crack of dawn each day. It thrilled Waymon to no end to ponder a valued customer's question or request while he took his shower and drove to the branch so he'd be prepared to call the valued customer the moment he got to the branch and give them the absolute best and correct answer according to Waymon Poodle and TrustTrust Banks. Of course, calling back valued customers was Waymon Boner's responsibility but he happily allowed Waymon the opportunity to enhance his customer service skills as Waymon seemed real freaked out to want to do it.

131

Waymon got an interesting message this morning that had been left at 5:45: A Bartwick Dilworth, Executive Vice President of Customer Service and the president of TrustTrust would like to see him downtown this morning as soon as possible. Okay, Waymon? Real important so soon as possible. Just come on down sometime before lunch to the president's office. Tenth floor. Thanks. Have a nice day.

"Lord God Jesus," Waymon breathed. Then hit the "2" button to replay it.

By car, from Mullet Luv to downtown Atlanta, was eighty-one miles and it usually takes almost two hours to get to Atlanta. Then you gotta throw in the traffic.

Of course, then you've got to find a parking space in one of those spooky parking decks and as you make your way to the building you've got to fend off homeless people and street preachers who pose complex philosophical or religious questions to you and follow you down the sidewalk or across the park until you give them an answer which was never correct in their opinion, even if it actually was the correct answer. This was once Waymon's personal experience. Of course, he could take the MARTA train but MARTA trains made him claustrophobic, especially when they went underground.

So instead of turning left out of the San Souci apartments toward Atlanta, Waymon Poodle, smiling, because he knew getting there real quick was the right thing to do as you never get called downtown by these people unless it's real bad or real good, not in between he had heard, turned right and drove half a mile to the Mullet Luv Helicopter Center. Come to find out the parking lot of the Mullet Luv Helicopter Center was already full of huge Mercedes and Dodge Vipers and Ferraris because Waymon discovered as he boarded a shiny green (an omen) helicopter, it was full of rich-type people who lived up there in Mullet Luv in some of those new rich-type neighborhoods and who refused to sit in Atlanta traffic and were willing to pay $150 per day, per round trip, weather permitting. They were all reading Wall Street Journals and golf magazines, more omens.

It was 6:08.

Waymon poked his head into the door of the president of TrustTrust Banks at 6:21. The seven secretaries weren't there yet so that's how he got in.

The president cheerfully said to Waymon his office had already been vacuumed and wiped off and whatnot. But thank you nonetheless and to go away and have a nice day.

"Sir," Waymon said. "You and Mr. Dilworth wanted to see me?"

The president made a strange expression. "And you *are?*"

"Waymon Poodle. Waymon Poodle of the Mullet Luv Publix branch."

The president looked around his office as if he were trying to find a prankster hiding behind one of his five sofas. Then he looked at his watch "How—"

"I took a helicopter. I thought I should get here as quick as I *could.*"

Although Waymon was sweating and his personal presentation was arresting, even more so at 6:21 in the early morning, the president walked toward Waymon with an expression of fear and appreciation all mixed together and wrapped an arm around his shoulder and led him to a chair, then whacked Waymon on the back. "You're an amazing animal, Waymon. Truly one of a kind of a human being. So good to *meet* you I think."

"*Thank* you." Waymon sat down.

"Now I mean that as a compliment."

"You bet, sir."

The president lurched forward and pointed. "Hey, I like your tie!"

"Hey, yours, too, sir."

They both smiled at each other and held their Augusta National Golf Club logoed ties in their hands and looked at each other's ties and smiled some more and essentially had a moment together. Then the president cleared his throat and called Dilworth on the phone.

"Good morning, Bartwick Dilworth the fourth, Executive Vice President of Customer Service of TrustTrust Banks. Thank you for calling. And how in the world can I help *you* today with *your* problem?"

The president cupped a hand over his mouth and whispered. "Cut the *shit*, Dilworth. You're not gonna believe who's sitting in my office at this very moment."

"Wonkka?"

"No, dumb ass—*Poodle*."

"No *way*. I just left a message at his branch not two minutes ago."

"He took a *heli*copter."

"Kiss my *ass*. He knows how to fly a helicopter, *too*?"

"*Dil*worth," the president said, "hang on a second."

"*Right!*"

"Uh, *Way*mon. Where's the helicopter now?"

"On the roof, waiting for me. There's a helicopter pad up there."

"Really?"

"Right up there on the roof."

"I did not *know* that. Well I'll be—*Dil*worth."

"*Yes*, chief!"

"Get *down* here."

"*Right!*"

While they waited for Dilworth, Waymon and the president kept fiddling with their ties and looking at each other, smiling uneasily.

The door opened.

"Ah, *Dil*worth!" The president shouted. "Waymon, do you recognize this fellow here?"

Waymon shook Dilworth's hand and smiled, as he was a very polite person, but had to admit he did not.

"Waymon, you met him Saturday at the branch. You had personal intercourse with him. A lot."

Waymon squinted a little harder. "Sir, I serve with joy an enormous number of valued customers every day, and I deeply apologize for not recognizing him. But I'll certainly make it a point to recognize him next time. Thank you."

Amazing.

"Well, Waymon, I'll just cut to the ol' chase here as we're all busy people doing things. Dilworth here put you on the spot Saturday and you passed an extremely difficult test."

Waymon's eyes widened. He looked at Dilworth and seemed as if he wanted to speak.

Dilworth whistled a silent tune.

Waymon's eyes widened some more.

"That's *right*, Waymon. But let's not rehash all the unpleasantness."

Waymon gazed at Dilworth with an odd look of admiration. "Lordy. Lord God Jesus in Heaven."

"Uhhhh, *right*. Now Waymon, let me ask you a question."

"Yessir."

"What could we do to reward you for your years of serving the needs of our valued customers? Especially Saturday. We'd like to promote you to branch manager or something."

Dilworth butted in. "Hey, I thought we were gonna go play—"

The president held his hand up.

Waymon straightened himself and took a big breath. "Sir, my life goal is—"

"Yes?"

"To *not* be a branch manager so that I can continue to serve, one on one, my valued customers in a face to *face* type way."

"Waymon, *really*," the president said. "Get a grip here. I know there's something *else* you want. Now tell me what it is. Let's be official about this, so so stand up."

Waymon stood up, but looked at his feet. "It's embarrassing."

"You can tell *me*. I'm your new *pal*. And stand up a little straighter!"

Waymon jerked his shoulders back. "Well, one day it's the most important thing in my life and the next day God punishes me for it. It's called desire, sir."

"Desire for what? Some Bermuda grass?"

"No, sir. I could have some of that anytime I wanted—actually."

Dilworth said stupidly, "Hey, way to go Way—"

"Shut up, *Dilworth!*"

"*Right!*"

"Sir, I simply desire to play Augusta National Golf Club one time before I die." Waymon took another big breath and looked as if he might cry.

"All *right. Now* we're getting somewhere, Waymon. Okay, now—how does Saturday, October the sixth sound, my boy? The first day of the season and the very first tee time." Puff chested, the president said, "I give you Augusta Country Club."

Waymon's heart dropped.

"I mean Augusta National, you know, *Golf* Club. *That* one. Sorry."

Waymon touched his head as if he had a sudden pain.

The president whacked Waymon on the back. "Just you and me and a couple of caddies. We'll have a great time. Just get there Saturday morning in time to hit a couple of warm up balls." The president pretended to hit a warm up ball.

"*Sir,*" Dilworth croaked.

"What *now?* Thus endeth my remarks, okay?"

Dilworth made a goofy expression.

"Oh, *yeah*, and Dilworth here. He might go, too." The president rubbed his hands together and produced some pretty obvious body language that communicated, unequivocally, the meeting was over and for them to get out. Then, when Dilworth and Waymon didn't get it, the president pushed them toward the door from behind. "Okay? Everybody okay with that date? Super *du*per. You fellows have a great summer—happy Fourth of July and Labor Day—and we'll see you *then*." He started to close the door.

Waymon suddenly stopped and the door hit him on the back. "Sir, I might have a slight problem." He touched his head again. This time the pain was real.

"*Way*mon? Your life goal we're talking about here. How slight can it be?"

"That's my wedding date."

The president whacked Waymon on the back. "Waymon, *no*body gets married in October. You get married in June."

"Yeah, *Way*mon. You get married in *June*," Dilworth said.

"Shut up, Dilworth," the president said.

"*Right!*"

Waymon said, "She's real headstrong, LaJuanita."

The president grinned. "La-wa-*nee*-ta?

"LaJuanita. LaJuanita Mumps."

"Sounds like she'd have some big hair, ol' LaJuanita," the president said. "She got some big hair, Waymon? Know what I *mean*? Credentials? Does LaJuanita have credentials?"

"She sure does, sir," Waymon said stupidly. He had no idea what the man was talking about.

The president squinted at Waymon. "I don't think you know what I mean, Waymon. This is hard *work*, communicating with you."

"She's got it going on, sir. She really, really does." Waymon felt like he hadn't breathed in the last fifteen minutes. His heart was racing like a sewing machine.

"*So*, Waymon. She play golf, *too*?" The president made another golf swing. He would have shanked it.

"Gosh, *no*. She thinks the wonderful sport of golf in general and the iniquitous allure of what goes on behind the gates of ootsie-tootsie private golf clubs are for flaming squids, bald fat farts, and mules."

Dilworth made a goofy face. "Say, what does iniquit—"

"Well, *hell*," the president bellowed, then pushed Dilworth out of the way and then whacked Waymon on the back, "Ol' LaJuanita's goddamn *right*!" The president began laughing so hard he ran out of air, then grabbed his throat with both hands so violently his toupee changed angles and his Augusta National Golf Club member newsletter slipped out and lodged into the cuff of his pants, and then he stumbled around his office knocking over chairs, some little tables, and three floor lamps, and then finally pulled down a nice set of Masters-logoed drapes.

In this delicate moment, Waymon and Dilworth thought the best course of action was to run away.

# A Purrsuasion

LaJuanita UNDERSTOOD. COMPLETELY. Sure she did. Six years of doing hair taught her a whole lot about mullets and human nature.

Waymon had figured it would be best to go ahead and tell her the news that night since the excitement of it would come through in his voice and mannerisms and facial expressions with great passion: Waymon Poodle had another definite date with Augusta National Golf Club. This one felt for real. It really did.

He had practiced what he was going to say to her in the bathroom mirror and Waymon thought it looked and sounded pretty good. So he lured her over to apartment 1931 with Wendy's food. LaJuanita loved Wendy's food. LaJuanita especially loved a Wendy's double with cheese and everything else and thought she looked sexy when some of the gook that got squeezed out of the cheeseburger ran down her neck and arms and sometimes onto her chest and between her boobs. LaJuanita was wrong about that, but that's what she thought. Waymon appreciated it when LaJuanita ate Wendy's cheeseburgers over his sink or bathtub or even the commode but she never would.

Just a second after Waymon hit her with the thing about meeting the president of the bank and him being a member and him being real proud of me and my teller work and him being a member (he purposely repeated that part) of Augusta National Golf Club and the business about the first tee time on the first day of the season and how that was also their wedding date and how he felt like he ought to do what the president of the bank told him to do and that was to play golf with him, then LaJuanita's mind went into quick action. She took a big bite out of the double. Then she said, while chewing, that—all right—they could change the date—to the next Saturday if Waymon would do one thing—for her that evening and any other—time she wanted it.

Waymon asked what she wanted, you know, him to do. Asking this question made him very nervous.

Even though LaJuanita was thoroughly "experienced," there was still something about Waymon that turned her on to the highest degree. Particularly the fact he had a steady job with a big company and he wanted to have fourteen kids, too.

Waymon asked her again what it was she wanted him to do as she was really making that Wendy's double disappear and wasn't answering his question.

LaJuanita said she wanted Waymon to finally fornicate with her, but after she finished eating and then he could go play golf at Augusta Country Club on their wedding day.

*Well* now.

Waymon, using everything he had beginning from vacation Bible school to the current lessons he obtained in Sunday School and all the sermons he'd ever heard in his life and watched on TV and most of the stuff he read in the Bible, especially Job, had to quickly rationalize how God might beat the hell out of him if he fornicated with LaJuanita, even if he didn't enjoy it.

The thought—fornication—did actually interest him. Waymon was Waymon, sure, but he wasn't a cave monk. He had been told once, by a nurse, while she held it in her hands, that his pecker was one of the biggest ones she'd ever seen.

LaJuanita could tell Waymon was really sorting this one out as she started in on the fries. Eight or nine shoved in there at a time. "Whatcha—th—ink?" she said with two good hiccups. She was eating that cheeseburger too fast. "We're definitely getting—married—so it's—ooooo—kay. I've been saying this to you—for the last six—months. If you don't want to get married then let's not for—ni—cate and I'll just go off and fornicate with soooooomebody—named Ken—or something. Or another

140

Pootie Tang named *Mitch*." Then LaJuanita burped. She'd been drinking Miller Lite in cans all afternoon, too, but God forbid if Waymon found out.

Waymon didn't quite understand the logic of fornication. But he understood his destiny. There had been too many omens. The president of his company, a member no less of Augusta National Golf Club, has made official plans and has official expectations I will arrive at the official appointed time and tee. So Waymon said, officially, "Let's do it."

"Do *what?*"

"What do you mean 'do *what?*' "

"I'm just making sure you—wanna—*do* it," LaJuanita hiccupped, then burped, then hiccuped again.

"I wanna *do* it."

"I wanna finish—my fooooood."

"Finish your food and we'll *do* it."

"But I wanna take a shower first, because I'm nasty down there. I'll get all hot and steamy, then you come on in the bathroom real slow and sexy and take off your clothes and wiggle yourself around while I *watch*." LaJuanita chewed for a moment. "Waymon, ho—ney?"

"Yes, LaJuanita," Waymon said flatly as he was thinking the correct shot was to fade it around Tea Olive's fairway bunker and not try to hit it right to left because if it didn't turn *left* for some reason you're dead in the bunker.

"Then, like in them sex movies," LaJuanita said. "You come on in there and soap up my boobs."

# Doin' It

AFTER WAYMON FRANTICALLY fornicated with LaJuanita, she left to go out to some bars with a bunch of friends.

Waymon went into the second bedroom and shut the door behind him. Because Waymon felt guilty about fornicating with LaJuanita and making her scream a lot, he felt he should punish himself. He turned his computer on, pulled up the Internet, and typed in that certain address given to him by his Christian psychologist, then hit Search. Shakily, wearily, and with extreme tension.

# PROFESSOR JEEVPIL BISWAPATI'S ULTIMATE! AND EXCLUSIVE! GIANT CICADA KILLER WASP WEB SITE

*http://www.georgiainstituteoftechnology.edu/Entomology/~biswa pati/KILLER.html*

*July 2014*

YES, MY DEVOTEES, entomology pays. I told you! Yes, I did! Pays good!

*Last evening at the Washington Road Hooters I used a little bit of my $800,000 "Super Whopper Location and Elimination" grant given to me by the Augusta Chamber of Commerce. If you have not been to one of these unique dining establishments then allow me to tell you it is hard to concentrate on your chicken wings.*

*I felt I stood out from the local patrons and perhaps was perceived as strange by my Hooters' food and beverage servant, Pam. She asked me what I was up to in this part of town and after I told her she said, "Creee-peee." I cannot blame Pam. I am creeped out by my discoveries here. That God forsaken Feckle.*

*As you know, I believe nothing is more beautiful than to see a giant cicada killer wasp drag a stunned cicada into its humid burrow, then suck its juices out. It is the same feeling I had watching my eleven children gain freedom from the humid womb. But this is no longer beautiful, my devotees. It is not beautiful to see a Lamar Feckle super whopper drag a* cocker spaniel or a flapping chicken into its lair. And then to hear their screams.

Upon meeting with the nice people of the Augusta Chamber of Commerce I stuck the check into a hole in my sari then asked them where might I find expansive areas of sandy, well drained soil in full sunlight in Augusta, Georgia, as this is where the super whoppers would have certainly ended up. I was directed to a place called Augusta National Golf Club. This is where Feckle's gob have come to roost and pulsate.

I have once seen a golf course in a magazine, but this is not what I expected. I understand wealthy men with prominent bellies and turkey necks follow around a little white ball and attempt to loft the ball into the air with a titanium device called a "club" onto a "green." A most difficult endeavor this golf must be. At Augusta National Golf Club the greens are protected by tents that must, I think, be used to deflect the balls into "traps of sand." Bulldozers also roam the golf course scooping up large wads of grass and dirt. Bodies of water are deliberately re-routed in an attempt to frustrate the man who is golfing. Large tree planting machines scoop up various trees—some over 300 feet tall—and move them only inches from where they once stood. Loud helicopters constantly fly over the golf course with photographers taking photographs of these various activities. Certain of these aforementioned greens are also dug up and replaced on exactly the place where they once were! They say they are "proofing" the course for a "tiger." I have not come to this place for tigers. I do not understand.

But this I understand: the caretakers of this golf course, who constantly chew and spit tobacco-laden saliva streams into the air and smoke Marlboro Lights—at the same time—are very nervous. Feckle's gob have chosen as their base of destruction and horror a place called the "twelfth tee," noted by the locals to be hallowed. These caretakers are meaty, sunburned men, but they are afraid of this twelfth tee and the perverted creatures who roam and rule the air space above, and below, this grass, or in their unique vernacular, "turf." Super whopper elimination is simple work, I have informed them. Take a tennis racket down there and whack the Feckle out of them. I'll watch from here. "Toby done tried that," one meaty fellow retorted. "And Toby ain't never come back yet."

*Toby, I know, is being cuddled in the arms of the mukhya nyayadhish. I, Jeevpil Biswapati, must regroup and really earn my cabbage as the tennis racket idea is my best one. I admit, I am also confused and afraid. Now I must ponder what drastic action to take.*

*Over another bucket of chicken wings at Hooters.*

# Waymon's Reaction to Professor Biswapati's Latest News

TALKING TO HIS computer screen in the eerie quiet of apartment 1931: "Professor Biswapati. You gotta get those thangs by October *sixth*. Oh my *Lord*."

# PART V

## SUMMER OF SOAP

# Sweat Equity

SO THERE WAS Waymon, all summer long soaping up LaJuanita's boobs and fornicating and trying as hard as he could not to daydream about super whopper giant cicada killer wasps at Augusta National Golf Club.

It was a long summer.

Waymon discovered LaJuanita enjoyed fornication with all the covers kicked down to the end of the bed and Waymon, covered with goose bumps wearing a purple Trojan "Magnum XL" condom covered with pleasure knobs the size of pencil erasures, on top of her for a while—over her, really—as if he were doing push-ups, then she'd flip over and Waymon would fornicate for a while that way, then she'd flip over and finish on up. LaJuanita never knew when Waymon was finishing on up as he never announced when he was finishing on up or made any finishing on up-type noises. He was so business-like about it.

LaJuanita wasn't so creative herself, but Waymon didn't know otherwise. Her key mid-fornication phrases, delivered in an fairly monotone tone of voice, while she stared at the ceiling fan's pull cord over Waymon's shoulder, were, "Give it to me, Waymon," and "That's the way—Waymon—to give it—to me."

LaJuanita, after a few sessions of fornicating, finally said to Waymon, "I finally figgerd out when you finish on up because you twist up yer face all funny when you finish on up. You oughta look at yerself in a mirror."

Fine, so I twist my face up. You burp and claw your fingernails all over my back.

While fornicating, Waymon would occasionally glance over at his Bible on the night stand and shake his head in shame and shaking his head would usually make a big drop of sweat fall off his nose and hit LaJuanita in the face, which sometimes was okay and sometimes not okay because it depended on the status of her makeup and if she had somewhere else to go after they fornicated whereas her makeup needed to be on right.

What really bothered Waymon the most about all this was that after the front nine he was always five over and it seemed his approach shot placement was getting him into trouble. You had to stick it near the pin, Waymon knew, or otherwise you were looking for trouble. Ten, Camellia, was a tough hole for him as it was for a lot of the invitees and he never seemed to have that much trouble with Azalea, but being eight over after Azalea got Waymon worried because there were still some tough holes ahead, like Holly. So when LaJuanita would flip over, Waymon would start back at two, Pink Dogwood, as he always birdied Tea Olive, and try to get his drive a little farther over to the right so he'd have a clear second shot, but not in that fairway bunker. They had moved the tee back Waymon knew, so he could really beat it down there, but that bunker was always in his mind's eye. Waymon loved the third shot on Pink Dogwood, usually with a lob wedge, to the second green.

LaJuanita yawned. She looked over at the clock radio.

Waymon knew there were two bunkers up there by the green but they didn't bother him. It was definitely a birdie hole. Then one evening, Waymon cold shanked his third shot on Pink Dogwood with his lob wedge, and that's all he needed to push him toward lessons. His secondary goal was to break the course record at Augusta National Golf Club and be well known for that and maybe after he did Nick Price, the current record co-holder, might call him up from South Africa and Greg Norman from Australia, the other current record co-holder, and congratulate him. Wow, the course record. It could happen. Could. They would up and call him.

That meant shooting a sixty-two. That meant he needed

149

some help. That meant he needed some lessons. Some lessons now.

LaJuanita, lying there, squirming a little bit, staring at the pull cord, while Waymon humped like a piston, finally said she finished on up about twenty minutes ago and she'd appreciate if he would too.

# Blind Devotion

THE WEDNESDAY NIGHT scene at the Mullet Luv Golf
Center was frightening to an outsider—mostly out of town
business guys staying at local hotels who come over to whack a
few balls in their expensive logoed golf shirts from their home
clubs or some resort they took the wife and kids to or the golf
courses near where they had a trade show. They have to make a
quick decision once they walk through the door whether to
proceed to the counter. Most do not proceed. The facility does
not smell nice.

But for the regulars there's a comfort to the place. Snort and
Billy there tonight, sure. Shirley as snack bar counter clerk,
referee. And there's Jim, now more than ever. He'd been fired
from IBM and had grown a goatee and gotten an ear ring and his
verbal inflections were growing more and more Mullet Luv even
though he was from New Jersey. And Waymon, the center of
attention more than ever. Every Wednesday night the clamor
about his Masters volunteer Bermuda grass grab-and-hold not
dying down, fading away, but getting worse. Waymon more than
ever a curiosity. His face and Bermuda grass-cupping hand on the
cover of seventy-two different golf magazines and they're
scattered on the big round table. Always being held up, pointed
at, shaken in Waymon's face. Bermuda grass grabber, man.
They'd worn out the snack bar VCR playing the moment of
Waymon's grabbing on CBS over and over.

Tonight Waymon was, like it or not, "The Unexplained."
Sweat drying, he'd hit two big baskets. Some balls solid. Some not

quite right and he was scared. The Unexplained, picking at the corner of a business card he'd pulled off of the bulletin board coated with the cards of real estate agents and chiropractors. LaJuanita had a few up there. Hers noted her experience in creating award winning Senior Prom mullets, Prison mullets, Probation mullets, Court Appearance mullets, Bass Tournament mullets, and Softball, Wedding, Divorce Court, Body Builder, NASCAR Race Weekend, and Biker mullets and she's just introduced to America a new six hundred dollar hairdo for women called the "Corn Cob."

THE UNEXPLAINED: "This fella here says he can improve your game in ten swangs. Angus O'Riley. Just *ten*? Now ain't *that* something."

SHIRLEY, from behind the counter: "Sugar, he come in here the other night. I sorta felt sorry for him, so I let him put his card up there. He's a little *diff*-ernt than most of them others what I let put their cards up there."

BILLY: "If he's diff-ernt, then him and The Unexplained outta get along just *fine*!"

SNORT AND BILLY: High fives. Adam's apple-bobbing gulps of beer. Fresh cigarettes lit with squinting eyes.

Different. A little different? Waymon wore his expressions on his sleeve.

SNORT: "*Unexplaaaaaained*, the dude's *blind*."

THE UNEXPLAINED: "That's *crazy*. How could a man teach a golf lesson if he was *blind*?"

SNORT: "And the dude hobbles around like a goat, *too*. I *seen* him, didn't I Shirley? I seen him come hobblin' in here with his cane and like he could see he trucked on over there and tacked his *biz*-ness card on the board and boogies his gimp ass right on *outta* here! It was goddamn *weird*. I shot him a *bird*."

SHIRLEY, distastefully: "Sure, *Snort*, you *seen* him. You was sittin' right there in a puddle of your own juices. So *what* you shot him a bird?" Shirley rolled her eyes. Drunk speak. Every so often it made sense, but not tonight.

SNORT, distastefully, as he banged his empty beer can on

the table: "Bring me another goddamn Miller Lite, woman."

BILLY: "Yeah, me goddamn, too. *Me* want one."

JIM, looking real Mullet Luv with that new goatee and the subtle beginnings of the local hairdo and a hard pot belly, born of robotic, nightly beer drinking with Snort and Billy at the Mullet Luv Golf Center: "Yeah, baby. I'm horny for one, *too*."

SHIRLEY: "*God*, you dumb country hick redneck sister marryers."

Waymon called the blind man when he got home and met him on the range the next night after a session of fornication. She skipped the boob-soaping-up part as they were getting tender after so much recent action. Waymon had skinny hands but they were strong.

A blind golf instructor. Waymon chuckled to himself. What the heck. And the blind shall see. Asked me did my clubs fit, like my shoes. Didn't teach people whose clubs don't fit.

A taxi brought him. He hobbled like a goat and used a cane and was blind. He brought a stool, a green Masters stool with the logo (another omen), and sat down next to Waymon's big basket. Not a word while Waymon took warm up swings. He was listening to them. Then he asked for twenty dollars.

Waymon gave him the money but he never put it in his pocket, just held it in his hand.

From a passing pick-up truck, someone yelled, "Five, ass-*hoooole!*"

Waymon didn't look. Eyes on the teacher there, sitting on the Masters stool.

"Ten balls," the man said. "Ten only."

"Okay. Mr. O'Riley, what club should I use?"

"An iron."

"Which one?"

"A *five*."

Waymon already had it in his hand. Couldn't believe he was doing this. Knew how stupid he'd look if he told the man his goal was to shoot a sixty-two at Augusta National Golf Club.

Snort and Billy and Jim, down a few stations, making faces,

belching, whacking. Beers drunk in two gulps then pressed into the forehead. Basketball shots with the pressed cans at the mesh trash baskets. Air cans.

Waymon: "Ready?"

He nodded.

Waymon hit.

"On the *toe*."

"Yeah, it was." Waymon looked at the clubface. A white smudge with stretched out dimple marks, like gaping, screaming mouths.

"Why?"

"I'm just swanging at it. I'm not trying to hit it solid."

He shrugged his shoulders.

Waymon hit number two solid. The third on the toe again.

"You *swung* too fast."

"I did."

"Then don't *swing* fast. Seven away from knowing everything."

Number four: fairly solid.

"Not quite?"

"No, sir."

"Why?"

"*You* know why. Next ball."

Number five: topped it.

"Why'd you *top* it?"

"This is making me nervous."

"What part scares you the most? You've never taken golf lessons from an old blind man?"

"It's knowing how to hit a golf ball perfectly but not doing it."

"You're not scared—you're lazy. It takes about two and a half seconds to hit a golf shot perfectly. Two and a half seconds, son."

"I'm not a lazy person. I'm really not."

"Then hit five perfect shots in a row, Waymon Poodle. I *dare* you."

# State Ammo

SIX WEEKS LATER Waymon Poodle won the Georgia State Men's Amateur Championship at East Lake Golf Club.

Waymon won it all right.

He did.

The Atlanta newspaper shouted his story in "Sports," then the next Sunday in "Living," on the front page with a big color photo of his face.

Who? *Who* won our prestigious state amateur championship?

The *bank* teller.

*Who?*

The guy who plays out of that butt hole Mullet Luv Golf Center. You ever gone up there and played that toilet? Rednecks in coach's shorts. Brains and shirts and shoes are *not* required. I been up there man, and it's scary.

The *weird* looking guy?

*You* know, the Masters volunteer guy. He was on the cover of every damn golf magazine grabbing that woman's Bermuda grass. And on TV, too!

Oh *that* guy. Yeah, he's an American *he*ro!

Waymon won it all right.

By five shots.

# Toby?

BECAUSE WAYMON FELT guilty about beating all those other nice fellows in the state amateur—the first golf tournament he'd ever played in—and then watched as forty-two of them, who looked as if they'd been preparing their entire lives to win this one single event, wept in the parking lot, he felt he should punish himself.

So he turned his computer on, pulled up the Internet, and typed in that certain address, then hit Search. Shakily, wearily, and with extreme tension.

# PROFESSOR JEEVPIL BISWAPATI'S ULTIMATE! AND EXCLUSIVE! GIANT CICADA KILLER WASP WEB SITE

*http://www.georgiainstituteoftechnology.edu/Entomology/~biswapati/KILLER.html*

September 2014

*THEY HAVE NOT found Toby.*

A new employee, Toby had not yet had his Augusta National Golf Club Employee Location Microchip surgically inserted under his scalp. They have a big electronic "course layout" on the wall in a place at Augusta National Golf Club called the center of golf course maintenance used to monitor the activities of these tobacco spitters and their machinery. This is one sophisticated place, my devotees.

Cuddled in the arms of the mukhya nyayadhish, I tell them, Toby is. They do not know who the hell the mukhya nyayadhish is. Or Toby is still barely alive and most likely being "cocooned" by the super whoppers in their underground burrow—the super whoppers slowly sucking out Toby's juices like in "Aliens" (see photo below courtesy of Warner Bros.).

Mukhya nyayadhish help me. I have decided to take on this super whopper elimination process myself. I am used to delegating to underclassmen as you know, but now I must, as they say in sports vernacular, "step up." The flame-thrower has arrived. It is a goddamn fire breathing dragon. In the get-to-know-each-other phase, I have already killed two bulldozers, what they call a "flag" "stick," melted my long *fingernails, and singed the tip of my jibh.*

*From far away, my devotees, I have spied the super whoppers with a pair of really powerful binoculars. And they have spied me. They wait for me at this place called the twelfth tee. I have been told by the locals and the tobacco spitters that the thang is a "par 3," the toughest par three in the world of championship golfing competition.*

*But this is no championship competition like you enjoy in your pansy-ass intramural volleyball games with your cold beers and gurgling hookah bongs and your bisexual girlfriends and your infected tattoos and eyelid rings when you should be studying about giant cicada killer wasps. This is a fight to the death. If I survive, you will find me at Hooters, cuddled in the arms of Pam.*

*My devotees, I will tell you this so listen the hell up—main vahan ja raha hun, you cow eaters!*

## *Waymon's Reaction to Professor Biswapati's Latest News*

TALKING TO HIS computer screen in the eerie quiet of apartment 1931: "Lord, I don't *want* to skip the twelfth *hole*. That's where I want to make a *bir*die. Now I've been telling you that for *years—dang it*."

# PART VI

## A DREAM COME BLUE

# Butler Cabin Fever

*We were intrigued by recent studies that prove golf really messes male humans up real good.*

*The golfer who has finally obtained a tee time at Augusta National Golf Club, we discovered, becomes immediately disoriented and might brush his teeth with his toenail clipper. The subject fails to wave "thank you" to people who let him merge into traffic. The infants of these subjects waddle aimlessly through their home, dragging around six pound poo-poo diapers. These subjects, who now frequently run out of gas, sit in the middle of an interstate highway, dislocomoted, and don't care one bit, even while a state patrolman taps on their window with the tip of his .357 magnum. The golfer's tendency, who now has this tee time, is to gaze into space and smile.*

—From the September 2014 issue of *Go Figure*, the monthly report of the American Psychological Association

AS IRRITATING AS it was to people, especially to those foreign people who bag groceries and always stare at Waymon, even while they're bagging groceries, and even when they're mopping up something they spilled because they dropped something onto the floor while they were busy staring at Waymon when they should have been watching what they were bagging, Waymon was bright and cheerful on Monday mornings when he got to work. God forbid they if they knew he was bright and cheerful before he got to work.

Waymon never had to worry about a Monday morning hang over and since he was the last to leave the branch on Saturday afternoon, he gladly finished up the last business and turned off the lights and the copier and the coffee machine and locked the door—so the slate was clean and ready for action come Monday morning and that made Waymon happy as he loved his job so much. Sometimes on Saturday afternoons Waymon might be all the way in the parking lot about to stick the key into the lock of his Diplomat and then all of a sudden run back and unlock the branch door and check the contents of the employee refrigerator just to make sure something turning to goo or spewing mold got thrown away.

On the Monday morning of the week Waymon was to play Augusta National Golf Club there he sat serving a multitude of valuable customers.

Very badly.

Which was unlike Waymon Poodle, the friendliest and most competent of any teller in any branch in all five states and the District of Columbia in which TrustTrust did business. He really shouldn't have been distracted and irritable. That summer he won the state amateur championship, just like Bob Jones did once, the founder of Augusta National Golf Club. Waymon's game was in perfect shape for the practice range and that big practice green they have and the sloping fairways and slick greens of Augusta National Golf Club. It was just that he didn't know yet what the plan was. Waymon liked to know what the plans were. The president of TrustTrust or that crazy Mr. Dilworth fellow or the Augusta National Golf Club head pro or that crazy Betty Simpson if she still works there hadn't called him yet. So Waymon was distracted and irritable—he was desperately thinking about why the phone wasn't ringing or why he hadn't got a FedEx delivery from Augusta National Golf Club or why the phone wasn't ringing or…

Just then, the phone rang.

Waymon wondered if the omens were still coming even though he was set, or supposed to be. A moment later, instead of with a perceptible level of obnoxia, but with an extreme level of obnoxia, Waymon called from the break room for Waymon to come get the phone.

Waymon trotted back there. Waymon grabbed for the phone, but Waymon jerked it back before he could get it. Waymon said, "It's your *golf* buddy—the president of TrustTrust Banks. Hoo-dee-*doo*."

"That's not nice, saying hoo-dee-*doo* like that. Give me that *phone*." Waymon grabbed for the phone again.

"I've been working at TrustTrust for twenty-three *years* and I ain't *never* talked to the president. And here's ol' Waymon Poodle just yakking it up with him. So, hoo-dee-doo-*doo*."

Waymon grabbed the phone and bumped Waymon out of the chair and sat down. "Now that I *really* don't like. Adding *doo*-doo to it."

"Then how about hoo-dee-*shit*-shit."

Waymon's eyes widened. "Now that's just downright sacrilegious—and dang *foul* mouthed."

"Hoo-dee-*shit*-shit, then."

Now Waymon's mouth hung open. His eyes were still wide, too.

Waymon pointed a finger at Waymon. "So what do ya think about *that*—you Bible thumper!"

"I'm a Bible reader!" Waymon pointed for Waymon to go up to the front and sort of wiggled his finger for Waymon to shut the door, too.

The moment Waymon got up to the front he hit the buzzer. *Buzz—buzzzz.*

Waymon sucked in a huge breath and then stuck the phone to the side of his face. "Sir, Waymon *Poo*dle here. I can't tell you how exci—"

"*Way*mon," the president said in a chilling tone, "I have some

163

rather bad *news* to deliver. Rather, well, bad—as *hell*."

Waymon scrunched his face up. "It's not about Saturday is it?" Waymon's heart was already racing. He cupped the phone and took another huge breath and began reciting the Lord's Prayer in his mind.

"*Well*, son. It's about Saturday *and* Friday."

Nothing.

*Buzz—buzz—buzz.*

"What's that damn *buzz*ing noise? You there, Waymon?"

"Yessir. What do you mean 'Friday?' "

"Well, I'm just afraid you might not like how I've mangled this whole thing *up*. You being so deserving to play golf at Augusta National Golf Club."

Resolved to it now. Never, ever question God's design. The fornication with that horny dang LaJuanita. Soaping up all her boobs. Waymon began to weep.

The president said, "I just hate you'll have to come down Friday afternoon instead of Saturday morning and stay in the Butler Cabin with me and Dilworth here and Jack *Nick*-lawse."

Nothing again. Waymon's expression like the moment of the revealing of the Bermuda grass. As if he'd seen a ghost. He didn't like it when people pronounced Mr. Nicklaus' name like that. But maybe that really was the way to do it. Now Waymon wasn't exactly sure. Now Waymon was real confused.

*Buzzzzzz.*

"Waymon, I keep losing you here. I'm a busy man doing things."

"Sir, I'm—did you say Jack Ni—"

"See, I'm just afraid you might not like to get on down to the ol' *golf* club on Friday afternoon and get settled in the ol' Butler Cabin, you know where they do part of the ol' TV thing down there, and have dinner with Jack and me and *Dil*worth. I'll show you our wine cellar."

"Sir, I'm—did you say Jack Ni—"

"*Right*. Now I got elected Membership Committee Chairman this summer and for God knows why the Entomology

Committee Chairman and at dinner with Jack on Friday night I'm going to tell him he's been elected to the membership since he might have been miffed we let Ed Fiori in a couple of years ago so that moment will be a hugely historic moment in the history golf and you'll be right there at the dinner table with him when I give him the good news. To get him to come we told him we were going to pay him ten million dollars to redesign a bunker and he cleared his schedule for two days. Hey, Waymon—you know they call Jack Nick-lawse the Golden Bear?"

Snickering heard in the background of the president's office.

*Buzz—buzzzzz.*

Waymon staring off into space. Mouth gaping. Tears of joy now. As we forgive those who trespass against us...

"And then Saturday morning we'll pack our bellies with a monstrously greasy breakfast and burp real loud and then tee it up with Jack. *Jack*, baby, Waymon. First tee time. First day of the season. You know you measly guests can't play from the tournament tees—we got this big rule that says measly guests can't play from the tournament tees—but guess what I finagled. Just *guess*. I really hope that sounds okay. I just hope I haven't mangled this thing up for you, Waymon." The president burped real loud.

Waymon wiped his cheek with the back of his hand. "No, sir. Of *course* not. Praise Jeesus."

"Yeah, okay, *Jesus*, sure. *Hey*, so bring a coat and tie for Friday night. You got a green jacket, Waymon?" The president wanted to laugh so badly but he thought he might burst an artery. Got a green jacket.

Dilworth snickering so hard he's about to pee in his pants. Both hands pressed over his mouth. Red faced, beating his shoes on the carpet as if he were stomping fire ants. And so happy he got invited. Had to kiss ass and lick crack and wipe crack and brown nose and suck up every day, all summer long. And beg. He was exhausted.

165

The president rolling his eyes. "*Way*mon? You there?"

"Here, sir," Waymon said meekly, wet faced.

"And *hey*, congratulations on that state am, Waymon. Aren't *you* the total package."

# *T.G.I.T.*

THURSDAY.

Because Waymon never got a transaction right all week, pretty much beginning Monday morning, Waymon fired him on Thursday afternoon.

Waymon waited for everybody to leave and as Waymon was pouring the tar-like goo substance of the office coffee into the sink, Waymon up and fired him.

Waymon turned around and gave Waymon a strange look. He didn't say anything at first, just like when LaJuanita hit him with the fornication ultimatum, so Waymon chewed on the situation for a moment. Surely, the last thing in the world Waymon Poodle would be accused of was being pompous or arrogant. But Waymon really did have a relationship with the president of the whole dang company. He thought at that moment, Here was a man who was a member of Augusta National Golf Club, the same gentleman who invited me to meet him at Augusta National Golf Club less than twenty-four hours from this moment to play golf and hang out with him and Jack Nicklaus at Augusta National Golf Club. So if Waymon had ever done the same thing with the president of TrustTrust Banks and Jack Nicklaus at Augusta National Golf Club then he would have made a big deal out of it for a month. This was a heady feeling for Waymon. Waymon said, with a slight bit of pomposity in his voice, "I don't think you can *fire* me."

Waymon waggled a finger at Waymon. "Oh, yes I *can!*"

Waymon had what are called "donkey smarts," and knew

when dealing with people such as Waymon who he felt like didn't have donkey smarts, not one bit, it was best to just to agree to whatever it was they wanted then shut your mouth. Use your donkey smarts. Call their bluff. So Waymon said, using his donkey smarts, "Okay then." And walked out.

"*Hey*!" Waymon yelled. "You can't just walk out like that! I just *fired* you!"

## *Bunkered Up*

*And there's one other thing.*

*Now that the golfer is on the property of Augusta National Golf Club to exercise this tee time he's obtained, we have discovered that a period of intense unreality begins and sometimes might not end, even after the golfer blows out of the front gate and back into the Real World.*

*This unreality, our research produced, can include an overwhelming feeling of what's called "heebie-jeebies," hallucinatory activity, and the possibility of actually beating Jack Nicklaus in golf. And a bunch of other stuff.*

*Therefore, we finally conclude, that those who have played Augusta National Golf Club, as compared to those who have not played Augusta National Golf Club, are distinctly different from those who almost played Augusta National Golf Club.*

—From the September 2014 issue of *Go Figure*, the monthly report of the American Psychological Association

WAYMON POODLE HAD the heebie-jeebies real bad.

Friday morning real early he was rolling around on the grass in front of his apartment as if he were on fire. Actually, it wasn't grass Waymon was rolling around on. It was more like hard packed red dirt with a few small rocks and bullet casings and bits of concrete blocks and clumps of hair with the skin still attached and a whole bunch of beer caps and an eyeball that kept getting pressed into his shirt and his kneecaps and some cigarette butts were getting stuck in his hair too.

Mr. Gable, of course, was watching this scene from afar with his Chihuahua and didn't see Waymon with a pistol in his hand with a silencer on it, or a rifle with a scope with a silencer on it, or a knife in his hand, or a sharp ice pick in his hand so he walked over to Waymon and asked him what the hell he was doing.

While he was still rolling around on the dirt, Waymon said, "I don't want these new—*golf* clothes—I bought last night at *Dill*ard's—to look too new. You know?"

"Not really," Mr. Gable said.

Waymon stood up and brushed himself off. There was a cigarette butt in his ear. "I just think I'll look like a hick if my golf clothes look too new when I pass through the holy *gates* this afternoon."

"Waymon?"

"Yessir. Mr. Gable?"

That Chihuahua barked specifically at Waymon then started gnawing on a flea on his leg.

"Can I tell you something that's been on my mind for a long time and you not get all messed up?"

"Well, *sure*, Mr. Gable."

"Waymon, you've got to be the strangest cat I've ever met in my life. And I've known loads of strange and dangerous cats." Mr. Gable squinted at Waymon. "But I love you, Waymon. You really are a dangerous country hick. A real perfect example. Like they use in the movies. You know what I mean?"

"No."

So Waymon went back inside and put his dirty golf clothes in the washer—cold, one rinse, delicate—and while his clothes were getting washed he called Waymon at the bank branch to make sure if he really was fired or not, just to make sure. To think he could have served some valuable customers from his bank branch window on the very same day he'd pass through the gate of Augusta National Golf Club, even though he'd have to leave work earlier than normal, delighted Waymon quite a lot.

"What part of 'You're fired' don't you understand, *Waymon?*" Waymon said real mean.

Waymon thought his heebie-jeebies might let up once he got on the road and started listening to gospel music, but they didn't. He didn't want to drive too fast because he didn't want to get a ticket, but he got a ticket near Siloam on I-20 anyway because he was driving too slow.

Waymon honestly thought all those people riding up on his tail in the left lane, then swerving around him and honking their horns and making arm and hand and finger and ferocious facial gestures, knew, somehow, he was traveling to Augusta National Golf Club to play golf. Waymon honestly thought that those who are about to play Augusta National Golf Club had an aura and it was real obvious. Even the aura of their cars.

Waymon took a right onto Berckmans Road and went down there to see if they had come and gotten the twelfth green, and it looked like they had, so he drove to the holy gates and stopped the Diplomat, which was hissing like a cat and steaming like a volcano, by the guard house. Waymon could not have cared less about his car about to blow up. He glanced over his shoulder to the back seat to make sure his golf clubs and his golf shoes were still back there and they were, and this made him feel very nice. Not that they would have gone anywhere. This was just the kind of things heebie-jeebies made Waymon do six hundred and four times, smiling oddly, during the drive down I-20 to Augusta in the left hand lane going real slow.

As he had hoped an enormous number of times in his life, Waymon's name was on a list with the guard in the guard house on Washington Road. Waymon asked the Lord God Jesus to drive him through the gate after the guard saluted him and told him how nice it was to have him as a guest and hopefully many times in the future. So Waymon drove through the gate after the guard saluted then and told him how nice it was to have him as a guest and hopefully many, many times in the future. The guard took down Waymon's tag number as he drove away.

Waymon, then, with the Lord God Jesus' assistance since his hands were shaking so violently, drove slowly, reverently, desperately trying not to run over all those weird looking magnolia pine cone things on the asphalt of Magnolia Lane even though there weren't any weird looking magnolia pine cone things on the asphalt of Magnolia Lane. But if there were, Waymon would not have run over them.

He did not go and have lunch in the men's grill, into the pro shop to say hello and thank them and to buy seventeen logoed shirts, onto the practice range, then onto the first tee of Tea Olive, however. Or to see that dang Betty Simpson.

He parked in front of the Butler Cabin and was immediately met by an ancient man in a white waiter-style jacket and a white shirt and black tie who took his suitcase and walked inside with it and took it to Waymon's room and unpacked it and saw a need to begin ironing his golf shirt and a pair of pants and was planning to steam this fellow's bright orange jacket as it had been crammed in there too. Waymon graduated from Clemson a year early and the orange jacket was a gift from his six different grateful, exhausted guidance counselors. It was the only sport jacket he had ever owned and Waymon thought it really made him stand out when he wore it to special occasions although this was Waymon's first special occasion in his life.

Waymon took a deep breath and blew it out as he stood in the living room. Even this gave him the heebie-jeebies as he thought taking a deep breath and blowing it out at Augusta National Golf Club, like those erections he had during the Masters, was rude and sacrilegious. Just then a bedroom door opened and a blond-haired man, shorter than Waymon, walked up to Waymon in only a pair of white grippies and a pot belly and introduced himself. "Hi there, Jack Nick-lawse."

Waymon didn't—couldn't—say anything for a moment. He just held his right hand out. Jack Nicklaus grabbed it. "Son, you got a *name*? You look like you'd have a *good* one."

"Nick-lawse?"

"No that's *my* name."

172

"*Poo*dle. Waymon Poodle from Mullet Luv, Georgia."

"Well then, it's nice to meet you, Waymon. You're playing golf here tomorrow?"

"Yessir. With you and two other gentlemen. I'm so exci—"

"Oh, no. I'd *like* to, because I really love to play golf, but the Golden Bear is here to look at redesigning a bunker. Ten million for it, but if that's what they want to pay the Golden Bear—dang let the dumb asses. Know what I *mean?*"

Waymon said, zombie like, "You're the greatest golfer in the *world.*"

"Well, that's what they say. Hey, the Golden Bear is hungry. You wanna go chow down?"

So Waymon Poodle went and put on his bright orange jacket and the Golden Bear put on his green jacket and they walked toward the clubhouse together. Waymon had prepared two hundred and sixty-two questions for the Golden Bear, but he found his throat had closed up and he couldn't speak. Waymon looked off to his left and saw a hot air balloon hovering over where the par three twelfth would be and thought it was a pleasant scene. Just then, from way down there, it looked as if someone poked a nice campfire and made it flame up for a second, but Waymon wasn't sure. Maybe the members had campfires and hot air balloon races out here when they had the club to themselves, Waymon thought. Could be. Who knows? Waymon had so deeply suppressed into the particular lobe of his brain that deals with this sort of thing, the knowledge of a particular Hindu entomologist who recently acquired a flame thrower who was using the flame thrower to fry a super whopper giant cicada killer wasp down around the twelfth tee at Augusta National Golf Club, that it didn't occur to Waymon at that moment what the "flame up" really was. Just so deeply suppressed.

The Golden Bear, as they walked near the practice putting green, could tell they had moved the practice putting green two feet and three inches to the left.

As they walked into the clubhouse, Waymon's heebie-jeebies

subsided just a little as he discovered he didn't think about super whopper giant cicada killer wasps one bit as they were walking unprotected across the grounds. But then as he thought about not thinking about them, then he immediately started thinking about them and his heebie-jeebies came back to the level they were a few minutes ago.

Waymon and the Golden Bear walked into the dining room and saw that the president of TrustTrust and Dilworth were already sitting at a table. Dilworth had the heebie-jeebies real bad, too, so he had slurped down eight scotches hoping that this would calm his heebie-jeebies down but it didn't. So he was drooling and he also had over two hundred questions for the Golden Bear.

"GENTLEMEN!" the president of TrustTrust screamed from across the room, then came jogging over. (Six pina coladas already.) "*Jack*, baby? You meet Waymon?"

"The Golden Bear met Waymon." The Golden Bear gave Waymon a pleasant look, then his face suddenly contorted. "Hey, I *knew* it. You're that fella who grabbed Betty Simpson's bermu—"

"Nice *jacket* by the way, Waymon," the president blurted out with pina colada breath, running his fingers along a lapel. "*Damn* that thing's orange."

"Thank you, sir."

"Really, it's orange *all day*."

"*Thank* you."

"Maybe until the end of *time*, Waymon—that jacket. You hunt deer in that thing?"

Waymon gazed down at a sleeve. "Thank you so much."

The president winked and nudged the Golden Bear with a knuckle. "Hey Waymon, I thought I told you to wear your *green* jacket."

"I don't own a green jacket, sir. Just this orange one."

The president whacked Waymon on the back. "Well not yet, right Waymon? I mean you could *get* one—one day, *right*? You just come on down here again and win the goddamn Masters, by God, and we'll give you a green jacket for *free!*" The president laughed real loud, then poked a finger into the Golden Bear's belly button. "Hell, Jack, baby, you got *six*. You don't wear them all at one time, do you? So why doncha run your ass upstairs and get Waymon one?" The president cackled so loudly the dining room manger and the sommelier and a guy with a broom poked their heads out of the kitchen door.

The Golden Bear gave the president a cool look. You really don't joke around about the jacket. Takes a lot of toil and pain and suffering to get one. Heck, you nearly die getting one. And those stupid questions you have to answer afterwards. Sacrilegious, really, to joke about, even a member joking about it. Like having an erection or something while you're here. Sure, I've had erections during casual rounds and even during the Masters. Had forty-nine erections back when I was reigning United States Amateur Champion right up there in the Crow's Nest. Erections are permissible at Augusta National Golf Club under the proper circumstances, okay, but you just don't joke about the green threads.

The president whacked the Golden Bear on the back. "*Jack*, baby—you know this guy in the orange jacket might have grabbed Betty Simpson's Bermuda grass on international TV. I mean, he grabbed the *hell* outta that thing, but did you know that he's also the best teller in my whole company?"

"The Golden Bear didn't know that. Congratulations, Waymon." The Golden Bear whacked Waymon on the back.

Waymon perked up. "Sir?"

"Yes, Waymon?"

"I'm not a teller any more. I got *fired* yesterday."

"Well *hell*, you musta wore that crazy orange jacket to work. You wear that damn thing to work, Waymon?"

"No, sir. I was sort of distracted all week because—"

"*Right!*" The president whacked Waymon on the back. "Because you were thinking about playing Augusta goddamn National *Golf* Club! *That's* what! Something imp*ort*ant. Hell, you'll probably find another job in a couple of years. So—*Jack*, baby. *Way*mon. Thirsty? Hungry?"

175

The Golden Bear looked at Waymon who looked as if he were about to faint, which he could do sometimes when the heebie-jeebies got to a critical level.

Waymon blinked a few times.

The Golden Bear whacked Waymon on the back. "It looks like we are."

After they got settled at the table the president of TrustTrust leaned down as if he were saying something real secret. Dilworth had passed out but had not fallen out of his chair. Under the table the president stabbed him with a fork where he thought Dilworth's left nut would be. Dilworth came to, but he didn't give the immediate impression he was focused. "Fellas, listen— we got a load of nine pound lobsters in today from Omaha or someplace. I hope you all like nine pound lobsters?"

"The Golden Bear likes a nine pound lobster."

"Me, too," Dilworth said like a little kid. "I *love* 'em. Nine pound loz-baters."

The president gave Dilworth a hard look, then stabbed him in the kneecap.

A waiter appeared.

The president of TrustTrust said to the waiter, "*Flap*jack, how *big* are those nine pound lobsters you got back there? Huh?"

Flapjack held his hands out as if showing the size of a fish. " 'Bout this big."

"*Naw*, they're bigger than *that*!"

"*This* big."

"Naw, they're about the size of—the size of *what*, Flapjack?"

"Small crocodile?"

"Nine pound lobsters, by God. That's what they look like, boys. A small crocodile." The president leaned over and nudged Waymon with a knuckle. "Waymon, you like a nine pound lobster?"

"I've never *eaten* a lobster, sir."

"Well, you are tonight. A nine pounder. Size of a small crocodile! Flapjack!"

"Yessir?"

"Nine pound lobsters"—he waved his arm in a circle—"all around!"

Knowing he was going to eat a nine pound sea creature with red claws heightened the level of Waymon's heebie-jeebies but the chardonnay they made him drink squelched some of it. The bread and the butter was real good so Waymon crammed a whole bunch of that in his mouth and listened to these men talk about matters of great importance to the wonderful world of golf and to the commerce of the global community of earth. All of a sudden, the Golden Bear asked the president what bunker it was he was going to be redesigning. "The Golden Bear thinks it's the one behind the green at five?"

"Naw, Jack, baby, the real reason we asked you—"

The nine pound lobsters were plunked down in front of them on huge platters. Waymon's heart began to race.

"Say, that big squiggly one," the Golden Bear blurted out, "in the middle of the tenth fairway? Redesign it? Or why don't we just get *rid* of it. Nobody ever uses it anyway. Huh?"

"Naw, shut up a second."

The Golden Bear cut off a huge wad of nine pound lobster and shoved it in.

"Now this is about to be a real historic moment in the history of golf and the private club industry, so pardon me if I'm a little formal all of a sudden. *Jack*, baby?"

"Mmmm?" He was chewing.

"Welcome to the club."

"Great—to—be here. I love a good lobster."

"*You* know"—the president winked and nudged him with a knuckle—"welcome to—the—club. Get it?"

"Really deli—cious."

Waymon Poodle, the chardonnay now coursing through his veins and arteries and capillaries like the Niagara, so frustrated at this wink-wink, nudge-nudge thing going on while the greatest golfer in the world was trying to enjoy his nine pound lobster, stood up as if he'd been electrocuted, then made golf history again by being the one who told the Golden Bear they had finally made him a member of Augusta National Golf Club, so welcome. If Waymon ever had bad heebie-jeebies in his life, he really did then. So right after he delivered the wonderful news to the Golden Bear in his squawking voice, he finally fainted—onto his lobster and his glass of wine and the basket of bread—then slid off the lobster and onto the floor and sort of quivered for a moment and then went limp.

So it was a real memorable moment in the history of golf.

## Sunscream

IN THE WORLD of golfing men, when the threesome and their loyal caddies step upon the first tee, that moment is always fraught with fresh heebie-jeebie-type emotions for all of those six people. It doesn't necessarily matter if it's the first tee of Augusta National Golf Club or the first tee of the Mullet Luv Golf Center. That's just the way it was in the world of golfing men.

Of course, an uninformed observer of the world of golfing men would think that since these peculiar people have spent time on the practice range warming up their minds and muscles for the day ahead and have temporarily re-trained their bodies to remember what to do, then it would seem that the moment spent on the first tee, or the tenth tee if the nines had been reversed that day because of something, would be a period of utter confidence about the whole deal.

Not really the case, though, with the first group on the first tee on the first day of the season at Augusta National Golf Club.

In the feeding frenzy of the evening, Dilworth forgot, after seven pounds of lobster had been gulped down, that he was allergic to shellfish, so his head swelled up right there in front of everybody in the dining room and itchy, red blisters emerged on one hundred and three percent of his body, and that morning he and his head and his body were still being watched in his room in the Butler Cabin by a physician Augusta National Golf Club had on retainer for when guests did stupid things when they played or ate there for the first time, which was a lot.

So Dilworth was out.

The Golden Bear had hit some really great practice shots with just his telescoping ball retriever, amazing everyone, after he stretched on the ground for nearly two or three minutes and had a belly packed with a monstrously greasy breakfast. So he was ready to go, even though he could have gone back home since he learned he wasn't really there to re-design a bunker for ten million dollars although the Ed Fiori thing sort of miffed him a little bit. But the Golden Bear really loved to play golf, so there he was. The Golden Bear burped real loud four times.

The president of TrustTrust, whose belly was also packed with a monstrously greasy breakfast, was still feeling guilty about Waymon just lying there under the table while they finished their nine pound lobsters and some fabulous tiramisu. Waymon was breathing, so that was good. They kept looking down there every once and a while to check. And there wasn't anybody else in the dining room so they all agreed it was okay for him just to rest until Flapjack tripped over Waymon and nearly gouged out one of the Golden Bear's eyeballs with one those little espresso spoons, which are fairly sharp. The president loved to play golf, too. He tried to match burps with the Golden Bear but instead gagged up part of his omelet which he just re-swallowed to save time.

On the first tee, Waymon, whose belly was also packed with a monstrously greasy breakfast, felt as if he was from outer space. His dream had come true in more incredible ways than imagined, and now that prosperity had arrived, and he thought he'd be joyous about it, instead he found he was twitching. Not much, but enough for his caddie to walk over, tentatively, and give him a wet towel. Waymon didn't look like he liked to play golf or even knew how. Waymon didn't even burp real loud—even though he could have and not gotten in any trouble at Augusta National Golf Club—because he felt like burping real loud at Augusta National Golf Club, especially on the first tee of Tea Olive, was as sacrilegious as the erection business.

As for the caddies, Waymon had indeed been assigned the best and wisest caddie at Augusta National Golf Club, just as he dreamed. The caddie was called "Albert Einstein," and he really did seem good at being a caddie and wise. In the pockets of Albert Einstein's caddie overalls were six disposable cameras from Wal-Mart Waymon had given him. Two cameras had already been used up on the practice range with one or two of Albert Einstein's fingers in all the shots.

The Golden Bear's caddie was the one he always asked for when he came up for a casual round and that caddie was called "Birdie Train." The president of TrustTrust's caddie, even though he always wanted Birdie Train but had to give him up for the Golden Bear this time, was a new kid from the local medical college whose real name was Mike, and who went by Mike, and who was an irritating know-it-all.

Everybody perked up when the president of TrustTrust all of a sudden said: "*Now*, before we begin to play this wonderful game of *golf*, I must give you all a little warning. As Chairman of the Augusta National Golf Club Entomology Committee, which was formed real quick this spring, I feel obliged to inform you people that we have a little *wasp* problem out here at the ol' club. Anybody ever heard of a super whopper giant cicada killer wasp?"

Waymon, still having the twitches, twitched violently. The twitch looked as if he were fanning cigarette smoke away.

"So *Way*mon, you've heard of these things."

Waymon twitched violently again. This time as if he were reaching out to shake hands. Twice.

The Golden Bear moved away from him just a little bit.

"Well *good* then, because for some reason that's real hard to figure, we've had an infestation of these fascinating creatures. And I'm sorry to say it's a particularly fascinating mutate form of these bugs called super whopper giant cicada killer wasps, and although our special super whopper giant cicada killer wasp on-site consultant tells me we're down to *one* now, and he's real *nasty*, they've indeed caused havoc and mayhem here at the ol' club. May we have a brief moment of silence for a maintenance employee named Toby."

They had a brief moment of silence for Toby.

"Now the last one of these things has been observed to be

holding fort at the tee box of Golden Bell and although I don't think we'll have to *skip* that hole—"

Waymon finally began to smile.

"—I just feel I'm pretty much off the hook *legally* since I informed you people of this pesky menace thing. Thus endeth my prepared remarks."

That caddie Mike rolled his eyes.

Albert Einstein silently prayed he wouldn't have to tangle with a mutate damn wasp because he had a date tonight with a nasty, freak bitch with long, curled-up fingernails.

Birdie Train sucked on a cigarette as he adjusted the position of his enormous two testicles merely by subtly shifting his weight. He learned the technique from Phil Blackmar in 1988 or maybe it was 1989 when they were in that playoff.

The Golden Bear gazed lovingly at the gallon milk jug-sized head of his new, never-before-tested, what-would-be-retail-priced-at $8,700, Japanese-made prototype driver called "The Lincoln Continental." The Japanese promised the Golden Bear he could hit a drive with this thing—even on the hosel or the ferrule—that would go four hundred and twenty-three yards with a pleasant fade and he'd never chicken hook again. That's what the Japanese told him, and then a bunch of them had bowed, and then he designed a course for them.

"So everybody feels they've been legally notified?"

Nobody really said anything except for Mike. He looked around at ever'ybody and finally said, "Mister, see—"

"Son, my name's not 'Mister'— "

"Well, whatever your *name* is, I really don't think just blabbing about this mutate wasp situation will stand up. See, mister, my father's a big fat lawyer and if somebody'll give me their cell phone I'll call him to check because I really don't think just bla—"

"Mike—*Mike*," the president of TrustTrust growled.

"Shit! *What?*" Mike said.

"Pinch my weenie. Everybody?"

Pleasant, expectant expressions all around, except for Mike's

182

"Game on."

Waymon eagled the first hole with a nice approach shot with an 8-iron so he was feeling a whole lot better even though he would have been enormously pleased with a birdie or a routine par or a tap in for bogey.

"Go easy on the Golden Bear, Waymon," the Golden Bear said to Waymon as they walked to the second tee, which took them a while since it had been moved, this time, forward by one hundred and fourteen yards and a quarter.

At the turn, Waymon was six under and the Golden Bear was not, so the Golden Bear was now mildly irritated. In kind of a sweet fatherly way, sure, but still irritated that this cross-eyed cat was whipping him. Then when the Golden Bear finally asked Waymon how he became so good at golfing Waymon told him that the fellow who'd been giving him lessons all summer really had to get a lot of the credit, even though he was blind. So that bit of information just made the Golden Bear even more mildly irritated and therefore he chicken hooked it at ten. He'd never chicken hooked in his life unless he was trying to. The Golden Bear gawked at the head of The Lincoln Continental as if the details on why he chicken hooked were printed on the face of the club.

The president of TrustTrust forgot to wipe the sunscreen off of his hands so now all that grease was on his grips and he was not having a good season opener at all.

Dilworth, still laid out in the Butler Cabin, was continuing to not have a good season opener at all either.

## The Ascension

WHEN SOME GUY was winning at golf more than the rest of the guys in his group, this situation has a habit of infecting the way he walks.

Most guys who are winning at golf walk as if they've had the scorecard pencil carefully placed between their butt cheeks and they walk in a quick-step, confident, from-point-A-to-point-B sort of way as if they're actually trying to keep the scorecard pencil from falling out and this way of walking is real irritating to those who have noticed and are not winning.

This was the way Waymon was walking to the twelfth tee after making a lip-out par on the eleventh as opposed to another person's double bogey in the pond (the Golden Bear) and another person's pick up (the president of TrustTrust).

But all was still good. The temperature of the air. Just a few cotton-white clouds that didn't threaten anything except continued meteorological aesthetic pleasure for those type of people who noticed and cared about that sort of thing. Like Waymon. Except that hot air balloon didn't quite fit in to the aesthetic pleasure situation at all.

Sure, it was one of those crisp October days, perfect for hot air ballooning, but Waymon wondered why it had to be hovering so low in front of the green of Golden Bell, right where the ball would go. Waymon gave one of those quick glances at the president of TrustTrust as if to say, Why aren't you doing something about this, you know, sir, since you're a member of the club and a committee chairman and all?

The president, whose raw nerves could have sensed if a dogwood tree petal fell onto the wooden bench way over at the fourth tee, was immediately irritated even more at Waymon for giving him such a snotty look but was also irritated at why a hot air balloon was right where the ball would go. If they were in trouble, then float the thing down—fine—then wad up the balloon and get the hell outta here. We're playing golf. You're where the ball would go.

The Golden Bear said, "Hello, Milt."

Milt waved back. "Hello Mister Nick-lawse."

The photographer up there in the basket with Milt, who had sixteen cameras hanging off of his neck, waved back too.

The president asked who in the hell was Milt.

"Oh, Milt *Limp*. The investigative golf journalist from the New Jersey *Oppressor*. He's real pesky."

"Well why don't you tell him to a-*scend* if he doesn't mind? There's nothing to investigate here at Golden Bell so just go over and investigate something over there at Augusta Country Club. Everything *here* is under control." Then he said real quiet under his breath, "I *hope*."

"Milt?" the Golden Bear said.

"Yes, Mister Nick-lawse?"

"Mind ascending? We're—" then the Golden Bear then made a series of intricate arm and hand and facial gestures that golfers, and investigative golf journalists, universally recognize as the series of intricate arm and hand and facial gestures that mean we're about to hit our golf balls if you don't mind because you're where the ball would go.

Just then Milt yanked on a cord and the hot air balloon air heater contraption made a loud noise that scared everybody to death, and even woke up Professor Biswapati who was sleeping behind the base of an enormous loblolly pine tree on the other side of the twelfth tee. Professor Biswapati fell over onto the flame thrower which was still fairly hot from an earlier shot at what he thought was that last super whopper but it was just a yellow-billed nuthatch. Which he obliterated. When the side of

185

his face and part of his beard hit the metal he shrieked in Hindi, "Jee-sus!"

"So, gentlemen," Waymon said, not to genuinely. "Are we playing golf or not?"

"Sure, Waymon," the president said, making a horrible and rude face at Waymon. "We're playing a form of golf."

# Thousands of Eyes

ALBERT EINSTEIN, JUST as Waymon had predicted, who had been complimenting Waymon on his swing—every single one of them, even his putting strokes and practice swings—and never once seemed to mind he was asked to take a picture of Waymon and his golf bag on every tee and by every green as well as when Waymon insisted he pause in front of a number of landscaped areas and clumps of azalea bushes that were particularly memorable, leaned down and whispered in Waymon's ear, "Be cooool, now, mistah Poodle. Stay in the zone. Don't think about them mutate bugs even though this is they crib, Mistah Poodle, right *hee*-yuh." Albert Einstein was suddenly struck at the faraway expression on Waymon's face. Albert Einstein stepped back about twenty feet.

Oh, Lord God Jesus, Waymon was thinking, how incredible it was to be finally walking on the other side of the ropes and six under as he stood on the twelfth tee at Augusta National Golf Club—remember to look at the top of the pine trees behind the green—and thank you Lord God Jesus for cleaning up all the trash and half chewed up pieces of pimento cheese sandwiches people spit onto the grass and the TV cameras and those awful TV tower things and the concession tents. Waymon knew the caddie would, by that time, instinctively know his game, and Albert Einstein did, instinctively. How by that time the caddie would know exactly what club to give him as he, Waymon Poodle of Mullet Luv, Georgia, stood there looking at the flag on the historic twelfth green, flapping lazily, with his right arm extended toward the

187

caddie and his ball freshly rubbed with a wet towel and his white tee—one of a handful of them grabbed out of a wicker basket in the pro shop—shining so brightly in the sun. How when he nestled his 6-iron behind the ball something wonderful happened: A little butterfly twittered around the ball, then lighted upon the ball. A butterfly. A little yellow one, innocent, never in harm's way as he sat on the golf ball of Waymon Poodle. Waymon watched the butterfly open and close its wings as it sat on the ball, Waymon's favorite type of golf ball, a Titleist balata 90 compression. Waymon loved the way the black Titleist lettering and the red number looked on the ball, so dang professional. He knew at that instant how he would explain the greatest moment of his life to his friends he played golf with. He would explain it in rich, somber detail. He might even tear up. Using his 6-iron as a support, Waymon leaned down to gently brush the butterfly away so he wouldn't kill it at impact, and reached out with his gloved left hand (FootJoy, light blue this time, medium) and...

"*Way*mon," the president said real quick, "as Chairman of the Augusta National Golf Club Entomology Committee, I think it's best you don't *mess* with that thing..."

The zone speaking. Waymon still leaning down, his face eight inches from the hymenoptera. "But it's just a little yellow butterfly."

Albert Einstein looked at Mike who was looking at the Golden Bear who was looking at Birdie Train who was looking at the president of TrustTrust. Then Mike looked at Birdie Train.

Black and yellow pulsating thorax. With a stinger.

"*Noooo*, mistah Poodle. You *voo*doo tawkin," Albert Einstein moaned, slipping a camera out of his pocket and up to his eye.

"*Nice* butterfly, just as I've dreamed my whooooole *life*," Waymon whispered as he stroked its wing. "Beau*uuuuu*ti*fuuuuul*."

The Golden Bear grabbed The Lincoln Continental out of his golf bag.

Birdie Train went wide eyed. "*Naw*-suh, Mistah Nick-lawse. You need the seven. It's a seven all *day*."

"Nice little yellow butterfly at Augusta National Gol

Club..."

"Waymon, *really*. As chairman of the Ento—"

The last of Feckle's beasts suddenly rose up and attached itself to the face of the Chairman of the Entomology Committee of Augusta National Golf Club, whereas he immediately went stiff and screamed, "HOLY LORD IN HEAVEN HAVE MERCY SWEET PRECIOUS JESUS!" which echoed through the pines like thousands of Augusta National Golf Club screams before him.

"*This* is attractive," Mike said.

"Oh, *Lordy*," Birdie Train said.

"Oh, Lordy, *Lordy*," Albert Einstein said.

"You got *that* right," Birdie Train said.

"You *know* I got that right, Albert Einstein said to Birdie Train, then touched knuckles with him.

"A real member's bounce," the Golden Bear said, head cocked a little as if he were reading a difficult putt.

"Sir," Waymon said in a faraway tone, "just gently nudge him with the tip of your finger and he'll flutter off. And then we'll play Golden Bell together. Nice butterf—"

"Goddammit, *you* gently nudge him with the tip of your—"

So Waymon walked over and gently nudged the super whopper with the end of the grip of his 6-iron instead of the tip of his finger.

The super whopper turned around and looked at Waymon. Waymon was looking right back at it, then all of a sudden discovered what a fool he'd been. This wasn't a little yellow butterfly not one bit. It was a super whopper giant cicada killer wasp, exactly one of those creatures mentioned on that weird web site. He'd been in denial. And consumed with desire. This was what denial felt like, coupled with consuming desire. Waymon Poodle in pure denial, consumed with desire, and had heebie-jeebies real bad, with hallucinations. Waymon all of a sudden burped real loud.

The super whopper turned and looked at the president again, hissed, as only the mutate form of these wasps could do, then jumped off his face and onto the rifle shaft (s-flex, low torque) of

Waymon's club. It started creeping up the shaft…

"*Way*mon," the Golden Bear said, "What club have you got?"

"The six!"

"Listen, Waymon, just drop it and hit an easy five. Or pull the seven and we'll hit it *hard*. I'll show you how to hit a hard seven. So let the *bug*"—the Golden Bear said in a rising tone of panic—"you know, have your *club*."

Waymon, frozen, gawking. Creeping over Waymon's hand now, the mutate, up his forearm, then his bicep…

Mike said, "Somebody tell me what's wrong with *this* picture."

The president said, "A golf tip on how to hit a hard seven iron from the Golden Bear, Waymon, at no less, Augusta National Golf Club, right here on historic Golden Bear—I mean Golden Bell. Oh, boy—be a real life memory." The president rolled his eyes so hard it hurt.

…and crept up Waymon's neck and over his Adam's apple and over his chin, then his quivering lips and onto Waymon's face at Augusta National Golf Club on the first day of the season on Golden Bell, tournament tees, one hundred and fifty-five yards with a slight right to right to left, then back to the right again breeze, with a swirl. Pin in the far right portion of the green.

The bunker was really in play.

Waymon was looking directly into thousands of eyes.

The super whopper was opening and closing its wings slowly, like a butterfly. The pulsating thorax was pulsating, sure, they do that all day, but the super whopper was moving its pulsating thorax around a lot, too, as if its thorax were searching for something important. Specifically, it was pushing its stinger down—and into—Waymon's mouth in hopes of finding the soft tongue of the human. It was sort of doing this like a cat does its tail. Working it. Real mean and sure and slow, like a cat does its tail right before it claws your eyeballs out of your head.

"Uncle!" Waymon squawked. "Get *off* me."

Albert Einstein snapped a couple of shots. The flagstick was in the background so it was going to make a nice photo, but of course his fingers were over the lens again so it wasn't going to make a nice photo.

Waymon also realized this super whopper wasn't seven inches long as the May report of professor Biswapati's Ultimate! and Exclusive! Giant Cicada Killer Wasp web site had noted. This one was a little bigger than that. Therefore, Waymon, real worked up, suddenly began speaking in tongues. And because all of the people in the group had heretofore in their lives never heard a person speak in tongues, what Waymon said next in a tone of voice extremely particular to when a person speaks in tongues while he's being stung on the tongue by a mutate wasp, was slightly unnerving. "Hala-sha-mamba…Walla-mon-hal-som-ba-ta-ta!" Waymon yelped something to that effect as he pranced around the tee box on his tip toes in circles.

"Hello Tokyo," Mike said.

"Son of a *gun*," the Golden Bear said. "Will ya listen at *that*."

"Oh, *this* is quaint," the president said, rolling his eyes some more.

"Hey, fellows," the Golden Bear chirped.

"Yes, Golden Bear?" they all said in unison except Waymon.

"Waymon's talking *back*wards. *That's* what he's doing," the Golden Bear said like a kid. "I heard this woman on National Public Radio one time talk *back*wards. Then she sang the dang Pledge of Allegiance—*back*wards. Will ya just listen at *that*." The Golden Bear pointed at Waymon. "And I remember one time I was up late after like the second round of the U. S. Open one time watching Jay Leno and he had that same woman on and she just starts in on 'Amazing Grace,' but *back*wards. And she was just as normal looking as *any*body. But there she was, just a singing that wonderful song from back to front. I'll never forget it as long as I—"

"Golden Bear, you *dumb* ass. It's that *tongues* stuff," Mike said. "See, when people of certain religious affiliations get all emotionally riled up they start squawking this stuff. Can't understand a dang word of it. Saw it one time in a snake handling documentary. *Tongues*, my friends—I promise you."

The president said, "Okay, then. Since everybody's got an opinion on Waymon—Albert Einstein, what do you think?"

Albert Einstein didn't say anything. He waved good-bye at everybody, and then ran off into the woods, missing the opportunity for Waymon to give him a big tip, which Waymon had been planning to do. Seventeen dollars.

"Birdie Train?" the president asked. "*Your* thoughts?"

Birdie Train decided not say anything either. He threw the Golden Bear's golf bag onto the ground, waved at everybody, then ran off toward that little building over there behind by the eleventh green you could see when Larry Mize hit that great chip to beat Greg Norman in the playoff. Birdie Train slipped and fell into the pond, then swam real fast across it and ran off into the woods behind Albert Einstein.

Now Waymon looked as if here were clogging.

Mike was now pointing at Waymon, which was rude and inappropriate for the particular situation Waymon was in. Mike was also cackling. Not pleasantly laughing or chuckling. Cackling.

The hot air balloon had caught one of those mysterious Golden Bell zephyrs and was now spinning like a carousel and the photographer was wildly buzzing away at the action at the tee box then Rae's Creek then the tee box at Golden Bell then through the woods at a foursome playing the ninth at Augusta Country Club and so on and so on and around and around.

Professor Biswapati, in a shiny silver fireman's coverall with some real funky looking goggles and his turban, and his flame thrower, and his beard which was smoking a little, started for them, shouting in Hindi, translated, which sounds exactly the same as in English: "Motor scooter! Motor scooter!" He got to about five yards from Waymon and pointed the business end of the flame thrower at Waymon's head and put his finger on the trigger. The nozzle of the flame thrower was dripping some fiery looking oil type stuff which was bright red and bright orange.

The president held up a hand. "As Chairman of the Entomology committee, I don't *think* so, amigo. Why not just get a butterfly net and capture it and study it. You thought of that?

Sell some advertising on your web site. Huh, you ever thought of the butterfly—*net*—idea?"

Professor Biswapati wanted to shoot that thing so bad he was spitting and foaming. "No. Not really."

"Malooka-sistawa-boom-sola-ta-ta-ta—ta-*ta*!" or something very, very much like that—and still clogging. Waymon's eyes were coming together just like his second grade teacher said they would when he grew up. But they were coming together too fast and now they were cross eyed the other way.

"So why don't you go *get* you one. There's got to be a hobby shop somewhere in Augusta or the metro area I'm sure. Get the yellow pages from Betty Simpson." The president pointed up toward the clubhouse. "Note your mileage and any food and beverage, job-related related expenses and the club will be happy to reimburse you."

Professor Biswapati started moping that way. He flung his flame thrower to the ground. "*Pam!*"

In championship competition, the Golden Bear was religious about having no more than one swing thought while he swung. And he was an undisputed veteran of championship competition. Absolutely undisputed. Occasionally he'd have two swing thoughts during a championship competition swing, but when he did, one swing thought was real big so then the other swing thought had to be real little. He was religious about it. But even when a golf writer asked him after a round in the press conference if he ever had two swing thoughts during the round the Golden Bear would clear his throat and drink some Gatorade instead of answering the question, or sometimes he'd just tell a story about Gary Player instead.

The super whopper finally found purchase in the soft flesh of Waymon's tongue, which Waymon had been violently flicking from side to side in hopes of avoiding the stinger part. Waymon now stood as stiff as a statue, feeling the claws of the super whopper tighten on his cheeks. Waymon suddenly thrust out his arms as if he were being crucified. He closed his eyes.

As the Golden Bear took The Lincoln Continental back like a

baseball bat to smash the super whopper on Waymon's face, the Golden Bear had a total of fourteen swing thoughts pulsating through his mind. All he wanted to do was to whack the super whopper enough were it would fall off and go away and not also smash Waymon in the face and they could keep playing golf but instead he smashed Waymon in the face real bad. "Darn it, Waymon. *Sorry*."

Waymon crumpled to the turf as the green and yellow guts of the super whopper gushed down both sides of his face. And some other weird material.

"*Wow*," Mike said.

"Seems we had—*no choice*," the president said distantly, thinking a shot to middle of the twelfth green was the prudent tact today. Why mess with the bunker or come up short in the liquid?

The Golden Bear was once again gawking at the head of The Lincoln Continental as if the details on why he had fourteen swing thoughts going on instead of one real big one and one real little one were printed on the face of the club.

Waymon was now turning purple. Just then, Toby's hand, with a Marlboro Light between his fingers, thrust through the turf. Very tightly, Toby grabbed Waymon's ankle and yanked him into the humid burrow.

## Where Screams Echo

BECAUSE THE AMBULANCE was bouncing around so much, the paramedic was having a hard time sticking the long, sharp intravenous needle into a nice blue vein on the top of Waymon's left hand. The paramedic would just about have it all lined up, then the ambulance would hit a pothole or a curb or swerve around a car and the needle would get shoved into one of Waymon's wrist or knuckle bones, or one time right there into the soft flesh between two knuckles real deep.

Waymon popped awake to find this going on and a clear plastic mask over his face helping to pump pure oxygen into him. "I had *tol'* myself," Waymon said with a swollen tongue, so it was real mushy sounding, "that I wasn't going to lay up at fifteen—and I didn't. Waymon Poodle, remember *this* sir"—wagging a finger—"did not lay *up.*"

The paramedic gave Waymon a forced smile typical to paramedics who are trying to concentrate on something important such as the life of their patient. "That's great sir. Thank you."

"But you can go into the water behind the green, too. Yesser-*eee*. You sure can. It's been *done.*"

"Is that a tricky hole?" the paramedic said. "Fif—teen?"

"Oh *yeah.* It's the final round death hole for so many invitees."

"Well ain't *that* something. A *death* hole. I had heard golf was a tough sport."

The ambulance turned into the emergency driveway of Columbia County Hospital. Waymon leaned up a little and looked

195

at the sign. Underneath the name of the hospital was a street address: 1931. "Hey, you know nineteen thirty-one was a big year for golf?"

The president and the Golden Bear swerved in behind them in the president's Rolls Royce. A hubcap popped off and hit, right between the eyes, a guy sitting on a bus stop bench who'd just been released from the hospital.

Milt Limp and his photographer and that hot air balloon were already hovering over Columbia County Hospital. The photographer was taking shots of the hospital. Milt Limp was already typing the story in his mind... *And this was where the powers of Augusta National Golf Club brought the unfortunate, innocent, purple-faced guest—I saw the Golden Bear make the worst golf swing of his long, historic career—so bad it had law suit written all over it.*

They wheeled Waymon into his own room in the emergency ward and about four people pounced on him and started looking at his tongue and his busted nose with little flashlights and started asking the paramedic a whole bunch of questions that included math and scientific words. So there was a lot of poking and prodding and squeezing and yakking going on.

And it echoed in Waymon's mind.

But he was at peace.

The president and the Golden Bear sort of tip-toed up behind everybody and started gawking. They were both really hoping Waymon wouldn't die. Again. They were convinced Waymon had died there on Golden Bell's tee box, until Mike, since he was a medical student, and even though he was studying to be a podiatrist, was asked, not too politely by the president of TrustTrust, to quit standing there cackling and pointing and give our very special guest Mr. Poodle mouth to mouth resuscitation as having crossed eyes and turning purple was a real indication he's not getting air.

Mike, even though he was new at caddying, exercised that innate ability given to people who decide to caddie at real nice golf clubs, to stand there with a blank expression on his face, for an abnormally long time if necessary, until his man handed over a bill, or bills, of some satisfying amount.

"Goddamn, *here*," the president had said, handing him a two dollar bill. "Now blow some life back into Waymon." The president had looked up the eleventh fairway to see if any other groups were behind them, watching his guest die. "This is embarrassing."

So Mike got to pull the dead carcass of the super whopper off Waymon's face. The super whopper had dug in there pretty good. It didn't come off so easily, and when it did it made a crunching sound. Then Mike placed his shaking lips onto Waymon's.

Waymon could see the president and the Golden Bear standing back there. "Nothing personal, Jack, baby," Waymon said to the Golden Bear. A nurse shoved Waymon's head back down.

"No of course it wasn't, Waymon," the Golden Bear said. "The Golden Bear should have hit you in the nose with the seven." The Golden Bear nudged the president in the ribs with his elbow and they both chuckled. Uneasily, however.

Waymon said, "I'll promise not to tell anybody I beat you and made you think about giving up golf forever and giving away all of your clubs and balls to inner city children. I promise."

The Golden Bear gave Waymon a strange look. "Beat me?"

"*Jack*, baby. You quadruple bogied eighteen, right?"

The Golden Bear looked at the president who shrugged his shoulders. "Uh, *yeah*," the Golden Bear said. "The Golden Bear couldn't get out of that—concession stand?"

"That's right. You were eating all the cheeseburgers. So I had a sixty-two and you had an eighty-nine, with a triple cheeseburger. So do you think Nick Price will call me from South Africa and Greg Norman from Australia to say way to go, Waymon?"

Just then the doctor who was fussing over Waymon turned around to see who was bothering Mr. Poodle. As far as he knew the patient had been stung on the tongue by a mutate super whopper giant cicada killer wasp then smashed real hard on the proboscis by a Japanese-made prototype driver not yet available in stores and then lost consciousness and then did not breath for a while and might have even been dead for ten or fifteen minutes and they had not played the rest of the holes at all. So according to the rules of golf, no scores could be officially recorded, he was fairly sure. Plus, Mr. Poodle was sunburned quite a bit. When the doctor recognized who was behind him, like a lot of people, he immediately told the Golden Bear for some weird reason what he shot last Saturday with his foursome (a ninety-seven) and congratulated the Golden Bear on him quitting smoking a few years ago.

"Thanks," the Golden Bear said.

The doctor also told the Golden Bear the next time he saw Arnold Palmer to tell him he said he was glad he quit smoking, too. That the medical community was pretty sure now that smoking was bad for you.

"Will do," the Golden Bear said. "You got it."

Waymon said from his gurney, "And I'm so glad we found Toby, *too*. Toby sure did *smell*."

"Listen, gentlemen," the doctor said, "we've got to give Mr. Poodle a reality check so he can deal with his situation and help himself."

The president of TrustTrust said, "No we don't."

The doctor squinted at him, adjusted his glasses, then turned around and told Mr. Poodle the poop. It took a few minutes.

Then Waymon said, "So Nick Price isn't going to call me from South Africa and Greg Norman from Australia to say, 'Way to go, Waymon?' "

The president and the Golden Bear glanced at each other, then the president said, "I wish the good doctor hadn't *done* that." The president stood on his toes to get a look at Waymon. "Hey, *Way*mon, you're not the—lit*i*gious type, are you?"

Waymon thought he had said "religious" type, so Waymon said, supremely unequivocally, confidently, with a passion that rumbled up from down deep, "Yes, I am—sweet precious *Jeee-sus*."

"*Damn*." The president rubbed his chin. "And while we're at it, I'll bet you think we oughta let some ol' *wo*man in?"

Waymon thought the president asked, "And while we're at it, I'll bet you think we oughta let some healing begin?"

"This *in*stant, praise *Jeee*-sus. This *in*stant," Waymon said in a tone that was pretty much supremely unequivocal for the second time. "Oh, praise Jesus."

"Damn a-*gain*," the president said. We're in a real *fix* here, Golden Bear. I'm looking at double bogey."

"The Golden Bear knows what we need to do," the Golden Bear said.

The president said, "Ain't gonna happen, mister master. You've never had a double bogey. You don't know what it feels like."

The Golden Bear said flatly: "He saved your life."

The president pressed down the left sideburn of his toupee, which had been bent in an upward position in the Golden Bell fracas. "Just a little wasp. I was about to yank it off, ring its neck, you know, Golden Bear, by whipping it around and around like country women do when they're ready to eat a chicken, and hand it to my caddie."

"No you weren't." The Golden Bear gave the president a cool look, with one eyebrow raised. "Say, I think the Golden Bear can play any time the Golden Bear wants, *right*? I mean, *heck*, I've won the Masters six—"

"Yeah, six times. The president poked him in the chest again. "But you've never won the par three contest so maybe you're not such a master after *all*."

The Golden Bear gave the president an even cooler look than the earlier cooler look, this time with both eyebrows raised. "And the Golden Bear already has my own locker, right?"

"Sure. *Sure* you do. Your own locker. Big shit."

"And I can scoot right on through the front gate without anybody getting all upset, you know, once the guard sees it's the Golden Bear and I do my little wave. You've seen it many times."

"I will now alert our guards to shoot your tires out." The president of TrustTrust pulled his cell phone out of his pocket but it slipped out of his hand and broke apart on the emergency room floor.

They both watched the parts skittering around on the floor.

"And you're the new Membership Committee Chairman, right?" the Golden Bear asked. "Sorry about your stupid phone."

"Uh, no, Golden Bear. I'm not even a member."

"Yes you *are*. You made such a big deal about it last night I almost puked and that would have been a darn good waste of some delicious lobster."

"They were really mutate crawfish. Like that goddamn wasp. I'm surprised you haven't grown a third eyeball by now."

"May I continue?"

"No."

"And you said Waymon's the greatest teller in company history, right? Loves golf. Loves Augusta National Golf Club. Loves the Masters. Reigning Georgia State Amateur Champion. Six under as he stood on the tee of Golden Bell today, so that tells you something right there. So why not?"

"*Was* the greatest teller in company history. He got fired because all he thinks about all day is golf. So let's go. I want to go back and play some more."

"Six under. First time out. Waymon was on fire. And whatnot."

"I'm waiting for your point."

"Here's my *point*." The Golden Bear walked over to Waymon and put a hand on his shoulder and made some more golf history. "Waymon, what size *jacket* do you wear?"

Waymon reached into his mouth and pushed his swollen, purple tongue out of the way. "*Lawrrrrge.*"

"No, Waymon. *Sport* blazer. You know—jacket. As in, you know, a *green* one like your Clemson *orange* one." The Golden Bear winked real hard, then smiled as if he'd won the par three contest.

Waymon reached back into his mouth and pushed his swollen, purple tongue out of the way again. "Forty-two—*lowng.*"

## *In Real Good Standing*

WAYMON POODLE WAS the new Executive Vice President of Customer Service of TrustTrust Banks, now making $978,000 per year instead of $12,250, with an amount of stock options that were downright socially and politically incorrect, a year-end bonus of no less than $1,000,500, and instead of driving a worn out Chrysler "Diplomat," Waymon zips around Mullet Luv and the parking lot of Sans Souci real fast in a slightly pre-owned three hundred and seventy horsepower, eighty-two thousand dollar Jaguar XKR coupe, "Phoenix Red," whose interior does not smell of luxurious Connolly leather but of roasted garlic.

Now, more than ever, no other human being on planet earth loves more than Waymon does the Masters, the golf course on which it's played, and the wonderful sport of golf in general, even though all those things recently happened. He wasn't necessarily interested in anything iniquitous anymore.

It's Monday morning, and Waymon, who almost played Augusta National Golf Club two days ago, had a satisfied expression on his face anyway, and enjoyed a life finally worth living. In a faraway place, screams no longer echoed. Waymon Poodle was a member, for free, of Augusta National Golf Club, and so was his fiancé, LaJuanita Mumps, for free, as all of the members of Augusta National Golf Club felt adding a surprise announcement about LaJuanita's membership status in Waymon's new member, 3-ring binder kit—which also included a monstrously detailed confidentiality agreement that was ten

201

inches thick for Waymon and LaJuanita to sign—was a fantastic idea as they were super, super eager to please him and LaJuanita. The binder was delivered to Waymon in Mullet Luv in a Brinks truck. About forty guys with shotguns and dark aviator sunglasses and ear plugs jumped out and were not smiling and were looking around a lot with their fingers on the triggers.

And now Waymon made golf history yet again, this time in the kitchen of apartment number 1931 of Mullet Luv's Sans Souci apartment complex, and this time by being the person to tell LaJuanita Mumps of Mullet Luv, Georgia, that after all the recent ruckus in the wonderful world of golf, that she was the first woman ever accepted into the membership at Augusta National Golf Club and they had been sort of against doing it for over seventy years. Waymon told LaJuanita she'd be the most famous woman in the wonderful world of golf for the rest of her life and have a lot of golf and fashion magazine articles written about her and the next time the phone rings it'll probably be that Oprah woman on TV wanting to interview you on her TV show. So congratulations, Waymon said shakily, and I love you. Waymon's head started to hurt real bad and a bad pain started up in his guts. Maybe it was really a bad pain in his soul he was feeling. He instantly regretted everything he just told LaJuanita. He sensed trouble as he looked at her. A Mullet Luv kind of trouble. Then Waymon added one more thing to what he sensed. He also sensed doom for his golf club. Doom, which was the most trouble a golf club could have, even over them wasps. He knew LaJuanita would eat that place up and probably get into a cat fight with that Oprah woman on her TV show if Oprah looked at LaJuanita the wrong way. Waymon gazed at what was squeezing out of her cheeseburger and oozing down between those big boobs. Waymon wondered why smart men made dumb decisions. But he was a smart man now. Very smart. One of them—they—those guys—us. Oh, Lord God Jesus. So Waymon started using his donkey smarts again. Waymon's expression, on purpose, was now as dull as a concrete cinder block. Even more impassive than a pile of beat up range balls.

LaJuanita had been standing there eating a Wendy's triple all the way with cheese, because she was real hungry. Quietly, she had also been appraising Waymon, but her expression was as dull as a concrete cinder block, too. Just as impassive as a pile of beat up range balls. Her very words were, delivered finally, and irritably, "Now, I don't wanna take no *golf* lessons. Every weekend I wanna go down there and I just wanna go play a couple of holes and then go eat and then go make love in one of those cabin things they got down there. Except we're going to have *drinks* with our food, too. They're called *cock*tails, Waymon. We're going to go get us some nice resort wear and look and act like fancy people once and for *all*." She poked the Wendy's triple at his face. "Don't screw this up." LaJuanita took another bite of the oozing triple, so vicious it made a crunching noise. Sure, the Mullet Luv Wendy's served fresh, crisp lettuce and pickles on their triples, but LaJuanita had big, dull-bottomed teeth that looked like concrete cinder blocks. When she ate a cheeseburger it was something to hear—and watch. "*Way*mon," she said, "you're creeping me totally out. What *is* it?"

"When did you learn about golf and golf lessons and where Augusta National Golf Club was and that they have cabins and all that?"

"You talk about golf and that damn golf club with yourself out loud in your sleep. Every night."

He had no idea. Now Waymon's donkey smarts told him to look real sympathetic at this point. Waymon made a real good sympathetic expression. "Sugar, I'm telling you, you won't *like* these fellows. All they do is play golf and talk about their score and whatnot in their snack shop."

"Like you do," she said. She took another chunk out of that cheeseburger.

"Well—and even though you're a smoking hot, foxy lady, they won't pay any attention to you. Not one *bit*."

She swallowed. "Like you do. Don't. Pay attention to me."

Waymon gazed at the slow moving ooze. He couldn't help it. He couldn't help but realize she had him figured out without much effort. He couldn't help but lean down and stick his tongue into her infinite cleavage and lick it all up.

LaJuanita gently pulled his head even closer. Then she stuck her mouth into his right ear. Very loudly, she burp-talked, "Baby, come to——*maaaaaa-maaaaaaahhh.*"

## *Old Mrs. Willard Again*

SO WAYMON'S AT his old window, the window in the middle even though he didn't have to do teller work anymore, waiting on his long-time customer, Old Mrs. Willard, who for the seven hundredth and twenty-third time has brought in a check to cash for $250, given to her by her brother-in-law for something personal. Even though she saw Waymon back there in the branch manager's office busy talking to a real strange looking fellow, Old Mrs. Willard made a big fuss about Waymon coming out to his teller spot to give her his great customer service.

By order of the president of TrustTrust Banks, Waymon was to immediately find an exact copy of himself for the recent Mullet Luv Confederate Victory Parkway TrustTrust Publix branch teller opening. Then Waymon could come and start work in the big office downtown starting at 5:30 every morning until he retired. And you've got to run in a bunch of marathons, starting Saturday in Iowa. So Waymon was interviewing his cousin, who was also named Waymon, who looked exactly similar to Waymon and had tremendous interpersonal skills, too. They were back there flapping their arms as they talked to each other.

And even though Waymon has waited on Old Mrs. Willard all those years standing there wearing his Augusta National Golf Club tie, today was the first time she'd ever said anything about it. It was a tie everybody else usually noticed. She didn't even say anything about his nose, which was a mottled orange, green, and purple color. And a lot bigger than it normally was.

"Oh, *Way*mon," Old Mrs. Willard said while Waymon was

flipping through the cash drawer, "so you're a member of the Masters?"

Waymon started to speak but his tongue got in the way.

"You know my oldest, Lucky, has always wanted to be a member of the Masters. Lucky told me he's heard it's real easy to get in if you act nice and know the right people."

Since his tongue was still swollen, but not quite as purple anymore, although it was still fairly purple, more turquoise than anything now, Waymon slowly, with sloth-like effort, told Old Mrs. Willard that a person isn't a member of the Masters—that that's the tournament—a person would be a member of Augusta National Golf Club—not the tournament—the Masters was the tournament they have down there at Augusta National Golf Club each year in April. Then Waymon did not make a huffing sound similar to the huffing sounds made by three year olds. He didn't even consider making a huffing sound not one bit. Or a gurgling one.

Old Mrs. Willard didn't understood a single word he said. So to be polite she told Waymon she'd go tell Lucky—since her next stop was to visit Lucky over at the county mental sanatorium—that Augusta National Golf Club was looking for new members. Then Old Mrs. Willard gave Waymon a nice wink.

Waymon gave her a wink back. A wink with deep meaning. A knowing wink, one that had some history, some real weight behind it, the best wink only a new member of Augusta National Golf Club could give without being found out he was a member of Augusta National Golf Club and getting in trouble with his new pals. Then Waymon handed Old Mrs. Willard exactly, exactly, $250 in cash and a big fat lollipop.

This time, a big fat green one.

## *EPILADY*

TWO MILES AWAY and a day later, LaJuanita had just done the Corn Cob on a mule. The hairdo looked like a six hundred dollar hairdo should look. And LaJuanita felt any woman who paid for a Corn Cob should not be called a mule any more.

Now the valued customer was reclined on a squeaking plastic lounge chair in the back room next to the water heater with her legs spread real wide, waiting for LaJuanita to quickly—very, very, very, very quickly—yank the two wax strips that would violently wrench, from the roots of her very quivering and sensitive flesh, the untamed wads of hair that surrounded her thing. The customer was having herself prepared for a vacation to Myrtle Beach with her husband and his big golf buddy. She liked to ride along in the cart in her bikini thong. Only.

The customer reached down and picked up the newspaper and started reading it, but also deliberately used the newspaper to block from view the impending and horrifying scene developing between her legs, while smoking a Marlboro Light 100.

And it just so happened, as certain things were sort of doing a lot of in Mullet Luv lately, that the front page facing LaJuanita had a big, three-inch tall headline on it. So big it caught LaJuanita's eye. With her head cocked a little sideways, she read it. The headline blared, "AUGUSTA NATIONAL FINALLY BLOSSOMS." The subhead, two and a half inches tall, blared something else: "AND SHE'S GOT NICE CREDENTIALS."

LaJuanita read the story real quick.

Everything it said about her was quoted by some man who

ran the club named Huge Pecker. LaJuanita couldn't wait to get down there. Grinning iniquitously, LaJuanita yanked the wax strips real, real, slow.

And all women screamed.

# Why Golf is so Exciting!

*to* Jack Sentell

*Who's never played alone because he's got too many friends*

Well now I don't read that daily news
'Cause it ain't hard to figure where people gets the blues
If they can't dig what they can't use
If they stick to themselves
They'd be much less abused
Say I know a little
Lord I do know a little 'bout it

—*from "I Know a Little" by Lynyrd Skynryd*


Golf is the strangest game in the world.

—*Byron Nelson, a professional golfer*


Bring out the gimp.

—*from the movie "Pulp Fiction"*

# The Night before Waddell Plays Golf

WADDELL TIDDYBUMPUS WAS lying or laying in bed. He never could figure out which one it was. But there he was in bed. In a prone position.

The ceiling fan was making that annoying clicking noise that beating on it with a mop stick could never get rid of.

It was Friday night.

Rubbing his stubble and looking at the clicking ceiling fan, Waddell was thinking that tomorrow afternoon all of his member buddies at his country club, Pine Cone Country Club, down the street from where he lived, would be crammed in the men's grill watching the third round of the Masters on that big new television that the House Committee probably spent too much money on because some guy named Bill Kratzert was leading the Masters by a record sixteen shots after only two rounds. The Golf Channel commentators said that Bill Kratzert's hybrid was on fire.

In Kratzert's big TV interview shown on the Golf Channel earlier that evening, Waddell watched the Kratzert fellow make a big fuss about how dang tired he was of being called the darkest of all dark horses in the illustrious history of the Masters and he said he was also getting dang *tired* of being asked by all of *you* guys if he could hold the *lead* for two more rounds under such incredible pressure and at *his* age and since Tiger was in second and seemed focused on winning his big deal eleventh Masters. I'm not worried about *no*-body, including—Kratzert sucked in a huge breath here—*Ti*-ger, and hell *yes* I can hold the lead and I don't appreciate the question—I've held a lead be*fore*, the Kratzert fellow said, if you just take the time to go look at some of my statistics compared to Jack

*Nick*laus on some things. Why don't you boys ask me how I got *into* the lead so much? Then the Kratzert fellow accidentally dropped his cup of grape soda and the entire contents of the cup splashed all the way back up onto his golf shirt on TV and all over his glasses, so bad it was dripping off of the glasses and he didn't even take them off.

"Dam-*na*tion," Waddell had mumbled at the TV screen. "What a fag." The Kratzert fellow looked like he was about to freak out, right there on TV, Waddell was convinced. Waddell had also read once where the guys at the Masters really take good care of the players and Waddell thought for a player to be able to get a grape soda was incredible.

After Kratzert wiped off his shirt with a towel somebody handed to him, he acted like he didn't want to answer a whole bunch more questions from the golf reporters, but he did anyway, and then he stomped out of the press room and didn't even give the towel back to Augusta National Golf Club or whoever.

A Golf Channel commentator said that the man is without a doubt looking like he's freaking out.

Well, its Masters' time, another Golf Channel commentator said.

And you know you gotta be able to handle the pressure of major tournament golf, another Golf Channel commentator said, especially when you have a slight lead of sixteen shots. Tiger's won *eight* Masters, by the way, the Golf Channel commentator said. Not eleven like Kratzert said, although Tiger will probably have eleven wins in the next couple of years, you know.

Another Golf Channel commentator said Kratzert oughta go ahead and slip the ol' green jacket on Tiger tonight and just go out there tomorrow and Sunday and use those rounds as practice rounds for next week's tournament if he's playing in next week's tournament. I don't know. Does anybody know if Kratzert is playing in next week's tournament?

The other three Golf Channel commentators said they didn't know.

Then all four Golf Channel commentators started laughing real loud.

# Why Golf is so Exciting!

Waddell thought Bill Kratzert was from Indiana.

Now scratching his left armpit so much it was making a noise, Waddell thought that if he played golf after three o'clock or so then he'd probably have the whole golf course to himself and he was thinking that would be a nice experience because it was rare that you ever had Pine Cone Country Club to yourself on a Saturday afternoon except if it was real cold and then sometimes when it was real cold they'd shut down the golf course and wouldn't let you play anyway. Pine Cone Country Club was the nicest country club in town and cost $95,000 to get in. Cart fees are $25 per eighteen holes. Waddell, retired after forty-nine years as a loyal muckety-muck with a multi-national, multi-billion, multi-multi conglomerate type affair that started out over one hundred years ago in the founder's chicken coop in his back yard became a member of Pine Cone Country Club when it cost $150 to get in and golf carts cost 55 cents per eighteen holes and had only three wheels.

Waddell was an operations man his whole career. Waddell loved operations. Executive Vice President of Operations those last twenty-two years. Yeah, boy, Waddell mused while automatically salivating while he rubbed his big gut when he thought about all that good free food all those years at the company headquarters' cafeteria. And those three o' clock chocolate chip cookies and sometimes peanut butter macadamia nut cookies we started in 1977. Or both kinds of cookies. Served warm and how when you'd pick one up it would fold over your fingers just a little bit. Offering cookies to employees at 3 o'clock was his idea.

Financially, Waddell and his wife and their children and their grandchildren were in safe shape if they ever screwed up because of Waddell's toil, but buying boxer shorts at the prices they were asking for these days at the mall made Waddell edgy. Waddell was what financial advisors called a saver.

In retirement, Waddell plays a lot more golf. He also goes to church on Easter sometimes, has two daughters and a son and two grandsons, six and three, from his son. One daughter was a lesbian but she didn't look like it.

3

People are always shocked when they learn where Waddell went to college and he had a record for something in college wrestling that still stands.

Waddell likes to wrestle on the floor and make faces with his grandsons. His grandsons love to do a thing called "talk-burping," which was burping and talking as loud as possible at the same time. It's amazing to Waddell how good they are at talk-burping, especially the three year old. The three year old's favorite talk-burping phrases are "bootylicious" and "holy guacamole." One time the oldest one did an incredible talk-burping job with "shiver me timbers" but never did it again and Waddell found he was disappointed about him never doing it again and when Waddell asked him to talk-burp shiver me timbers again the kid got all huffy about being pestered about it.

Waddell thought sometimes you couldn't figure kids out no matter how many books you glanced through about it.

His grandsons also love to "cut the cheese" when they're with their "Wad Wad" as Wad Wad sort of encourages it when the women aren't around. Wad Wad was very, very tempted to show his grandsons how to light farts. But Wad Wad knew if he successfully showed his grandsons how to light fights—he knew the timing of the letting out of the fart and the thickness of the underwear and how close you held the match to your anus area had to be absolutely perfect—and if the women found out he was trying to teach them, even though he knew deep down in his heart that seeing a fart lit successfully under those three critical conditions was one of the funniest things to see ever in your life—ever in your life—then the women's reaction could only be described with one word, and that word was: apocalyptic. Their reaction would be apocalyptic.

One time the little one said out of the blue in the middle of his explanation to Wad Wad about what he wanted the Easter bunny to put in his Easter basket the phrase "apple pie molester" and Wad Wad didn't know what to do or say, so he distracted the little one by pulling a twenty dollar bill out of his thick, old, brown wallet and gave it to him. A week or so later, after the other grandson found out about it, and also knew that twenty dollars was a lot of money to give his fart wad brother, he seemed to go nuts and tore up his room and dumped his aquarium down the stairs.

When Waddell's not playing golf or at the club hitting balls on the practice range or practicing his putting and chipping or hanging out in the golf shop not buying anything, ever, Waddell likes to watch golf on television, read his golf magazines over and over and just glances at the local newspaper's headlines because he knows in his heart after all these years the local newspaper likes liberal Democrats better than conservative Republicans.

Waddell is also fond of an Irish whiskey during the local nightly news—or two Irish whiskeys some nights—especially when the stock market isn't doing well or the chairman of the Federal Reserve is being asked questions and they're showing it on TV and the chairman is not really answering their questions. Maybe three Irish whiskeys.

Waddell worships and pampers and hand waxes a lot and drives no faster than fifty-nine miles per hour in any intrastate or interstate traffic condition the greatest and most formidable automobile ever built: a 1996, cranberry red, Buick "Roadmaster." About once a month Waddell has a dream in which he's driving the car slowly—up and back, up and back, with fantastically slow and smooth U-turns—on the tree-lined street where he grew up. The only way Waddell could describe the way the car felt during the U-turns in his dream would be by describing the U-turns as "delicious." Waddell knew the emotions a man felt in his dreams were the most pure.

His member buddies at the country club tell him he looks and acts like the actor Walter Matthau. Waddell's a little hunched over and comes across as grumpy to those who don't know he's really not that grumpy. He laughs like Herman Munster—with the flapping hands and everything. Waddell says to his member buddies he looks more like Tom Cruise if the way he looks and acts was going to be compared to some goddamn movie actor.

Waddell's wife's name was Lucille. Lucille Poovey-Tiddybumpus. Lucille looks and acts like her mother. The grandsons call her "Poo Poo" because they think it sounds French. Lucille's an old real estate agent with Re-Max and she was lying beside Waddell in the bed with her mouth hung way open. Lucille had surgery for her snoring two and a half months ago and the surgery hadn't started working yet.

## Waddell Gets to the Club

WHEN WADDELL GOT to the club on Saturday afternoon he went into the locker room and scraped some ball markers, a few old tees, and a ball repair tool off of the top shelf of his locker and into his left hand and then put all that into his left pocket. A couple of tees fell onto the carpet and Waddell squatted down there real quick, as if someone else was jumping down there for them too.

He changed into his golf shoes and a pair of wrinkled, sweat encrusted, khaki golf shorts he kept in his locker. Waddell wears brown and white golf shoes that are twelve years old. His golf shoes were also sweat encrusted.

Out back a young bag room attendant handed Waddell his bag and Waddell mumbled something to him that the bag room attendant didn't understand although he expected it as Mr. Tiddybumpus was well known among the bag room and golf shop staff of assistant professionals and the pro shop merchandiser girl for mumbling things no one understood. God forbid if the Pine Come Country Club head pro was ever around.

On the wall, the bag room staff kept a chart on a piece of paper that showed how many times that month and with what member they had a remarkable interaction. The bag room staff had an ongoing debate about the mental stability of a lot of members, but about Mr. Tiddybumpus in particular the debate was whether he was drunk all the time or just had a jaw muscle or nerve problem, or both, that kept him from speaking clearly to them. The debate was still unresolved. That afternoon, on that piece of paper, Mr. Tiddybumpus got another check for mumbling something they didn't understand. Mr. Tiddybumpus was leading that particular category for the month of April of all the members of Pine Cone

Country Club and it was only the eighth day of the month.

Waddell walked to the practice range and in less than ten minutes he hit six balls with his pitching wedge, topped four balls with his 8-iron, and hit fifty-four balls with his driver way over to the right. Waddell thought about hitting two or three practice putts but changed his mind. He changed his mind because when he looked over at the 1st tee he saw there was no one on the tee or in the fairway of the 1st hole and this made him excited because he felt like he predicted it the night before while he was scratching his left armpit.

As he walked by another member hitting balls on the practice range, Waddell didn't say hello or mumble anything to the other member and he avoided eye contact with him because he had a feeling the fellow would ask to tag along and Waddell did not want him to tag along as Waddell knew he was an incessant joke teller. The fellow was also a left-handed golfer and Waddell disliked playing with left-handed golfers as he felt that was a peculiar, almost unchristian, way to play golf and having to play golf with a left-handed golfer, Waddell also felt, messed him up bad, concentration wise. The other member's name was Jerry Crowder and he owned a local heating and air conditioning company. His television commercials looked as if they were directed by drunk monkeys. Crowder was not above holding a barking Poodle or wearing an Elvis costume. Or both at the same time. Even the dog one time had on an Elvis costume made for a dog.

Even at his age, Waddell sort of enjoys carrying his own golf bag, although he was part of the group that ragged Phil, the general manager, for five or six years about buying some pull parts, but Phil always said talk to the Golf Committee. None of the complainers, including Waddell, ever talked to the Golf Committee. They kept complaining about it to Phil.

So, carrying his own golf bag makes Waddell feel like a purist, one with golf, and thrifty. And here he was on the 1$^{st}$ tee and he hadn't even hit his drive yet and he'd already saved $25.

## Waddell Plays the 1<sup>st</sup> Hole

ABOUT TWO YEARS ago, the Greens Committee at Pine Cone Country Club decided to create another set of tee boxes.

They already had the "red" tees, the "white" tees, the "blue" tees, and the "gold" tees, but a Greens Committee member had seen the idea of playing eighteen holes on a mix of blue and gold tees at another club whose name he didn't mention, and since he thought the other club's idea was a super great idea, he enthusiastically proposed to the Greens Committee that Pine Cone Country Club offer up a mix of blue and gold tees and call the new set of tees the "Cone Cobb" tees in honor of the Pine Cone Country Club designer, a guy named George Cobb, long since dead and never honored at Pine Cone Country Club with anything. Club legend had it that Mr. Cobb might not have ever gotten paid, but so many years later, and with Mr. Cobb being dead, no one in the accounting department could ever track that legend down.

The Golf Committee, the biggest committee meeting drinkers of all the committees at Pine Cone Country Club, even the Ladies Golf Association Committee, in the first unanimous vote in the history of committee meetings at Pine Cone Country Club, had talked-burped in unison, as was their tradition, then voted to call the new set of tees the "Cone Cobb" tees and to also reprint new scorecards with the following information down there on the bottom left side of the scorecards, underneath the front nine scoring boxes:

**The Cone Cobb tees, in honor of our golf course designer, George Cobb, are a new and extremely**

**exciting mix of blue and gold tees that plays 6,729 yards. It's more challenging than the blue tees, but more forgiving than the "tips." Play the pine cones signified by the blue/gold paint. Have a great day of golfing activity!**

At Pine Cone Country Club, the tee markers are huge pine cones spray painted by maintenance workers either red, white, blue, gold, or for the Cone Cobb tees, the top of the cone gold and the bottom of the cone blue. A lot of people steal tee markers from nice clubs but at Pine Cone Country Club they never had that sort of trouble. The course from the Cone Cobb tees was sloped at 128 and was rated at 72.5. Other than Golf Committee members, most other members don't play the Cone Cobb course because they later found out the idea came from the rival club across town whose members the Pine Cone Country Club members considered to be Cro-Magnons.

The 1$^{st}$ hole at Pine Cone Country Club was a downhill, dogleg right par four, and from the Cone Cobb tees it plays 412 yards.

When Waddell got to the 1$^{st}$ tee he hoisted his bag off of his shoulder. Waddell's golf bag was one of those bags that have the two legs that pop out when you drop it on the ground and it forms a tripod. When these bags are propped up like that it makes it easy for golfers to pull out the golf club they want to use. Waddell pulled out his driver. Waddell's lesbian daughter's lesbian partner, who was in the Marines and stationed in Pakistan and plays golf on the course at her Marine base back in the states, and has actually played golf all over the world, gave him the bag for Christmas a few years ago. She had Waddell's name embroidered on the side of the bag in big, blue, curly letters: Waddell Tiddybumpus. Waddell was speechless until Lucille jabbed him real hard in the side with a fingernail.

Waddell pulled a ball out of his pocket and looked at it. Written across one side of the ball was "PRACTICE." Waddell chuckled, "How'd *that* get in there?"

# Why Golf is so Exciting!

Waddell teed the ball up on the far left side of the tee a few feet from a blue and gold spray painted pine cone and all of a sudden decided, just like the pros he watched on TV, to stand behind the ball and pick an object on the tee box like a broken tee or a divot between him and where he wanted to hit it. Waddell picked a cigarette butt. So Waddell did that: he looked down the line and hoped, by the time he got all ready, he wouldn't forget he picked a cigarette butt as opposed to a broken tee or divot so he could get everything lined up straight when he took his stance. His member buddies often told him he had a crooked stance. They often said we're here to play golf, Waddell, not chop wood. Then Waddell decided to take a couple of practice swings just like the pros did before they hit. He had the time. He had the whole golf course to himself. He never took practice swings before he hit a shot because he always concentrated so hard anyway. But just as he took his first practice swing, Waddell began wondering what Tiger Woods mumbled when he missed a putt. Every time Tiger missed a putt—putts that seemed like Tiger could make real easy since he was the greatest golfer in the world—the camera would always zoom in real close to his face and there would be Tiger mumbling. In all the years of watching Tiger play golf on TV, Waddell could never figure out what he was mumbling. It looked like Tiger was mumbling, "Mip, mip—mop," or something like that. Most of the time when he and his member buddies missed a putt they would yell, "Damn!" or "I missed it!" They let each other know how they felt when they missed a putt, without obscurity. One time, Waddell remembered, as he was watching golf on TV, Lucille had walked into the den right when the camera was zoomed on Tiger's face and there he was: "Mip, mip—*mop*," and Waddell asked Lucille what she thought Tiger was mumbling. After she told Waddell what she thought, Waddell decided he'd never ask Lucille anything like that about golf again.

Waddell also liked the way the pros took a backswing and stopped the club for a second and looked up there to see if everything looked all right. Waddell did that. But off in the distance, on the practice range, that other member Jerry Crowder, was dramatically making the universal gesture that nonverbally said, "Me and you?" Jerry was pointing at Waddell with his pointing finger, then he would point back at himself with his thumb. He did this several times. Waddell thought about the jokes Jerry Crowder told. How Jerry would work his latest one over on every member of the club and once he'd told the joke to everybody, he'd go around the clubhouse or the locker room or the men's grill or on the practice range or even stick his head into a committee meeting and cackle just the punch line, then nearly fall down laughing. Just the punch line. What an annoying habit. "Don't know. I've never looked!" was the latest one. "Don't know. I've never looked!"

Do you smoke after sex, Waddell thought. It wasn't even a golf joke. Those were the best kind of jokes in the world. Golf jokes. With a hand on your shoulder, Jerry had started in on everybody, "Yeah, Darrell, I was with this ol' woman the other night and I asked her..." Or, "I was with some ol' gal named Lucy on Friday night..." Sometimes he'd be with a "Veronica" or a "Darla," a big ol' fat gal who was super hairy everywhere. "Yeah, Morris, I was with this big ol' fat gal named Darla who had a super hairy petunia on Saturday night and I asked her..."

Waddell, buddy, she told me she never looked.

Jerry was still performing the universal gesture.

Waddell thought for a moment. Then he came up with an idea. He dropped his driver and started wildly waving his hands around his face, then around the back of his head, and then he started running around on the tee box. He kicked his left leg up in the air a couple of times. Waddell remembered the time they had to haul Jerry off of the golf course in an ambulance after Jerry got stung by a bee. Jerry had gone into some sort of coma. Waddell tried to remember if it was the 14th or the 6th hole that they had hauled Jerry off of.

Running along the right side of the 1st fairway was a creek. Waddell hit his tee shot into the creek.

# *Waddell Plays the 2ⁿᵈ Hole*

ON THE WAY to the second tee a Mexican maintenance worker in a little pick-up-type cart, called a "Carry All" by its manufacturer, drove by Waddell. Waddell had to walk along the top of the cart path curb for a few steps to get out of the way. Waddell saw that a rake and a shovel were hanging out the back and bouncing around pretty good and he thought the shovel might bounce out but it didn't.

The 2ⁿᵈ hole at Pine Cone Country Club was an uphill par three, and from the Cone Cobb tees it plays 198 yards.

One hundred and ninety-eight yards was a pretty long par three tee shot for Waddell. He really didn't like anything over one hundred and ten yards but he was committed to the Cone Cobb tees today. The hole was uphill and you didn't want to come up short because the creek that ran down the right side of the 1st hole also ran in front of the second green and it was even wider at that point. Club legend had it that Civil War troops floated on the creek from there all the way down in front of the 12ᵗʰ green at Augusta National or something like that but no one at the club could ever track that legend down either. At least that's what he was told when he joined one million years ago. And that late at night you could hear their ghosts singing Civil War refrains as they rowed. The creek was called "Big Creek." So you didn't want to come up short.

Waddell pulled out his 3-wood and pulled out the ball he had finished up with on the 1st hole. Waddell gazed at the ball and said to himself, "How'd *that* get in there?"

Waddell teed the ball up and had already forgotten he wanted to stand behind the ball and get all lined up and then get up to the ball and take a couple of practice swings. Right before he started to swing, Waddell looked back behind him toward the cart path to see if Jerry Crowder was coming but he wasn't. Waddell sighed and then squinted at the ball, which he immediately thought was teed up to high, but then he wondered why he wouldn't just reach down there and push it down a little then get set again. It would take five seconds. But Waddell didn't do it. He told himself to concentrate really hard and if he did then he'd probably be okay. Waddell took a long look up to the hole and looked at the flagstick and a rake poking out of a bunker and a cloud. He caught a fragrant whiff of something. Then he gazed at the two grass-covered humps—one in front of the green and the other one sort of off to the right. All of his member buddies called the humps "moguls." Some of his buddies called them "mounds." But whatever they were, they constantly reminded him of the time when those two women marched into the men's grill, sat down at a table—the table Waddell was sitting at figuring up his scorecard by himself. Then they took off their golf shirts and their bras. So right there in the men's grill on a busy Friday, Waddell was all of a sudden sitting in the men's grill, figuring up his scorecard, right across from two women who had taken their boobs out.

# Waddell Plays the 3<sup>rd</sup> Hole

THE 3<sup>RD</sup> HOLE at Pine Cone Country Club was an uphill par four, and from the Cone Cobb tees it plays 378 yards.

On the 3<sup>rd</sup> hole, what was a creek a long time ago was now sort of a shallow ditch with grass. It runs across the middle of the fairway and from the Cone Cobb tees Waddell figured he was three hundred yards from the ditch or whatever it was so he relaxed too much and hit it into the ditch. "Holy guacamole," Waddell said. Waddell looked at the face of his driver, then back down there at the ball in the ditch, three hundred yards away. He burped: "Bootylicious."

Waddell's approach shot to the green from the ditch went into another creek in front of the green. It seemed to Waddell that Pine Cone Country Club had more creeks than pine trees, the very plant that begat their club mascot, or logo, or whatever it was. Waddell pulled a "Top-Flite XL" golf ball from a pocket on his golf bag crammed with dirty balls. Waddell dropped the ball at his feet so he could try again. He immediately thought of Lee Trevino who endorses the ball in television commercials. Waddell never could decide if he liked Lee Trevino or not and thought one day he'd finally have to decide. All of a sudden Waddell remembered the club didn't allow golfers to hit multiple practice shots on the golf course because hitting multiple practice shots damaged the turf. This was what it said in the booklet all members were given when they joined and the rule hadn't changed as far as he knew. Waddell thought he was the only member who read his monthly newsletters. Pine Cone Country Club was well known for having the nicest fairways in town. Of course, Waddell knew the rules of golf fairly well and technically he could have considered this to be his penalty shot but he also knew he could go down closer to the creek and drop his ball and this would give him a shorter shot to the green. But he was pretty mad he hit the ball into the creek and he wanted to see if he really could hit a shot onto the green from where he was. Waddell was seventy-eight yards to the middle of the green. So Waddell pushed a tee into the fairway and placed the ball onto the tee. He did this so he wouldn't damage the turf but he took a huge divot anyway and felt sort of bad about it as he walked to the creek to find his two golf balls which were sitting beside each other wobbling in the water which reminded him of those two women again who came into the men's grill. Waddell constantly wondered about women. Sometimes you can figure them out real easy then sometimes it's real hard.

"How's it going?" That's what Waddell had asked the two women who had taken out their boobs. Up until that point no one had said anything to them and there was obviously a lot to talk about. The only women ever allowed into the men's grill were the three little Nicaraguan cleaning women who came to vacuum in the middle of the night and wipe everything off. The other members were mouth-open gawking. This boob thing was getting uncomfortable, so Waddell asked the two women how it was going. The best conversation starter he'd ever learned when attempting to have a conversation with a woman. Ask a woman how it's going and they'll tell you—that was Waddell's creed.

The one on the right, Mickey Johnson's wife, June, said it wasn't going well at all. That her and Maxine had an issue.

Waddell knew her to be a complainer. Her boobs hung down quite a bit and poked out to the sides a little and the bottom half of them were real white looking.

The other woman, Maxine, Jerry Crowder's wife, said they were staging a *pro*test to air out our issue. Waddell knew her to be a Chardonnay fiend. One eyelid was closed and the other eye was floating around in its socket. Sort of going upwards.

"A protest about what?" Waddell had asked Maxine whose boobs were completely tanned and were the size of African elephants and the color of footballs.

And Maxine had said, "Because you *allll*—have a *grill*—and we *don't*."

16

# *Waddell Plays the 4<sup>th</sup> Hole*

THE 4TH HOLE at Pine Cone Country Club was a par four, and from the Cone Cobb tees it plays 421 yards.

The hole goes way uphill right after the landing area. It's also a pretty good test of a golfer's driving skill because you tee off from a hilltop to a narrow landing area and you're not filled with enormous confidence as you look at all of it while you're waggling. This hole was the reason Waddell hit so many balls on the practice tee with his driver because you have to hit a nearly perfect drive in order to have a decent shot to the green because the club members never had the guts to vote to cut down a huge, three hundred year old oak tree right next to the green, whose position up there meant you had to place your drive, in order to get the only good angle to the green, on a place in the fairway about the size of a trampoline. As old and imposing as the tree was, it wasn't associated with a club legend. Except four years ago, the club had an arborist come by to look at it and two hours of him looking at it and climbing up in it and measuring it with a tape measurer and him poking a tool in the ground near it cost the club $1,500.65.

Waddell had hit his approach shots into the big oak tree many times over the years, even when it was younger, and knew it was hard to make an eagle, or a birdie, or a par when you do that.

Waddell hit his ball into the oak tree.

The ball fell out of the oak tree and bounced three times and rolled into the cup but Waddell didn't see it since he was way down in the fairway and was already fiddling with trying to get his bag on his shoulder and figured it was just up there somewhere and that he'd find it. Waddell never had an eagle in his life. When he did, he vowed to himself to spend the money and have it put in one of those frame things with a little plaque with his name and the date and the hole engraved on it in curly letters, like on his golf bag.

When he got to the oak tree, Waddell urinated onto the base of the tree and then onto an ant hill for a minute, then back onto the base of the tree. While he was urinating, Waddell knew in his heart what he was doing was a little crass and considered stopping and holding what was left until he got to the on-course restroom and weather safety shelter, but at his age he knew he just didn't have the muscle power to do it. Some of the ants had crawled onto his right shoe, up his sock, and onto the side of his leg and began stinging him. Waddell jumped and urinated all over the front of his khaki shorts and into his golf bag.

Just then, Waddell heard a golf ball whiz over the green and into the woods beyond the green, and not five seconds later saw Jerry Crowder come riding up the apron of the green, over one hundred yards past those little signs in the fairway that said no carts beyond this point. Then Jerry stopped and looked to see if anybody was around. He looked at the oak tree but Waddell had scooted around it, still holding his dripping wang-doodle in his right hand, and was out of sight. The base of the oak tree could have hidden three good-sized men or good-sized women and their golf bags. Waddell peeked around the side of the tree and saw Jerry drive his cart onto the green, all four tires, and stop. Jerry got out of the cart, and looked around the green for a moment. He said, "Then get off the *side*walk."

Waddell knew that to be the punch line of the joke he plastered the club with around the time of the Christmas party. The set-up line was, "If you don't like my driving."

Jerry looked around in the greenside rough for a moment, and then walked over to the cup and looked in there.

# Waddell Plays the 5<sup>th</sup> Hole

THE 5TH HOLE at Pine Cone Country Club was a dog leg left par four, and from the Cone Cobb tees it plays 377 yards.

Down below all the tee boxes was a little oval pond and before Waddell pulled out his 3-wood he gazed at the pond. Something was moving around in the water but Waddell wasn't sure if it was a fish or a duck.

Waddell then gazed up to the bend in the dog-leg, three hundred or so yards away. He could see that the drink cart had stopped next to Jerry's cart and Jerry and the cart girl were on the other side of the drink cart. The blue and white canopy of the drink cart was blocking the view a little bit, but it looked like Jerry and the drink cart girl were standing real close together but Waddell wasn't sure.

Waddell, if anything on the 5<sup>th</sup> hole, always topped it into the pond. Waddell reared back, thinking that he always topped it into the pond, then topped it into the pond, so he didn't care that much. Waddell then took out his 3-iron and hit it into the fairway. He always hit his 3-iron into the fairway from the 5th tee.

As Waddell walked to his ball, the drink cart was coming down the cart path to Waddell's right. Lucy, the drink cart girl, edged off of the cart path and into the rough a little bit, then stopped and honked the drink cart horn two times. Lucy, of all the different drink cart girls in all the years at Pine Cone Country Club, was the only one who ever honked the drink cart horn. The horn was activated by a foot button down there near the gas pedal. Lucy never honked it while you were in the middle of your backswing, but she used it a lot to get your attention. Waddell had heard from a waiter that Lucy's goal was to get every group she honked at to buy something, no matter how many times she saw you during the round, which might be seven or eight times. She drove the drink cart around the property as if she were in one of those car races that plow through the Baja desert. Sometimes she honked the horn and then flashed the lights. Sometimes at the same time. The waiter told Waddell she cleared more in tips than Pepe, the shoe shine guy who drove one of those new marshmallow white Cadillac conversion truck eyesores with the chrome wheels that spin.

Lucy screamed over to Waddell and asked him if he would like anything. Waddell always thought sodas were priced too high so he never got anything. Although Lucy and the other girls who drove the drink cart knew that Mr. Tiddybumpus and a large number of other members never bought anything from the drink cart the general manager asked them to always stop anyway and politely ask. Cover your bases with these old guys, Phil told them. Before Waddell yelled out that he'd get some water at the next tee, he suddenly thought about all that might be wrong with golf. In a word, there was too much mystery, wasn't there? Too much of it. And it was an expensive recreation. These could be desperate times for golf. No one really knew the golf swing. There was no way. The only thing they really knew, these TV instructors, was the last two feet before impact. Everybody was the same. Maybe the Tiger kid had it close. Snead was said to have had the deeper understanding, the simple, shucking kind of deeper understanding that country folks have. The Harvey Penick fellow, enough to keep notes on it. Hale Irwin had the little tufts of hair that poked out from underneath his hat and poked out over his ears. He'd sported the hair tufts for years. Why? Why didn't he ever cut those things or shove them back behind his ears? Was he in a cult or something? The guy on the Golf Channel with the mustache. Until next time, keep it in the short grass. Keep it in the short grass. Keep it in the short grass. Easier said than done, sitting there in your air conditioned studio in your nice makeup and those nice suits provided by—whoever. The credits always went by too fast. Why? Why didn't he change his offering to something really useful to the viewers? Until next time, take it back real slow. Take it back real slow. Waddell yelled over to Lucy that he'd get some water at the next tee.

Lucy stomped on the horn one good time. "Mr. Wa-*ddell*," she screamed, "Water's for *ass*holes. I've got that new green Powerade you like so much and a delicious ham sandwich!" Then she flashed the lights. She jumped off of the seat and started around the cart to pull out a green Powerade and a ham sandwich and run it out there and force it into his hand but her shorts fell down to her knees.

Waddell watched her jerk her shorts up over one of those wedgied-up thongs, hop back into the cart and peel off. God only knew how much those Powerade's cost, Waddell thought. They were the ones in those huge plastic jugs that clogged up creeks and landfills and the throats of seagulls. They weighed five pounds. Not like a Coke in a bottle—like the old days where they fit into your hand and satisfied in three good gulps. The best when they were thirty-three degrees—ice, ice cold. Now you rarely see them in the grocery store, and always at the end of the isle, out of the way. Santa Claus still on the sides of the cartons in July. Maybe two or three six packs for sale, not obnoxious walls of them. You could return the empties, too. Get a little money back. Three cents a pop adds up if you were serious about it. A novelty item now, appreciated only by those who know *what was what* about liquid refreshment. And how she thought he preferred green Powerade over a purple one was a new one. Oh, suggestive selling, Waddell thought. But it wasn't going to work on him. Nothing mysterious about that. Tough as a rock—my wallet is impenetrable, Waddell thought as he stood over his ball, a 5-iron in his hands, waggling, thinking, pondering why all the big framed pictures inside the clubhouse were of other holes at other clubs. Over the fireplace in the main dining room, number thirteen at Augusta National. What did Pine Cone Country Club have to do with Augusta National? In the golf shop, the pro sold framed prints of holes at Pine Valley. To hell with Pine Valley. Those Jersey Yankees sell pictures of our range ball picker? On the wall between the doors of the men's and women's locker rooms was a huge oil painting—God only knows, Waddell thought then and now, how much we paid for that—of the

5th at Mid-Ocean. Waddell remembered the day it really got to him. He was standing there glaring at it. Jerry Crowder had walked up and slapped him on the back. "Whatcha doin' there, Wa-*dell*, glaring at an innocent oil painting like that."

"Where's *this* hole?" Waddell had grunted. "It ain't on *our* golf course."

"Oh, that's the famous nineteenth hole at—Hairy Petunia Country Club, Wa-d*dell*. You oughta apply for membership." Jerry slapped him on the back again and walked into the women's locker room, then poked his head back out the door. "They'll let anybody in."

"Not *me*," Waddell had absently mumbled. "I wouldn't join a place called Hairy Petunia Country Club."

In the distance, the drink cart horn honked two times.

Waddell cold shanked the 5-iron into the right rough.

# Waddell Plays the 6<sup>th</sup> Hole

THE 6<sup>TH</sup> HOLE at Pine Cone Country Club was a straight away par five, and from the Cone Cobb tees it plays 526 yards.

As he walked to the 6th tee, Waddell mumbled, "Take it back real slow. Take it back real slow." As he pulled out his driver he mumbled it for the third time as he'd heard things become habits after saying them to yourself for three times right before you did whatever it was.

As he squeezed the grip of his club real hard he remembered he didn't get a drink of water, so he walked over to the water cooler.

Just that morning he had read in the newspaper that health inspectors were finding rat droppings in iced tea dispensers in fast food restaurants all over town and had even heard it on the news in his car and Waddell thought about that as he gulped down eight cone shaped cups of three-day old warm water. Waddell talk-burped real loud, "Bootylicious!"

Waddell stood back over his ball which he had left teed up on the tee. It made Waddell feel great that while he was over there drinking water that no one had run out from behind a tree or whatever and messed with his ball. That out here on the golf course you were embraced by safety and solitude. Not like when you had to go into the city. Looking around while you locked your car. Always on alert. On the golf course you were on alert for friendship and camaraderie. Yes sir. Millions of memories are made on a golf course. Relationships begun. Strengthened. Sentimental words expressed through the facial expressions of your fellow competitors, and in match play, your opponent. Yes sir, Mister Golf. Mister grass and trees and mister cut grass smell. You listened to the water of a creek running over rocks. Even listening to a crow was nice. Watching him balance himself at the top of the tree on a golf course, the tip bending and him working his little claws on the flimsy branch to stay steady. Listening to his caw-caw.

Waddell popped his tee shot up when a crow in a nearby tree cawed real loud.

But it's in the fairway, Waddell thought, holding his finish. Made it to the fairway and that counts as one of those fairways in regulations. The PGA didn't have certain sections of the fairway roped off. No sir. You were in the fairway or you weren't. Lady, make a crisp little check on your clip board in the "fairways in regulation" column for Waddell Tiddybumpus of Pine Cone Country Club on the par 5 6$^{th}$. And I took it back real slow so give me a check for that, too.

The crow cawed again.

Waddell knew if you had to pop it up real bad it was better to pop it up on a par five. He was once told by the head pro of Pine Cone Country Club, a little munchkin-like fellow who could hit it a long way, that on par fives you were allowed by the gods of golf one indiscretion. Waddell remembered the conversation took place in the drive-through line at the Taco Bell two months ago. Waddell had thought at that moment he saw the pro more out of the club than in it.

Waddell walked to his ball and found it in what they call the "intermediate rough." But it was sitting up. Sitting up good enough where he could hit his driver. The pro had written in the club newsletter last year about how to do this. But only hit your driver off the fairway when there's not much trouble out there in front of you.

It was all trouble out there, Waddell thought. Had any one aver designed a golf course with no bunkers or creeks or ponds or lakes—and greens that didn't have a ridiculous part? Where every hole invited a better score? More confidence? Not all of us are trying to get on the PGA Tour, you know. The leave-the-rake-in-the-bunker-or-out-of-the-bunker dilemma would never have to be contemplated ever again. Waddell wondered how much money it took to make a golf course. He knew of a piece of land. But it had two creeks on it.

It'll scream real low and probably curve left to right, so compensate for that, the pro's newsletter column went on to say. So if you're looking for a lot of roll and distance, and if the aforementioned conditions are available to you as a golfer, then go for it and have a great day of golfing!

Waddell aimed to the left and swung. The ball screamed real low but it didn't curve that much and ended up in the intermediate rough again. A crow—Waddell didn't know if it was the earlier crow or a new crow—flew down and picked the ball up with his beak and took off, but immediately dropped it. The crow turned around and floated back down to the ball and pecked at the ball and rolled it around for a moment then flew off toward the 7th hole and cawed. Then a deer ran across the fairway with an arrow dangling from its neck.

## *Waddell Plays the 7$^{th}$ Hole*

THE 7TH HOLE at Pine Cone Country Club was a downhill par four, and from the Cone Cobb tees it plays 347 yards.

And there's a round bunker in the middle of the fairway right where you'd want you're ball to land.

Waddell eyed that bunker as if he were trying to get somebody's license number. It looked as if he were prepared to throw it a punch. But that bunker just sat there, with its nice white sand. Raked. The rake in the bunker. Would make a nice photograph if you were into that sort of thing. A photograph of a bunker for your bathroom wall. But Waddell had heard it from a rules authority that technically these things are called sand bunkers, because there were grass bunkers, too. So when you say bunker to your fellow competitors or playing partner, whatever the case may be for that round of golf, always qualify it. Sand bunker. Grass bunker.

At that moment, Waddell thought in all his years playing golf he'd never seen anyone's ball hit a sprinkler head.

Boy, the stuff that rules authority said. None of it made any sense. They had invited him to speak at the second annual Pine Cone Country Club "Evening of The Rules of Golf Discussion and Cocktails." Waddell liked the cocktail part, but thought they were priced too high at Pine Cone Country Club. The man had on a tweed jacket, no less. The kind with the elbow guards. His claim to fame was making a ruling on Ballesteros in the Masters. Waddell saw it right there on TV. The man didn't back down when the Mexican whined and moaned and pointed and waved his arms around, right there on CBS. When he got asked a question the rules authority eyes rolled up in his head and he quoted, verbatim, the numbers these rules have in that book—then let us have it with the explanation. All that smoke in the men's grill, too. The guy looked like he was going to pass out. But open the door and let in thirty-seven degree air. He kept sipping his water. The questions—his answers—then the giggles—more cocktails—then it turned into sniping. From all sides, literally. Why he chose to stand in the middle of the room, surrounded by bared teeth, and not on the stoop of the fireplace, like the last rules authority they had in there, Waddell never knew. The man looked like a trapped animal. Understood pretty quick this crowd at Pine Cone Country Club regarded the rules of golf on their own alien terms. Not quite making it up as we go along, but close, except for the club tournaments where we got watched. Golf rules: we thought for ourselves, comprised in mutuality, and had fun. The general manager over in the corner silently mouthing, "Oh, dear god. Dear god." Phil wiping his forehead and rubbing his eyes. That just made it worse. Just egged us on. You may just work here, but you're implicated. You let us act like this.

The rules authority was finally asked what was the one golf rule golfers abused the most.

"Just *one!*" somebody screamed.

The haw-haw-haw was deafening.

But you had to give the rules authority credit. He stood there and glared back, answer ready when we shut up. But his forehead and upper lip were coated with silver beads. This final question was his queue. He knew he could bolt when he told us. He told us it was where we put the ball back on the green where we marked it.

That Jerry Crowder. He stood up as if he'd been electrocuted. "Do *what!*"

Where you put the ball back where you mark it. The rules authority seemed to be quivering. Amateur golfers, he nearly whispered, usually don't put the ball back—typically—uh—in front or behind the ball or to one of the sides of the coin, exactly where it was. It has to go—exactly *back.*

Haw-haw-haw!

Cigar and cigarette and pipe smoke, thick as concrete.

Suffocating.

Haw-haw-haw! Even louder.

"You come to *our* club..." Jerry blustered, pointing his finger at him. "Our *club*. Right here in our fuckin' men's *grill*..."

The rules authorities eyes are as wide as they can get.

Go Jerry. You tell him, buddy. Tell this cat the way it *was* at P.C.C.C.

"...and accuse *us*!"

# Waddell Plays the 8ᵗʰ Hole

THE 8ᵀᴴ HOLE at Pine Cone Country Club was a downhill par three, and from the Cone Cobb tees it plays 169 yards. It's what everybody calls the "signature" hole because it's real pretty.

It's got a lake behind the green and over across the lake to the left was the green of the 13ᵗʰ hole and all its sand bunkers behind the green. Also behind the 8ᵗʰ green, over to the right, was a view of the 9ᵗʰ fairway that was real pleasant. To the left of the 8th green was a big bunker and behind the bunker was this one real tall pine tree that hangs out over the green like an gigantic flower that got struck by lightning eighteen years ago and it never did die so that added to the allure. Lightning struck the tree in the middle of the night but over the years approximately forty-two members said they were on the green picking their hole-in-one balls out of the cup or tapping in their birdies when the tree got struck by lightning and how they got pelted with butterscotch colored, razor-edged resin chips that had been solidified by the heat and thousands of twirling pine cones, our beloved club mascot, while the hair on their arms and legs and head and eyebrows and knuckles stood straight up.

Waddell let his bag drop off of his shoulder and then he swatted at a gnat flying around in front of his face. His hand went right through the gnat. He swatted at it again, but it made no difference. His hand went through it again. He swatted at it again, this time with some spastic fury, with both hands, going at it like a corn shucker, then realized it was one of those things floating around in his right eyeball and not a gnat. Waddell looked around to see if anybody was watching him. How embarrassing. I bet I looked like a lunatic he thought as he looked at a squirrel who had been watching.

Then he heard a cell phone ring in the distance. Waddell jumped as if the pine tree got struck by lightning again. Everything had been real quiet up to that point except for the thrashing noise his hands and arms had made as he swatted at that thing floating around in his right eyeball. *Cell* phones, Waddell thought. Now that was a club management dilemma. But not with me, Waddell thought. I don't sit my phone by my ham sandwich as if I'm expecting some emergency every minute. No sir. Not me. I'm not tied to technology. Not like these other guys. Not like that Crowder. Two cells phones and a pager clipped to his belt like some sort of old nerd. Answers the phone on his backswing. Always told whoever it was on the other end that he was in a meeting. So why did he answer it? And why do you need a pager if you've got a phone? God, not me. Not tied to Palm pilots and laptop computers and raspberries or whatever. Of course, that's the way these people run their companies these days. Call their secretary on the laptop or whatever. Let the secretary run the company.

Waddell's cell phone kept ringing.

And who's the creep who keeps letting his cell phone ring? Dang, I can hear it way over here. Probably one of those young, hot shot types we keep letting in. No respect. Rules are for other people. Rules are meant to be sniffed at.

Waddell's cell phone kept ringing.

Waddell took a practice swing with his 6-iron. Decided it was too much club, so he stuck it back into the bag and felt the bag vibrate.

Oh, *my* cell phone. Waddell scrambled for the zipper. He yanked it down, grabbed the phone and looked at the incoming phone number. It was the main number of Pine Cone Country Club. Cell phones made him a little nervous. He didn't want to be that in touch, but Lucille insisted he be in better touch so she went out and bought him one and some personal, business-style cards. "Waddell Tiddybumpus," Retired Guy," they said, and his new cell phone number. Remember, you're retired, she said as she handed over the wad of stuff. You're old and liable to seize up any moment the way you grump around and play golf so strenuously. Everybody's got one now. You don't sit in your office anymore next to a phone and a secretary. What if you have a heart attack? she said. If you have a heart attack—she grabbed back the cell phone and held it up and wiggled it to get his attention—*call* me. Stick it in your golf bag. You can call the club and order root beers from the 9th tee. See here, you can punch in frequently-called numbers. Have a heart attack. Punch my number. It's got voice mail.

Waddell didn't want to punch in frequently called numbers.

He punched the answer button. "This was Waddell Tiddybumpus," he said tentatively, "on the eighth tee—out here."

"Super," a voice said.

The voice was familiar, but Waddell wasn't sure. He never could remember who he gave his special cards to. "Who's calling the great golfing amateur, Waddell Tiddybumpus?" Waddell loved cell phone humor.

"It's Lamar. In the golf shop."

"My favorite golf professional." Waddell liked Lamar the best of all the assistant golf professionals. A new one every couple of weeks. Lamar had passed the test of four months. Seemed to be trying to make a career out of it. Gutting it out, selling overpriced shirts. Giving cheap, but good lessons. Waddell's grip had been all wrong for just ten dollars.

"Just wondering how you're doing out there, Mr. Tiddybumpus, and where you're at. You're pretty much the only one out there, believe it or not. Well, except for old Mr. Ming in the pool again. Did you know we call him 'The Exotic?' "

"I didn't know that. What do you guys call me?" Waddell knew they had to call him something. He just knew it.

"Sophocles."

"Oh."

"See, you're a thinker, Mr. Tiddybumpus. We all know you know stuff, but you never act like it."

"I'll accept that as a..."

"*Right. Any*how, The Exotic was doing his thousand laps with that goofy rubber cap on. That water must be thirty-two degrees,

I'm here to tell you. Boss, that water is ice…"

"Lamar?"

"…and you know the pool ain't even officially open yet, but oh God for*bid* if any of us *little* people goes and tells a rooster struttin' *mem*ber no you can't crawl over the pool fence because the pool is *closed* until Memorial day *wee*kend and I can't believe with all of his money why he doesn't build a pool in his own damn yard…"

"Lamar."

"…or come to think of it, uh, Mister Member, uh, no you can't just walk right into the kitchen and grab a crab cake when Hulio's gone to the toilet or you really actually gotta pay for stuff you sneak into your pocket from the golf shop or—"

"Lamar. *Son.*"

"Yes sir, Mr. Tiddybumpus? I just can't figure out all of you rich people. Sorry."

"You get old, Lamar. You get nuts."

"Yes sir. Okay. You people go nuts."

Waddell pondered The Exotic. Old Simon Ming. Half Scandinavian and a lot of Chinese. The creamy white skin—and the green eyes. Nearly seven feet tall. Had won Olympic gold in Helsinki? In the butterfly? Or was it the crawl? Was ambassador to Malta in the fifties? Had about nine doctorate degrees. Spoke a bunch of languages, they said. But didn't play golf, so he was exotic as hell. Uneducated, then. Golf was the greatest darn sport on earth. Now Waddell pondered Crowder. "What about Crowder? He's lurking around."

"Mr. Crowder's standing right here, wondering where you are. What hole did you say you were on again?"

There was only one thing Waddell liked about cell phones: locality anonymity or whatever. "I was kidding with you, kid. I'm back home already. Folding clothes."

# Waddell Plays the 9<sup>th</sup> Hole

THE 9TH HOLE at Pine Cone Country Club was a slight dogleg right par five, and from the Cone Cobb tees it plays 567 yards all the way up to the back of the clubhouse. You have to hit your drive over a lake.

After Waddell got to the tee he gazed at the lake. Something was moving around in the water and this time Waddell was sure it was a duck. Actually it was two ducks, and Waddell watched them play with each other in the lake. It would have been perfect golf picture if one of the ducks had quacked, but neither one of them ever quacked. Maybe these kinds of ducks didn't quack. Waddell liked to eat duck, and wondered if all ducks tasted the same. Wondered how ducks were raised for food. With chickens? Had never heard of a duck farm. So it was likely. Ducks and chickens associating to make our food. Waddell at that moment, on the 9th tee of Pine Cone Country Club, thought the world was going to Hell. If some fast food joint introduced a "Duckin" sandwich he thought he would probably faint.

Then his cell phone rang again.

Then he was reminded why he was here in the first place: to rip another three hundred yard drive right over those ducks and down the fairway. Waddell wanted his ball to hit hard and bounce down there three or four good times, real high, with some authority, just like the pro's tee balls did on TV every time. His just stopped. Sometimes they bounced backwards.

Waddell pressed the green button on the phone. It was the main number of the club again. He put the phone to his ear. Now I'm in the back yard tending to my bulbs, Waddell thought. Waddell didn't think to say hello as his mind seemed to be racing

33

with various thoughts.

"Hello? You there, Mr. Tiddybumpus?"

"Tiddybumpus speaking."

"Lamar here again. You're really not folding your underwear, are you Mr. Tiddybumpus?"

"No."

"I'll bet you're on the ninth tee, aren't you Mr. Tiddybumpus."

"Who wants to know? You or Crowder?"

"I do. Mr. Crowder creeped off somewhere. I think he went to hit some more balls."

"Great. Crowder making more divots on the range. Did you teach him his swing?"

"He's a lost cause. I fired him. Some customers you don't want."

"Why do you think I'm on the ninth tee?"

"Because I can see you from the golf shop. Wave."

Waddell waved.

Lamar waved back. "Then that's you."

Waddell was struck by the kid's tone of voice. Sounded like he called just to chat again. He thought about asking what in the hell did he want, but he was a good kid. Waddell never forgot a ten dollar lesson. "So..."

"Well, Mr. Tiddybumpus. I actually called to ask you a favor. You know I'm doing my PGA apprentice school stuff and I'm required to take a guy and make him a case study while I give him a whole bunch of lessons..."

Waddell thought that sounded like the lessons would be free to the guy who got to be the case study.

"...and all the time we spend together is free."

"Count me in."

"But my case study is going to be a little different. Since your club's head professional is such a dork, I never can get out of the golf shop and on my off day all I want to do was spend it with my girlfriend, you know, catching up on personal business, so I thought I would do something different and use today's cell phone technology and work with a guy over the phone while he played."

"That's different, all right. You said this would be free, right?"

One of those ducks quacked.

"See, you take a look at a guy like Furyk."

"I can't do it. Too strange."

"But you see—it works. It's not *how*, it's the results that matter. So all we'd be concerned about was your results. You swing at it any way you goddamn want. I don't get distracted, I don't get mad, you don't get embarrassed, and we just concentrate on the results. But you're gonna have to keep your cell phone charged up."

Now the ducks started to make love. The flapping and quacking was obscene.

"Are those ducks doing it?" Lamar asked.

"Wow. Yeah."

"Anyhow, you just go around and play and I talk you through things and you ask me swing and course management questions as your teacher and then I can write my thesis or whatever on how it turns out."

"What if I use a cart?"

"Free. See, I just punch a special golf cart charge button on the cash register. Boop. *Free*."

Count me in more. "But they don't want us out here yakking on our cell phones, holding up play."

"I talked to Phil."

"And what did he say about your thesis idea?"

"He thought it was the stupidest idea he'd ever heard of in all his thirty years in the club business."

"So let's do it," Waddell said.

"Okay—okay," Lamar breathed. "Okay. Great. This is *great*. 'Golf Digest' material."

"What do you want me to do?"

"Okay. Tell me what you're thinking as you're about to hit your tee ball there, then put the phone down by the ball and hit, then pick up the phone and tell me sort of what happened, then we'll rap about it like teacher and student."

"But you'll be able to see what happened from up there."

"I already thought about that. I'm gonna turn around and look at the logoed balls in this fish bowl on the counter."

"What I'm thinking ain't gonna happen."

"You gotta always tell me what you're thinking. You can't be embarrassed. You gotta fess up, man."

Waddell fessed up.

"Okay—okay. That probably ain't gonna happen. Would you be satisfied with a tee shot of two hundred yards, over the lake, right down the middle?"

"What do *you* think?"

"Right, Mr. Tiddybumpus. That's the attitude. You're a *great* student. So pull out your three wood."

"I wanna hit driver."

"Throw it in the lake. Hit the three."

Waddell's cell phone began beeping. "I'm about to lose the charge. Or the power. Or whatever you call it." Waddell shook the phone a couple of good times, then clunked it on his forehead once.

"Okay—okay. So just hurry up then. Pull the three and hit it smooth. I'm watching you. It's called the charge, by the way."

"Driver."

"Three wood."

"Driver."

"It's the—*three.*"

"Fine, okay."

"Swing slow. *Slow.* Watch the clubhead hit the ball. And tell me where the tee went after you hit. Okay—go—I've turned around and I'm looking at the logoed balls in the fish bowl."

"Fine, okay." Waddell teed a ball up, dropped the cell phone on the grass by the tee, pulled his driver out, settled over the ball, gripped the grip as hard as he could, swung as hard and as fast as he could, and skipped it across the water right by the ducks making love, bounced it into a floating log on the far side of the lake, rolled it over the ladies tees, through the rough, and into the fairway on the other side where it bounced on a sprinkler head and got about thirty more yards. Waddell picked up the cell phone. It was still beeping. "See that?"

"No. I told you we were interested in just the results." Lamar turned and looked out of the golf shop window. "Hey! Is that it down there, right in the middle of the fairway, Mr. Tiddybumpus? You da *man*."

"Yep. Sure was. Right there in the middle of the fairway."

"Where did the *tee* go?"

"I believe it disintegrated. I swung with such passion."

"Wow. *Wow.* Disintegrated. This is *ground*-breaking!"

# Waddell at the Turn

TO GET TO the 10th tee, Waddell had to walk up close to the back of the clubhouse.

He always liked to stop at a spot on the cart path below a stone wall where he always caught a whiff of what they were cooking in the kitchen. Today it smelled like they were cooking fried chicken. Then a moment later it smelled like they were cooking macaroni and cheese. And right when Waddell remembered that time when he was seven years old that his girlfriend at a church homecoming had successfully slipped a macaroni up his nostril and how, in his surprise, he sniffed the macaroni up his nose instead of snorting it out of his nose, the bag room attendant walked over to the top of the wall and put his arms on the top of the wrought iron fence and asked Mr. Tiddybumpus how it was going and if the course record for the front nine was still intact.

Mr. Tiddybumpus didn't immediately answer. He was rehashing how his mother had grabbed a clot of his hair to keep him from squirming while she tried with the other hand to pull the macaroni out with a pair of tweezers in front of everybody.

The bag room attendant asked Mr. Tiddybumpus again how he was doing. The attendant was really hoping hard Mr. Tiddybumpus would mumble something again so he could run back in the bag room and put another check by Mr. Tiddybumpus' name. There wasn't a lot going on. All the member slugs and slobs and drunks and complainers and phonies and blowhards and assholes and cheapskates and thieves and liars and adulterers and cigarette eaters and cigar nursers and child and wife neglectors and whiners and gossipers and gamblers and drooling nouveaux riche rednecks and tip stiffers and freak shows and monthly statement connivers and

38

twitching morons were in the men's grill watching the Masters.

Waddell sensed someone was talking to him. He looked over to this right.

"Up here."

"Right," Waddell said, gazing up at the attendant. "I got it in the crosshairs."

The bag room attendant appraised Waddell for a moment, squinting his eyes. There really wasn't a category he could check where a member said something philosophical, so he huffed back to the bag room and told them what Tiddybumpus said and the other bag room attendants didn't know what to think so the more senior bag room attendant after a long moment of weighing the situation—said let's just continue to keep an eye on Tiddybumpus.

Waddell stood there for a moment longer and then smelled what he thought was a fresh fart.

## *Waddell Plays the 10<sup>th</sup> Hole*

THE 1 0TH HOLE at Pine Cone Country Club was a dog leg left par four, and from the Cone Cobb tees it plays 365 yards. It's the one hole on the course that's so easy that the members of Pine Cone Country Club felt that if even the worst golfer didn't make a par then he was stupid.

Waddell pulled out his three wood, which was trusty, and planned to hook it around the corner, but Waddell knew every time he tried to hook it he sliced it. So Waddell thought of something he'd heard or read in a magazine or seen on the Golf Channel or whatever. The thing he'd heard or read or seen on the Golf Channel was a tip that said that when you're in bad trouble with your golf game, just do the opposite. If you swing slow, in other words then start swinging real fast for a change and see what good things happen! If you have a narrow stance, then work your feet way out there like a Sumo wrestler. Replace your spikes. Go back to a normal putter. Wear red pants instead of your normal brown. Waddell thought he'd try to slice it on purpose, so of course, he'd surely hook it. As he stood there squeezing the grip of the three wood, hard, like an axe, Waddell heard a golf cart pull up, then stop right in front of him. Without looking up, Waddell could see the bottom half of it and finally realized that getting away from Jerry Crowder was impossible. People who are obviously alone should be left alone, Waddell thought. If a guy was swimming alone way over to the side of an ocean full of members, then it would seem that the guy wanted to be alone. Waddell prepared himself to tell Crowder to beat it. Waddell looked up. It was The Exotic.

Waddell noticed that The Exotic was still dripping pool water.

Waddell also noticed that The Exotic was still wearing his orange Speedo and his rubber cap. Waddell noticed that The Exotic had a rental set of clubs strapped to the back of the cart. The rental set bags were unmistakable: they were lime green, ultimately meant to discourage the use of them. But the Jap guests loved them. Always asked if they were for sale, but God forbid that doofus general manager Phil see the unique revenue opportunity and tell the head pro to make some easy cash and keep our damn dues down.

And Lamar's stupid face up there in the pro shop window looking down there at them. A clownish grin and a thumbs up.

Waddell reached down and grabbed his ball and the tee, hoping this subtle gesture would show this oddity that he could play through. No problem. Just play right on through real quick. Please play on through real quick.

The Exotic, nearly seven feet tall and not an ounce of fat on his browned, lean, age-spotted body, gave Waddell an elegant nod. He looked like something from some science fiction movie. Clumsily, The Exotic gave the universal "me and you" gesture. It looked as if was the first time he ever did it. Then The Exotic said he had never played golf in his life and all of a sudden after his swim he had a flaming urge to give it a college go. He didn't have any shoes on either. He had long looking feet, like bird claws. Or pelican feet.

Waddell said under his breath, "Oh, shit."

The Exotic said in that weird accent, "Good sir—come again?"

Waddell said, "Uh, go *hit*." Waddell swept his left arm toward the fairway.

"Oh, I imagine I'll do some hitting, all right!" The Exotic came toward Waddell with his left hand out.

Waddell caught himself stepping back just a little and thought about where his manners were. The thought of The Exotic not wanting to play through and The Exotic wanting to play nine holes together made Waddell deeply depressed. Maybe he just wanted to play one hole. Waddell knew that super smart people who led lives of nerds most of the time just wanted to sniff the experience a little and make a quick decision so they could run back to their laboratories and eat their boogers. He had managed men like that

41

who designed devices and chemicals that saved people's lives.

"Sir Simon Ming," The Exotic said.

"Tiddybumpus. Waddell *Tiddybumpus*." Waddell figured some queen somewhere gave him the sir business. Read somewhere it was hard to get one.

They shook hands. Waddell had never felt anything like that hand in his life and he'd shaken a few hands, even left ones.

"I will venture to say," The Exotic said loudly, as if he were giving a speech, "that you've never played golf with a man in bathing trunks, a rubber cap, and no shoes."

"Nope."

"And I would also venture to say you're the type of man who would immediately tell me, without hesitation, if I were imposing on you in any way. In any way."

"You just want to probably play one hole, right?"

"Well done, Mr. Tiddybumpus. I'll briefly contact the experience and then make my pronouncement. I'm sure one hole is all I need. Possibly two."

"Well that'll be fine. Just fine, then."

"I can tell by looking at you, although I'm sure we've already met a number of times at the club's finer social functions, that you're the man to help me. You look like a golfer. A man who can play this game."

"I'm sort of a work in progress my-self." Waddell forced a laugh he tried to make sound like a sincerely blurted-out laugh and discovered he wasn't an actor one bit.

"Well said, Mr. Tiddybumpus."

"Thank you."

"So—shall we golf?"

Waddell looked down the fairway a little stupidly. "This is the tenth hole here."

"Ah—numbered—so golfers can find their way back!"

Lamar thumped on the pro shop window.

Waddell looked up there.

Lamar gave him another goofy thumbs up.

Waddell said, "I never thought about it that way."

The Exotic stepped closer and put that hand on Waddell's shoulder. "Then let's think and act in different ways this afternoon. Let's do it together."

"Just this one hole, huh?"

The Exotic reached down and took Waddell's ball and tee from his hand. "I shall lead the way!"

Waddell looked up at Lamar, who was really laughing hard now. Waddell could tell Lamar's arms were wrapped around his belly.

The Exotic pointed down at the tee box. "Begin here?"

"Right. Just sort of shove the tee into the ground and put the ball on top of it."

"Exactly as I thought." The Exotic teed it up in front of the Cone Cobb tee markers.

Waddell shuffled over there real quick. "Mr. Ming—you have to do all that behind these things."

"Ah. Immediately, a rule."

"There are a lot of damn rules out here."

The Exotic rose up and gazed down the fairway. "Are they ever broken?"

"All the time." Waddell pointed down at the tee box. "Right there is perfect."

"Yes. Certainly. So that's one rule against me?"

Waddell started to pat him on the back but pulled his hand back. "Well, not exactly. If you had of hit it while the ball was in front of the tee markers then it would have been—well, you would have incurred a penalty stroke, or maybe it's two penalty strokes." Waddell suddenly thought about how complicated that must sound to The Exotic. Hell, it sounded complicated to him.

"In-curred a penalty stroke. I like the way that sounds," The Exotic said. "Are the men and women who develop these rules fair minded people?"

Waddell thought for a moment. "Yeah, sure. The rules of golf are fair enough."

"That's exactly my impression so far. And I'd like to add at this moment that your sportsmanship is of a colossal size."

"Okay, right. Sure. So now just go over to your bag and grab, say, a seven iron. That's a pretty easy club to hit." Waddell really wanted him to hurry up and go get that 7-iron or go ahead, and maybe even better, to decide that golf wasn't for him and go discover the mysteries of some other sport with some other member.

"But what club have you got there?"

Waddell was looking up at Lamar who was making the universal gesture with his hand by his ear that meant "call me."

"Mr. Tiddybumpus—your club there. That's what you've chosen in order to begin this hole?"

"Oh, sure. This is what you call—a three wood." Waddell noticed he was speaking slower than normal, as if to a child.

The Exotic gestured toward it. "May I examine it?"

Waddell handed it to him.

The Exotic examined it.

"Three wood," Waddell said.

"May I?"

"May you what?"

"Who teaches the teacher?"

"I don't know."

"In other words, would you allow me to use this club for my beginning shot? If I'm to learn the way it is, then I should follow your example exactly. You're not using a seven iron for your beginning shot."

"You got a point."

"And how should I grip the club? I'm aware, at least, there are a number of preferred methods among amateurs and professionals."

"That's a big one. They say the grip is where everything good or bad starts from."

"Then let's start it the good way. Here." The Exotic handed the three wood to Waddell. "Show me your grip."

Waddell showed him his grip.

The Exotic leaned in.

Waddell moved his hands and club around in a number of angles.

"Fascinating," The Exotic said. "I believe the goal is to form a unit."

"You sure you haven't played golf before?"

"Never." The Exotic was really, really looking at Waddell's grip. "Fascinating." The Exotic lifted one of Waddell's thumbs up and then pushed it back down.

Waddell felt slightly uplifted, as if he were a famous Tour professional being observed by someone doing research on the game of golf. Slightly uplifted.

"Am I irritating you in any way?" The Exotic asked while he kept looking at Waddell's grip.

"No, of course not."

"Am I wasting your time in any way?"

"No—I'm flattered you'd like my help." Waddell was still moving his hands around.

"Did you know the staff members of this fine club have given most every member a nick-name?"

"Yep."

"And do you know mine?"

"I was told it recently."

"Do you agree? Am I—strange and unfamiliar?"

Waddell sucked in a deep breath. He gave this man another good looking over. "Yes. I would really have to say yes to that."

"And your nick-name?"

"Sophocles."

"And would you agree with me that the application of a nickname might actually crystallize and reveal the exact, true nature of us, as potentially impolite as the sophomoric practice is?"

"I have no idea who Sophocles was or what he did or even if he got his head eaten off by a lion. You know? I think they just like the way it sounds."

The Exotic leaned back up. "You're not a Sophocles."

"I'm not?"

"No. I know my Greek history, and you're not a Sophocles. He wrote plays. Do you write plays, Mr. Tiddybumpus?"

Waddell slowly shook his head.

"May I confer upon you your new nickname?"

"Hell, I guess."

"You're 'The Total Waddell.' "

"Well—okay then." Waddell looked pleased. "Okay. Yeah."

"Do you understand why?"

"Help me with it."

"There's no phoniness about you, Mr. Tiddybumpus. I can tell that you are purely you, a Waddell. So you it makes me happy and want to be a better human being just by taking a golf lesson from you. You are crystallized before me. Do you make believe all day— or do you do?"

Waddell thought for a moment. "I'm a doer."

"You are a doer, The Total Waddell."

"Thank you. Thanks a lot."

"All we're doing here is hitting a little white ball down a prepared, grassy playing field and into the bottom of a little hole as quickly as possible and in as few strokes as humanly possible?"

"That's the crystallized version, The Exotic. You're right on the button."

"The Total Waddell, may I use your three wood, which is obviously made of metal?"

"Knock a good one. You can do it."

Lamar banged on the window again.

Waddell glanced up there and saw that Lamar was now standing on a chair.

Lamar turned around and pulled his pants down and pressed his butt cheeks, very firmly, onto the glass window of the golf shop. Waddell could tell Lamar farted. He could see the bottom of Lamar's butt cheeks separate and flap and quiver for a few seconds.

"How's my grip?" The Exotic asked.

"It's just about perfect."

# *Waddell Plays the 11<sup>th</sup> Hole*

THE 11TH HOLE at Pine Cone Country Club was a par four, and from the Cone Cobb tees it plays 381 yards.

Waddell swung real hard. At the moment of impact, Waddell jerked his chin up to see if that would do any good, rather than dipping his head down real low behind the ball at the moment of impact, which never did any good either. Waddell hit the ball on the toe of his diver and for a while the ball floated off to the right, but then Waddell watched it curve back to the left a little bit. That made Waddell feel good—the ball curving back to the left a little bit—because there was an ad on TV one time that talked about how the faces of drivers, and our driver in particular, are designed to make your toe shots curve back to the left a little bit and Waddell never believed ads on TV about anything. The ball hit the fairway and bounced into the white and black-striped 150 yard maker post Pine Cone Country Club had stuck in the middle of all the par 4 and par 5 fairways about three weeks ago. Waddell learned from some of his other member buddies who served on all those committees that no one knew who decided to buy and place those 150 yard markers out there so everyone decided that maybe the pro or general manager just up and did it without permission and whoever it was who did it, one member buddy told him in this real serious whisper as if he were sharing a national secret, was going to be in trouble and there was a big investigation underway at Pine Cone Country Club. A real big investigation.

Even from as far away as the tee box, the ball looked to Waddell like it settled right down there at the bottom of the marker—with the marker between the ball and the green. Waddell stood there a moment with his driver in his hand and started thinking about what rule there was that said you could get a free drop away from things like that, but changed his mind and started thinking about the former LPGA star, Annika Sorenstam. Waddell thought about the former LPGA star in a way that was not related to golf, but related to something else. This produced an erection...while he walked toward the 150 yard marker, which made it worse in a way. And then when Annika didn't quite do it for Waddell, he started thinking about the former Olympic gold medal-winning gymnast, Mary Lou Retton. Waddell thought about Mary Lou Retton while he stopped and stared at an odd-looking patch of yellow mushrooms in the woods. Waddell knew he was in dangerous territory here, age-wise, with Mary Lou Retton, so he began thinking about Elizabeth Taylor. Waddell couldn't quite remember if she was the actress in *Gone With the Wind* or not. Clark Gable, Waddell thought, was a man's man, though. Waddell thought Clark Gable would be a popular member at Pine Cone Country Club and would love to be his regular golf buddy.

Waddell stopped staring at that odd-looking patch of yellow mushrooms in the woods and started walking toward his ball again. What about Mary Tyler-Moore, Waddell thought. Farrah Faucett? Waddell thought of a tropical scenario with Pam Grier...or maybe something much like the *Spartacus* jail cell scenario, with the same amount of skin oil. Then his thoughts turned to Dyan Cannon...then Morgan Fairchild...and then Dolly Parton. The mysteries of Dolly Parton. The planet that is Dolly Parton.

Waddell finally got to his ball. Just as he thought. It was lodged up against the bottom of the 150 yard post between the post and the green.

Waddell took sort of a club length drop and then grabbed his 7-iron out of the bag. He hit the approach short a little low and into the hill on the left side of the green and the ball bounced down the hill and it looked like it might have made it to the green but there was a hump on the left side of the green and the ball went behind that so Waddell couldn't tell if his ball made it onto the green or not. Waddell looked at the face of his club and decided not to clean it because he was still very busy thinking about Dolly

Parton. He shoved the club into his bag.

Waddell hated to think he'd never mated with anyone else but Lucille but that was the cold reality in that big department of the life of Waddell Tiddybumpus. Nobody's fault but his own, so Lucille had always been the lone recipient of his skills. He remembered the first time they slow danced in high school when they were seniors. Lucille was a real catch then. Waddell had boned it up and was rubbing it on her leg on purpose while they slow danced because he could get away with it since he was the captain of the wrestling team and captain of the football team and vice president of Student Athletes for Jesus. Lucille had finally said after about ten minutes of him rubbing it on her, "Watcha got in your pants, Waddie? My father's revolver?" Lucille's dad, at that moment, was a decorated agent with the Federal Bureau of Investigation. Before that he had been a decorated state patrolman in west Texas.

Waddell cringed. The moment still made him cringe. Madeline Kahn made him cringe. She busted in on him and Dolly Parton. Then Waddell had to eliminate Cloris Leachman. Louise Fletcher he could just not embrace in the act of love, especially while he was playing golf. And especially after Dolly Parton fired his revolver.

Waddell chipped it in for a birdie. Waddell had never chipped it in for a birdie in his life. Waddell all of a sudden started thinking about Vijay Singh's mole.

# Waddell Plays the 12<sup>th</sup> Hole

THE 12TH HOLE at Pine Cone Country Club was a par three, and from the Cone Cobb tees it plays 174 yards.

Waddell was thinking about Vijay Singh's mole because every time he played the 12<sup>th</sup> hole it made him think about an afternoon a lot like this one twenty-three years ago when he was standing on the tee box just like now all alone when all of a sudden a guy pulling a pull cart came walking up out of nowhere and asked if he could join up. The guy's name was Dieter von Heidelberg and he had a big mole between his eyes. The mole was so big that Waddell knew for the rest of his life he would always remember the moment he first saw the mole when he walked up onto the tee box of the 12<sup>th</sup> hole and every time he did in the last twenty-three years he was right. But now he was thinking about two moles: Dieter von Heidelberg's and Vijay Singh's.

In addition to the thoughts about the moles, Waddell had something else on his mind on the 12<sup>th</sup> hole and he thought that if the designer, George Cobb, rose from the grave that he'd ask him why he, and some of those other people he might know who design golf courses, make greens real small looking from where you hit your approach shots and from par three tee boxes, like this one at Pine Cone Country Club. The part of the green where the flagstick was looked real small but when you walked onto the green that part where they had the flagstick looked real big. Waddell wondered if golf course designers did that as a trick on golfers and he finally decided they did it as a trick and was going to do something about it once and for all because Waddell wondered at that moment how many more years he had in him and was determined to finally figure this particular dilemma out before Lucille found him one day dead and all dried out in his easy chair not watching golf on TV anymore with the channel changer clutched in his hand.

Waddell looked back behind him down the cart path so see if anybody was coming up. There wasn't anybody coming up. Waddell let his golf bag drop off of his shoulder and then Waddell started walking toward the green. What Waddell decided to do was walk all the way up onto the green and look around because he wanted to convince himself even though the portion of the green where the flag was looked small from the tee box that it wasn't small at all and that when he stood over his ball to hit his tee shot in a minute or two that he would be more confident and not nervous about it and try to guide it, which was a killer. Trying to guide your golf ball. Waddell cringed when he played with other guys who were guiders. Waddell thought they looked spastic and was embarrassed for them. Waddell thought, too, how stupid this whole exercise was because in his casual estimation at that moment he figured he had played this hole thousands of times and there was a time when he was real confident about hitting it onto what looked like the small part of the 12th green. What he tried to determine at this point was when he lost his confidence which led him back to thinking about how confident Dieter von Heidelberg has to be, not while playing golf, but in life in general because the size of the mole between his eyes was big enough to be safely excised. Waddell knew some moles weren't big enough to be safely excised because he played nine holes one time with another member who was a dermatologist and Waddell asked the dermatologist a lot of questions about skin and if he had ever met another member named Dieter von Heidelberg and had he noticed the mole on the guy. The dermatologist said he really didn't get out to the club as much as he wanted, but if he ever met Dieter then he would have probably noticed the mole if it's as big as you say and so public. The dermatologist's words: "so public."

Oh, it was public, all right, Waddell had thought. Waddell further explained to the dermatologist that you should see the mole on his wife's face, too. It's just as big. Their moles are so big that looking at them and thinking about why they don't go and get them excised makes you angry.

The dermatologist had said he understood Waddell's frustration, then sort of raked in a four foot putt and left a four foot long scrape mark on the green in the process.

Waddell said we got seated next them one year at the New Year's Eve dinner and I couldn't concentrate on my food.

Completely natural to feel that way, the dermatologist had said. Large moles have indirectly started wars.

Waddell was so flustered by all this that when he got back to the tee he decided to skip the damn hole.

# Waddell Plays the 13<sup>th</sup> Hole

THE 13TH HOLE at Pine Cone Country Club was a par five, and from the Cone Cobb tees it plays 552 yards.

Waddell walked onto the tee box and took a deep breath. He knew this was an important deep breath because it was time to get re-organized after that last horrible hole and if he had accidentally sucked in an insect then he would have packed it in for the day. Waddell's son had sucked in an insect when he was eleven years old right when they walked outside after church on the front steps of the church and his son was thrashing around because he said he could feel the bug crawling around in there and the kid was scratching at his throat and the incident so affected Waddell that after the emergency room doctor got the bug to come out and the kid quit gagging he asked the doctor to sedate him, too. But Waddell didn't suck in an insect and a moment or two after his deep breath he started to feel pretty good about the holes ahead. Waddell chuckled to himself, "*Sex of them.*"

Then Waddell had a thought. The thought was so powerful it made him giddy and made him unconsciously walk around in a circle on the tee box. Waddell decided to go join that other club across town and see what the reaction of all of his member buddies would be. Waddell was really thinking about it. He was getting more giddy. But it really wasn't across town, now, wasn't it? That's just what all of his other member buddies said to make the place sound like it was a butt hole or something. Waddell thought it was about five miles away, but he had never ever played there or wanted to. Never, ever. And he didn't know why. He said the name of the club out loud as he was walking around in that circle: "Sweet Gum Golf and Country Club." Waddell thought the name might be even better than theirs and it actually had the squiggly 'and' in there between 'golf' and 'country.' Waddell thought about what that thing was for about a minute. An *am*persand, Waddell thought. Waddell thought that even the word 'ampersand' sounded wonderful, like something you might put in a gourmet dish of food.

Waddell was still walking around the 13<sup>th</sup> tee in a circle

"*Sweet* Gum Golf and Country Club," Waddell said again. "*Pine* cone. *Sweet* gum." He couldn't help himself. "Cone. *Gum*." How would a place so nice sounding have members who were Cro-Magnons?

Waddell felt uplifted again. Waddell stopped walking around the tee box in a circle and teed a ball up and decided to make a birdie because that would be two birdies in a row kind of. Waddell felt like swinging hard and he did. He swung hard and topped this one, too. He topped it every time he swung hard in his life. But Waddell Tiddybumpus could not have given a damn about topping his tee shot. He was going to go join Sweet Gum Golf and Country Club on Monday.

He'd tell Digby first. Digby would drop the biggest brick. Digby would scrunch his face up like he just swallowed sour milk. Hell, Waddell thought, Digby looks like that all the time, like his spit's sour milk instead of regular spit. Waddell remembered one time he told Digby he ought to go get all the other nine hundred other grumps from Pine Cone Country Club and form the Angry Men's Club of America and leave the rest of us alone by moving to some island in the Caribbean. Waddell remembered Digby told him he ought to read the news more, Tiddybumpus, and then he'd be with the program—or notice how members were treated around this place and then he'd finally be with the program. That was Digby's response. Waddell finally noticed how Digby was more hunched over than him .

*Sweet* Gum Golf & Country Club. With an ampersand.

Oh, boy, Waddell thought, as his heart began to thump with even greater excitement. Delmo would have to be next. He'd ease up to Delmo in the men's grill and tell him the good news. And he knew Delmo would say he'd played there a million times with a podiatrist and it was a butt hole even when Waddell knew he'd never played there because he had another friend who palled around with Delmo who confirmed one time that Delmo was definitely insane but you wouldn't know it by the way he dresses. But, Delmo's friend would say, because he'd always end every damn conversation about Delmo with, "But you know the bastard's got fifty million. *Fifty* million." One time Waddell remembered Delmo's pal said it was ninety million. Waddell thought at that moment that Delmo's friend might be insane, too. Or a fag for Delmo. Not a real anal intercourse type guy, but the kind of old creep that seems to have one friend, and that was Delmo, and that's the only guy he ever hung around: Delmo. Like those guys who suffered the last months for Howard Hughes. Waddell had seen the movie. Waddell had traveled the world and had seen the awful truth a million times: weird old men couples at golf and country clubs. Waddell shivered for a moment thinking about the possibilities on that one. Delmo and his pal. And Delmo's clothes. He looked like an old Italian gigolo fag.

Waddell's mind raced through the roster of fellow members who would need to be told this important news. Revolutionary, really. Sturkey would not and could not care less. They hated each other. Sturkey was still a sandbagger, a flaming cheater, no matter how many letters he wrote to the chairman of the Tournament Committee to protest his reputation.

Yoder would immediately ask how much it cost. Yoder asked how much things cost every time you talked to him. Tell Yoder you went to see the new Tom Cruise movie and he'd ask you how much it cost. Hell with Yoder, but he'd tell him anyway.

Oh. Crowder. Crowder would have a field day with this one. Waddell, he'd say, that's a mighty brave *move*, ol' cowboy, but you know everybody over there has super hairy pussies? You know that, *right*?

Even the men, huh? Waddell would say.

Even the men, Crowder would say. Even the *men* over there have super hairy pussies.

Clinkscales, a committee freak. Had to be on every committee and even bragged about it—about how much he got done for the ol' club all these years—oh, boy—his big grand legacy was he was the one who found and hired that worthless general manager Phil— he'd drop an ostrich egg knowing I stroked a big check made out to Sweet Gum Golf and Country Club. Yeah, Clinkscales, call me a traitor, you cup of New England clam chowder soup slurpin', saltine collector old hag. There're more saltines in your pockets than golf balls. Your wife's pocket book, too. And those oyster crackers, too. You oyster cracker and ball marker hoarder. You go tell the Traitor Committee about me joining up over there at Sweet Gum Golf and Country Club and have them form up in my front yard and I'll shoot you pussies with my shotgun right in your worn out ball retrievers. Or maybe I'll step out there and shoot your old turbo diesel Mercedes Benzes, you bunch of cheap half a sandwich ordering hunchbacks.

Waddell suddenly remembered he was out of shotgun shells. Waddell knew he could get a box of them cheap at that new Bass Pro Shops. He had a bunch of coupons.

# Waddell Plays the 14<sup>th</sup> Hole

THE 14TH HOLE at Pine Cone Country Club was a par four, and from the Cone Cobb tees it plays 375 yards.

Waddell stood on the 14<sup>th</sup> tee, looking way down there at the creek that crosses the fairway, and felt a little bad about being so critical of his old member buddies. He felt bad for about ten seconds and decided to move on. He knew he needed to have some feeling of satisfaction in some form and in some facet of golf here pretty soon or paying these big dues every month was equivalent to flushing money down the toilet. His plan to make a birdie on the 13<sup>th</sup> hole didn't work out so well and he was determined to see if he could concentrate hard enough on just making a par. Pars are great sometimes. Waddell suddenly had a vision of all the male members of Pine Cone Country Club assembled and sitting there real quiet in a big amphitheater and then all of a sudden some old dead famous golfer comes floating down over the stage to ask them one simple question and then he'd float back up to heaven without needing to hear their answers because there was only one correct answer to the question and he didn't have time for the hot air of complainers and hagglers and hypochondriacs and cynics. Waddell decided that the old dead famous golfer would be Walter Hagen because he'd probably get their attention better than some of the other dead famous ones. He seemed to have had some personality. Walter Hagen would ask that pathetic, mumbling group, "Gentlemen golfers of Pine Cone Country Club, thank you for showing up. For the rest of your golfing life would you be satisfied with making a par on every hole? Not a bogey or a birdie, but a par? Would you be okay with that?" Then Walter Hagen would elegantly touch the bill of his hat or cap or fedora or whatever he wore back then and then float back up to heaven or over to some other amphitheater full of golfers from some other country club who needed a reality check.

So Waddell broke it down real quick. The dilemma of how a par is made on a par four. Waddell knew that the word "dilemma" wasn't probably the right word but it sure did feel like it. Waddell looked way out there at the flag on the 14th hole. The flagstick had been placed that day in the easiest position for a golfer of any skill to get his ball close to: right there in the dang middle of the green and it was a big green so you could hook it or slice it in there with no problems maybe. The flag flapped in the breeze once, then went dead. The flag didn't have a number on it—14—but it used to, Waddell remembered. When was that big brouhaha. 1988? That time when the universe was filled with so much hot air emanating from the conference room of Pine Cone Country Club it produced what's now known and feared as global warming. That's where global warming came from, not from George Bush and his White House. It came from the members of Pine Cone Country Club. From those blowhards who were all upset that when one of our beloved flags with a number on it got real dirty or ripped or whatever and had to be replaced with some plain old flag in some plan old color for a while—for like forty-five minutes—and that it severely embarrassed us and nearly permanently damaged our reputation as the best club in town because when you had a guest out for a pleasant round of golf and they saw that when our flags had numbers on them that were the same number as the hole you were playing it made them real impressed with Pine Cone Country Club but by God when there was a flag all of a sudden without a number on it and then the guest was not impressed with us at Pine Cone Country Club. And to think that whole new committee was formed to attack the problem. And then they just went ahead and decided, after nine meetings, to form a budget and have some flag company make all the flags look the same. That wouldn't it be logical to put the club logo right in the middle of a bunch of flags and put them out there? Waddell had hoped none of these committee members where denying time with their families or companies or their personal health. Waddell looked over at a crooked tree by the tee box—and remembered another committee had been formed to investigate the idea of instead of having flags out there with the club logo on them that they instead put white flags on the flagsticks on the days when the cup was on the front part of the green and blue flags on flagsticks when the cup was sort of in the middle of the green that day and yellow flags on the flagsticks when the cup was way on the back of the green that day. That that would save the golf staff from having to print up those sheets where the cup was on the green that day and hand them to everybody who came out to play because there were also a number of members who threw them on the ground anyway. Waddell pondered that crooked tree for a moment longer—and remembered that the whole flag decision process took about two years and that the whole time the competing committees were ultimately debating, they said, the very future of Pine Cone Country Club with this awesome decision that a maintenance worker had replaced the original flag in question a couple of years earlier. And when they found about it both committees accused the nice old course superintendent of insubordination.

So tee shot pretty much in the fairway way down there, Waddell calculated, but not in the creek. Get on the green or the fringe with the next one so I can use my putter, so the fringe would be okay. Really, really, really concentrate hard on getting the putt within about a foot or a foot and a half near the cup and no more. Then tapping the ball in for a par. Walk off of the green to the next hole and not get all worked up about it. Just adopt a slightly satisfied, businesslike feeling about it and repeat on the next hole which was also a par four. Even shorter than this one.

Waddell decided to tee a ball up, and then go through it again. He teed a ball up and stood behind the ball just like he did on the first tee, but realized he'd forgotten to do it on every tee after that, but went through the dilemma again. This time the mental visual of how he'd make a par on the hole was even better—aesthetically and theoretically—so he stepped up to the ball real quick while he was filled with some satisfaction and right at the top of his backswing Waddell decided to swing down slower and the drive he hit might have been the finest he'd ever hit in his life on any hole of any golf course he'd ever played. But he decided to not name the drive the best in his life because he felt like he wanted to save something to look forward to in the future, like if he played in a club tournament and needed the finest drive of his life in front of his friends. This drive satisfied the moment, in other words.

Waddell hit his approach shot with a 9-iron and hit the ball on the toe of the club, but the ball still made it to the front edge of the green and rolled and rolled and even if you were blind, Waddell thought, then you could see that Waddell Tiddybumpus just hit that golf ball up there to within one or two feet. Waddell's heart started thumping again. He stood there for a long time looking at his golf ball up there, then down at the odd looking divot he made, then back up there at the ball. Of all the off center shots a man could hit, Waddell hated the most the feeling of hitting a golf ball on the toe of any of his clubs. It was such an unsatisfying feeling on so many different levels. But there was that ball right up there by the hole. One of Waddell's favorite golf sayings was, "There aren't any pictures on the scorecard." Waddell wished he would have made it up it himself it was so good. He said his favorite golf saying out loud.

Waddell took the flagstick out of the cup and let it drop onto the green. He liked the sound of the flagstick dropping onto the green. He liked that slapping sound because when he dropped the flag onto the green or when someone else did it—it really didn't matter to Waddell—well, that slapping noise was a signal to him it was time to get hunkering down to the ancient art of putting. Waddell stood over his ball with his putter in his hands and figured the distance between the ball and the cup was thirteen inches. His plan had worked and Waddell felt extremely proud of himself. Here he was, working hard just to make a par and now all he had to do was give the ball a little tap and he'd make an easy birdie. Waddell quickly went through his two previous strokes on the hole to make sure he did everything within the rules. He decided that he did. Then he decided since he was the one who cooked up the member meeting with Walter Hagen and that after Hagen had asked the question he answered immediately, and with an unequivocal—"Yes, *sir!*"—that giving this ball a little tap and making a birdie would be the most ridiculous decision of his life. So Waddell deliberately tried to shove the putt a little right and hoped he would still leave himself an easy tap-in for a par but instead the ball rolled into the cup.

# Waddell Plays the 12<sup>th</sup> Hole Again

THE 12TH HOLE at Pine Cone Country Club was a par three, and from the Cone Cobb tees it plays 174 yards.

This information had not changed since Waddell had not played the hole about thirty-five minutes ago—but there he was, standing on the 12<sup>th</sup> tee again when in a normal golfing scenario Waddell probably should be standing on the tee of the 15<sup>th</sup> hole at this point figuring out what club to hit off the tee because it was one of those holes where you could use anything from a 6-iron to a driver and be pretty much okay because it was one of the those holes where the green was sitting there on the left across a lake so it didn't matter how far you were out in the fairway as long as you were in the fairway. Just somewhere out there.

But Waddell Tiddybumpus was not standing over his approach shot in the 15<sup>th</sup> fairway or on the tee of the 15<sup>th</sup> hole, especially in the mood he was in right now. He was standing on the tee of the 12<sup>th</sup> hole again feeling invigorated like crazy.

There were a number of reasons for this. Waddell was a hero, not a destroyer. Heroes could be depended on to do the great and wonderful thing that might affect the life of one individual or billions of them. Destroyers did everything the opposite. A destroyer would be standing smugly on the 15<sup>th</sup> tee right now, probably thinking he could jack it across the lake and onto the green even though it was 298 yards in the air to do that and he'd seen a bunch of member buddies come up short and destroy the lives of a number of ducks and even the meat of the thigh of the left leg of a Mexican maintenance guy who was weed whacking the edge of the lake near the front of the green that one time. You could hear the smack sound even over the weed whacker.

Waddell was a hero and enjoyed doing the right thing when he could, and that was completing the round of golf in regulation. For hundreds of years you played eighteen holes and not seventeen. That's the historical, heroic way, and old Waddell Tiddybumpus was like Spartacus, ready to do the heroic thing no matter how awful it might be. Plus, with the way the golf course of Pine Cone Country Club was made, the 12$^{th}$ green was near the 14$^{th}$ green and all Waddell had to do to feel heroic was the walk up a little hill, after putting out for birdie on the 14$^{th}$ hole, to the 12$^{th}$ hole. By God if he was going to let two people and their resistance of not excising their enormous facial moles make him skip a hole of golf on a Saturday afternoon on Masters' weekend when he had the whole golf course to himself. Waddell had to include Dieter von Heidelberg's wife at this point, after he really got to thinking about the total number of people he knew of who had public facial moles, so now he wasn't going to let three people do this to him.

Waddell heard Lucy honk her drink cart horn from way off somewhere. "Honk on *this*," Waddell said as he swung his 3-iron into the ball and watched it fly way up into the air real nice and real straight toward the flagstick. "Oh—*oh*," Waddell breathed. "Go *in*."

## *Waddell Finally Plays the 15ᵗʰ Hole*

THE 15TH HOLE at Pine Cone Country Club was a par four, and from the Cone Cobb tees it plays 358 yards.

Waddell decided to hit his 3-iron again while it was hot. He didn't know many other members who still had a 3-iron, but he did, and he decided right then and there that he would keep it in his golf bag for the rest of his life. Those hybrid helper clubs were for money spenders. Searchers. The easy way out, right there in the pro shop for two hundred dollars—or more.

So Waddell swung that 3-iron again and at the instant he made contact and watched the way the ball was flying around he knew that hitting a 3-iron perfectly, or even hitting it pretty good, involved an enormous amount of luck.

Waddell walked out to his ball which ended up in the fairway near another ball that was already out there, which always spooked Waddell when that happened. Waddell walked over to the other ball and didn't immediately pick it up. He leaned down and looked at it a while longer than someone else would. Then he raised back up and looked around, and then leaned back down and looked at it a while longer. A little black bug lighted on the ball then flew off so quickly it looked as if it just disappeared. Waddell kicked the ball with his foot.

Waddell stood over his approach shot with a 7-iron in his hands and felt wonderful his essay on how to win the Ryder Cup out of eight million entries worldwide won two real big prizes from *Golf Digest*. The prizes were that he could read the essay on the Golf Channel during the news show which was in prime time and the other prize was that the essay winner would be the next captain and what he said to do was the law on this thing finally.

# Why Golf is so Exciting!

Waddell Tiddybumpus, the critics and letter writers to the editor were already saying, seemed like a simple, typical, country club golfer, but with ideas that will change the course of American team golf, at least for this one time unless there's another essay contest. That this Waddell Tiddybumpus had the plan. Not *a* plan, but *the* plan, like in the rules of golf business. *The* ball was usually a lot better situation than *a* ball for those who knew what was what in the world of golf. That letter was from the president of the United States Golf Association, no less.

Waddell waggled his 7-iron, which he loved, too, like the 3-iron which he kept together in the same compartment in his bag because of his love for them even though it didn't look quite right with them being in the compartment Waddell liked better for his trusty long irons.

After he had made love with Annika he was going to lay in bed with her, for hours, and go over his essay if she hadn't already read it, but surely she had read it, and see what she thought about it as a women golfer not from America, but that business with Charlotta walking into the hotel room and catching them just moments before the heated coupling began spoiled everything and made him hungry instead.

But the Hall of Famer would have certainly said—after they told Charlotta to go down to the sundries shop and browse the trinket selection for a while, and after they finally did it real quick, which was sometimes the best way to do it—"There's something on your mind. I can always tell with you, Waddie." Said while she was leaned up on the headboard, stroking his thick, rough eyebrows with a pale white hand, her golf glove hand. There might have been a cigarette in her other hand, but Waddell wasn't sure. You never knew with some people.

But she would have said that. Annika knew me, Waddell knew. She knew how much I admired that 59 she shot.

And he would be gazing up at the ceiling. So thoughtfully. So much was said between two people, post coital. He had done well today in this hotel bed in Des Moines, Iowa. He had been majestic. So many thoughts expressed in soft tones, was Waddell's experience in life, post coital. Waddell started to go over the critical points of the essay, as if they were bullet points so he could get through them faster. He opened his mouth...

But then Annika would giggle. And she'd say, so lovingly, "Waddie, your *eye*brows—darling—are like *hay* bales."

And Waddell would have to agree. He would have to. No denying these things of his, so public they were, the two of them. His father and mother had eyebrows like hay bales and their fathers and mothers before them. Eyebrows like hay bales. He would relate their trials to this LPGA dominatrix. The trials of the Tiddybumpusses who ate life and were action people and adventure lovers and food eaters while those eyebrows said to the world I'm different. I'm human like, but back off a little.

"I see that in you, Waddie," she would breathe into his ear. "I had a caddie like you once. He knew what was *what* with me. But then he hankered to tote for one of the new Asian girls and he was gone. The next week they won in Knoxville by eight shots."

Waddell closed his eyes for a long moment and then opened them slowly.

"He left me with my bag hanging, Waddie. You won't do that will you?"

Waddell asked his lover, "You want to order a bunch of food?"

"Sure, after I make love for the second time in, like, twenty minutes, to the man who will fix the Ryder Cup problems for the American team."

Said in that voice. In that voice! Waddell grabbed his heart. "Oh, my God."

"*Then*—we'll feast."

# *Waddell Plays the 16ᵗʰ Hole*

THE 16ᵗʰ HOLE at Pine Cone Country Club was a par five, and from the Cone Cobb tees it plays 508 yards.

Waddell stepped up onto the curb with his suitcase and waved to Lucille and went inside to get his ticket for the trip down to Orlando where the Golf Channel studio was. They were flying him down there in first class but not on the way back for some reason. A producer had called the day before, who sounded like she was fourteen, and told him he would sit there on the set and read it from the Teleprompter and they had his essay all typed out in large letters on some sheets of paper to read from if the Teleprompter goofed up. Actually, she was the one who typed it all up herself and she said thanks for what you've done for America.

Waddell said you're welcome.

They'd have a limousine driver waiting for him near baggage claim holding a sign that said "Waddell Tiddybumpus" and the limousine driver would say to Waddell thank you, sir.

Thank you for what? Waddell would say back while he sort of looked around for a toilet.

For making us not look like spastics any more in international golf competition. That essay, man. How you must have thought it up, man. Why don't you sit up here in the front seat with me so we can talk like men, like golfers who know what is what.

Waddell sat up front in the limousine and they talked while the limousine driver patted with his hand on his issue of *Golf Digest* sitting on the bench seat between them containing Waddell's essay. The limousine driver said he'd driven Mick Jagger around one time for about four days but Waddell Tiddybumpus was the most famous person to have ever been in this damn limousine now.

Waddell wasn't surprised that the people at the Golf Channel knew he was the type of man who liked an Irish whiskey at the end of a hard day. There was a bottle of his favorite Irish whiskey in his room with a note: "Bring it Back Home, Mr. Tiddybumpus."

The limousine driver, the same one as before, drove him to the studio and began where he left off. "And you're still the most famous person in the world to have ever been in this damn limousine still. I just dropped off that guy who played Hans Solo in those Star Wars movies at Disney World with his grandchildren." The limousine driver handed Waddell the *Golf Digest* issue. "Autograph your name, sir, right here, and make this the most significant moment in my life."

Back pats. Shouts of his name as he entered the studio and into the makeup room. "I cannot improve this man," the makeup woman said.

Somebody put a thing in his ear so if one of the people in charge in that room with all the screens and buttons said something to him while he was reading his essay Waddell could hear it. Waddell hoped it wouldn't be too loud and blow out his eardrum or something on national cable TV.

Waddell looked the American people in the eye—but then a guy behind the camera he was looking into pointed to the other camera so Waddell looked the American people in the eye in that one.

Tom Lehman's wife told him to sit still and quit squirming. That you had your chance.

Waddell told America if they had their copies with them, like having their bibles during the sermon, and if they wanted to read along with him then that would be fine.

All of America said okay—thank you, Waddell Tiddybumpus.

Millions of wankers in pubs across England and sheep-shaggers in Wales and potato eaters in Ireland and grape stompers in France and pasta breaths in Italy and Zorbas and kangaroos and other supporters of the other side said in all of their irritating accents and languages, "Turn blue, Waddell Tiddybumpus." One porridge wog in a pub in Scotland who didn't even know he'd urinated and vomited at the same time all over himself two minutes ago said, "Smell me monkey, ye Yankee bastard."

Waddell cleared his throat real loud. "The title of my winning essay is, 'Not Nice.' Thank you. And here's the essay which I will now read: I just got finished watching that movie called *Road House* where that actor Patrick Swayze plays a guy named 'Dalton' who's what's called a 'cooler.' A cooler is another word for a bouncer in a bar. He's definitely a tough dude because he didn't want any pain killer while he had a big knife wound stapled up by this foxy doctor woman. Dalton, this American hero said, 'Pain don't hurt.' In the movie there was this scene where he was making some personnel changes at a disco where he just got hired by the desperate owner who said they have to clean up the eyeballs on the floor every night and he was tired of it and wanted his customers to act nicer. America is a desperate owner of a bunch of confused little golfers in matching golf outfits who like to yell and scream and jump around and even hug the guys on the other team and it's time to make some sweeping, and I mean, sweeping changes in these petunia goings on. Dalton said something to the employees that will become our Ryder Cup battle cry in 2014. Dalton fired a bunch of the slackers, and then said to the ones he thought were still worth a crap, 'I want you to be nice until it's time not to be nice.' So folks, it's time for Waddell Tiddybumpus to not make some nice."

The camera operators reached over and high-fived each other.

"First, the wives are fired. They can't come. I've pretty much had it with all of those pampered bitches sitting by the side of the green with both hands on their faces all the time. Know what I mean? All that wasted emotion on you guys is repulsive and phony and embarrassing to America. So they get to stay home and do home school or whatever it is they do. And during the Ryder Cup, wives, you may not call your husbands or boyfriends and you may not e-mail them or overnight letters. You may call only if your children are bleeding out of their ears or something. Go get your roots fixed, too. Three of you need to lose some weight.

Second, this matching golf outfit business is over. You want to look like a Pan Am stewardesses then go fly with Pan Am. Now you're flying with Waddell Tiddybumpus. Wear what you want—but wear what makes you feel like an asshole.

"And third, I'm going to run it down pretty quick here so listen up: we're not going to any more pre-Ryder Cup dinner parades in fancy suits or hug fests with the other team and zoo visits and have a team room where we play board games and we're not going to make a big deal out of all us playing the course the week before or whatever. The course ain't the problem, America. If those of you who are getting picked by me haven't played enough different golf courses in your lives then you don't understand the basics of golf. Here are the basics of golf: you get the yardage for the shot you want to hit and then you hit the club that makes the ball go that far. It's the same thing on every golf course in the world. It'll be the same with me except in 2014 you're going to hit it closer to the hole, every one of you, every time.

So who will represent the United States of America in 2014? Well, I figured it wasn't the golf courses that have screwed us up—it's the damn golfers. You can stick the points accumulation thing in a dark place that really smells bad. My player picks are based on personality and grit, because if there's one thing I learned in all my years is that personality and grit is the best thing to have in life which is a lot like golf."

"Awesome, Waddell. Awesome," the director said into Waddell's ear thing. "Get hot. Emote."

"Player number one will be Tommy Aaron. Remember this cat from north Georgia? Sure, Tommy's got some fine personality, but you'll really remember him as the guy who didn't have enough common sporting courtesy to make absolutely sure what Roberto DeVicenzo had on the seventeenth hole that year in the Masters as all he had to do was ask him what he had on the hole while they were walking off the green. If you keep the other guy's score card in a golf tournament, then by God keep it. So Tommy gets picked to be on the team because this will be his chance, from me, to make up for that monumental zombie whack job moment in golf sports history once and for all. I've had it with having to live with that for thirty years. I speak for all fans of the Masters on that one: here's your chance at redemption you dumb hick.

"Next we're going to fill out whatever form we have to for Billy Joe Tolliver to be a golf professional. He was a member at my club for a while and anybody who comes in on Monday and shows us all on the driving range his hematomas from the game on Sunday is on my team. He dips chew. He cusses. He probably shoots rats at the local dump in his spare time. This, desperate America, is the type of golfing man I'm talking about.

"Call me crazy, but I'm pretty convinced Hale Irwin needs back on the team. Personality? Questionable, sure: he's about as interesting as a bowl of warm water, but he's one gritty golfer. I think the only pressure this perfect veteran will feel will be on the sole of his golf shoe when he's stepping on some geek European's neck.

"And Steve Pate. Damn I like this kid. America, go look up pissed off and angry in the dictionary or on the Internet or wherever and his angry and pissed off face will be right there looking back at you. Welcome to the team, Steve.

"I'm pretty damn convinced Larry Zeigler's going to kick some ass for us. I played in a pro-am with him one time and on every tee box he'd rant and rave about how bad the hole was designed. So guess who was also in the group with us? Right, the golf course designer. These are the personalities we need."

Larry Zeigler's wife called from their media room where he was making her vacuum up his popcorn, "Larry, get your ass in here!"

"Call me socially or politically incorrect or try to read anything into this or whatever you want, but you know having Jim Dent and Jim Thorpe teamed up against two pink pants wearing pasty faced bitches from England will score beaucoup points all over the world. So welcome Jim and Jim to the team, my ni—."

"Brilliant, Waddell," the director said. "Gutsy."

"And Lee Trevino. Do I need to say anything more?

"I have a personal affection for people with bad swings, but bad swings that work good so Allen Doyle gets my nod and I'm not changing a thing.

71

"Johnny Miller, it's time to come out of the booth and tell it like it is with your clubs. I met you one time at a corporate outing and I felt your fever. Remember?

"How intimidating will it be to put Steve Pate and J.C. Snead out there? J.C. invented pissed off and angry and all I want you to do, J.C., is to get even more pissed off and angry and peak for three special days in late 2014. I can just imagine what match play mind tricks you could pull with that little schizoid Sergio.

"And finally, my anchor, America's anchor, who's a living, breathing example of every one of the qualities I'm looking for and a couple of others who will come in handy at night in the bars: John—damn—Daly..."

Waddell felt a rumbling under his feet. He felt America move. He had created something here, and all he did was watch *Road House*, in which he re-wound Denise's strip scene three or four times, sure, sure, but there's truth in cinema. You just have to know which movie to pick out at Blockbuster.

The director said, "I just got word from Arnold Palmer, who is one of the owners of the Golf Channel, you know and everything, and he wants you every week—your own *show*, to be called 'The Waddell Tiddybumpus Golf Show.' We'll talk terms after you finish up—now end big. Make your face red. Drool just a little—or if you can shoot some spit from out of your mouth on the camera lens that'll be great, too."

"And I'm going to say this just once—Tommy, Billy Joe, Hale, Steve, Larry, Jim, Jim, Lee, Allen, Johnny, J.C. and John—*men*— after you miss a putt you will not make any gestures with your hands about which way the ball went. We *know* which way the ball went, okay? And we can see for ourselves it damn sure didn't go in the hole, which is what you're put on this planet to do and that's to make your ball go in the hole. And after missing a putt you will not look over at your caddie, either, and make some stupid face and loll your head around. You got that?

"Now let's talk about a couple of you boys who have what's called 'man boobs.' I don't like them. If you've got man boobs and you don't do anything about them by the tournament then you're off the team. You make all that money and to think you haven't noticed them in the mirror or gone and had them looked at by a plastic surgeon makes me sick. So go get your boobs cut off.

"I almost think the thing that's worse than having man boobs is this new thing of putting the back of your hand on the other guy's neck or on the side of his face when one of you guys thinks he's done something great and wonderful on the golf course. You want to cup your hands on some other guy's face and get your face all close to his and say sweet and supportive golf things to him and act like fags with your teammates then go join the other team and act like a fag with those other fags. We all know that everybody from England is a fag.

"I've always heard that," the director said in Waddell's ear thing. "Just listen to their accents. Some of the women are fairly good looking like that gal in the werewolf in London movie or whatever."

"And you think you're going to take your hat off when the match ends and you've lost when you're playing for Waddell Tiddybumpus? If so, I'm going to ask the other team captain to instruct his players that if you lose your match and you take your hat off then the player from the other team can bury his putter head in your skull."

The director said, "I love your anger issues. This is what we've been needing a little bit more of. Crenshaw? Angry? With that hot wife with the boobs? He had them wear some nice golf outfits though. Remember those wildly elegant Bobby Jones shirts? Damn nice. I can't believe you can't find them anymore. I should look on E-Bay. Although I think a guy who used to work with Crenshaw on the shirts—a guy named Jeff Rose—now that guy makes some nice stuff but it's expensive as hell. Sometimes Tiger will leave our names at the guard gate and we'll go over to his club here in town and go buy some nice stuff in the golf shop."

"Oh, and after missing a putt if you immediately tap your putter onto the green like there was a spike mark or something that made your petunia golf ball not go in the hole I will walk onto the green on international TV and shove my walkie-talkie nine feet up your anus and up through your duodenum and out your mouth and talk on my walkie-talkie to somebody while you dangle off of my arm.

"And you'll get some really nice free clothes, too, when you come on board with us," the director said. "I think it's Dockers crap."

"And in closing, America, here's something else Dalton the cooler said and you better stick it in your memory bank right now members of the United States of America Ryder Cup team for 2014 if you want to win. If you want to win—'I'm telling you straight—it's my way or the highway'—but I think you've got that figured out by now."

Waddell pulled out his driver and nailed it.

# Waddell Plays the 17<sup>th</sup> Hole

THE 17TH HOLE at Pine Cone Country Club was one of those breathtakingly scenic, downhill par threes, and from the Cone Cobb tees it plays 208 yards.

This was the one hole at Pine Cone Country Club that makes everybody nervous, even the occasional PGA Tour pro or movie star who got on because he knew a member, which happens about once every twenty years because the members really had a strange thing about PGA Tour pros and movie stars and other people. They knew that to be considered truly exclusive a club had to adopt the attitude that it wasn't who you let in, it was who you kicked out and kept from playing.

As good as the 17<sup>th</sup> hole was, and it was good, the 8th hole at Pine Cone Country Club was still considered to be the club's "signature" hole because you just can't ever take a good picture of seventeen, even if it's got snow all over it.

There's a creek that runs across the front of the green that's real narrow to begin with and the green itself was two-tiered so you want to land your tee shot onto the tier where the flagstick is because if you don't you stand over your putt knowing you don't really know what to do because you never thought to practice this type of putt. Sometimes going up the green, the ball, if you don't hit it hard enough, will roll right back to your feet and if you're up on the top part putting down hill and you hit it too hard the ball will roll right off the green and into the woods or the creek. Waddell stood on the tee pulling a long hair out of his ear thinking about all the times over the years his putts had rolled right off the green and into the woods. One time, he remembered, in 1972, a putt had rolled right off the green and into the woods next to a turtle with two heads. Or it might have been 1982. Yanking the hair out his ear made his eyes water. Then Waddell sneezed.

Nine years ago, Waddell bought a 9-wood just for this hole. And after a while Waddell discovered it was the most versatile club he'd ever owned. He could hit it on seventeen, but he could also choke down and chip with it, he could hit a ball out of the rough real easy, and he could hit a ball off a real hard and tight fairway lie with no problem whatsoever. He also liked the way the 9-wood looked. It looked like a biscuit. Waddell loved biscuits. Waddell loved a sausage biscuit with cheese, then he'd put a little yellow mustard on it and could usually get the thing down the feed pipe in two bites. Waddell wished all of his clubs were so easy to get along with. Waddell reared back, and at the top of his backswing, felt it was time in the round for him to either be personally responsible for the outcome of his golf shots or to either be blessed by the fickle forces of luck which he also knew to be the moment preparation and confidence and justice had come to an intersection. Waddell also believed, after many years of paying dues, that being a dues paying member did occasionally effect the outcome of his golf shots. At this intersection of his membership tenure, Waddell didn't think it was a pleasantry anymore, the thing called a "member's bounce." Yes, Waddell Tiddybumpus, at the moment of impact of his tee shot with his 9-wood on the $17^{th}$ hole, very deeply believed in the concept of a bounce of a member of a nice golf or country club. The ball hit the green below the cup, bounced once, then rolled at the cup and then clipped the edge of the cup and stopped eight inches behind the hole. Waddell gazed at the pretty white ball on the rich, green green and wondered which concept he'd pondered was actually responsible for the outcome of this super great shot because this made him so happy he was willing to give them all the benefit of the doubt. After a long moment, Waddell decided not to kid himself any longer about the counsel he read in his golf magazines and about what he heard and saw on the Golf Channel or during broadcasts of professional golf tournaments on TV. He knew his recent success in golf was because he had paid all those obscene monthly dues for all these many years. There was absolutely no doubt about it.

Lucy squinted at Waddell while he delicately shoved his beloved 9-wood into his golf bag, and then hoisted the bag onto his shoulder and started across the tee and down the hill on the walking path to the white tee before she honked the drink cart horn for five or six good seconds.

The sudden exploding of the happy feeling Waddell was enjoying from almost making another hole in one that afternoon, this time from one from two hundred and eight yards away with his 9-wood, discombobulated him so much that when he looked back to see why someone honked a horn at him he misstepped and fell onto the white tee box and scratched the side of his face on the pine cone tee marker. There are sharp, little pointy tips on the end of the Pine Cone Country Club pine cone tee marker cone wings. As sharp as surgical needles, actually. Maybe sharper.

Falling down in front of someone was extremely embarrassing to Waddell. Waddell hardly ever fell down. So Waddell assessed the situation as quickly as he could. For one, he didn't mind so much that Lucy had seen him fall down. Lucy didn't seem like one to blab about old members falling down. Secondly, Lucy's gasoline powered cart was as loud as a jackhammer and the fact that Waddell didn't even notice she drove up behind him while he was swinging made him feel as if his powers of concentration were finally getting stronger after these many years of practicing his powers of concentration. So that was a positive. Waddell got to his feet, then grabbed his bag and hoisted it onto his shoulder. So, except for the blood dripping down the right side of his face and off of his chin and onto the front of his shirt, Waddell was pretty much okay with the whole deal.

Lucy let the drink cart ease down the path on its own. The gears made a grinding sound until she jammed her foot onto the brake pedal. Her pack of cigarettes and her lighter slid off the seat and onto the floorboard. She wasn't more than ten feet away from Waddell, and like you should communicate to old people or foreigners, the same rule applies to people who've just had some sort of accident: Lucy felt the need to yell. "I GUESS YOU DON'T

WANT ANYTHING FROM THE DRINK CART, DO YOU MISTER WADDELL?"

He said, "No, Lucy. I'm okay." Waddell felt a wave of hilarity wash over his being. Waddell made the mildest expression humanly possible for someone who was not a trained actor: "I'll just get a swig of water from the creek down here."

"I DON'T HAVE ANY BAND-AIDS OR GAUZE!" Lucy pronounced "gauze" like this: gawwwz.

"I'll just mop up with my golf towel," Waddell said. Waddell held up his golf towel toward Lucy.

"YOU'RE GONNA GET YOUR WOUND INFECTED IF YOU USE THAT DIRTY TOWEL TO MOP UP YOUR WOUND WITH!"

"Don't worry about me. Go take care of the other members." Grandly, Waddell swept his arm toward the golf course.

"DO YOU WANT ME TO TAKE OFF MY SHIRT AND GIVE IT TO YOU SO YOU CAN PRESS IT ON YOUR WOUND? IT'S CLEAN. IT'S GOT THE CLUB LOGO ON IT!"

"Your assistance is appreciated."

"I DON'T HAVE A BRA ON!"

"It's all right. Please go and serve the other golfers." Waddell's expression was still mild.

"OKAY, THEN, MISTER WA-DDELL!" Lucy jumped out of the cart and came around toward Waddell. As if she were accompanied by friends celebrating Mardi Gras in New Orleans, and as if she were asked by her friends or even strangers to pull up her shirt for a moment in order to show other people her boobs, Lucy pulled up her shirt while Waddell watched. Appreciatively. He was no more than three feet away. She had it sort of wrapped around her head when the old and beloved and long-time Pine Cone Country Club membership director, Vern Johnson, with someone else in his four-seater golf cart provided to him by the club in which to tour prospective members of the club around the grounds and the golf course, came over the rise near the tee and honked his horn. Vern, like Lucy, loved to honk his horn at members. Actually, Lucy had learned it from Vern.

# Why Golf is so Exciting!

At that moment, a thought occurred to Waddell. He had heard or read or seen on TV that some people possess a personal or psychic "magnet," if you will, that attracts singular incidents to occur, constantly, to only them. In other words, Waddell had a friend who could never successfully pass his car over an indecisive squirrel. Never. The rest of Waddell's friend's day was always shot. A friend discovered, after years of travel, that his plane always docked at the gate farthest away from the elevator to baggage claim. Always. The friend had told Waddell that the whole thing went from irritating to comical and currently it was at a mystical level. Waddell was now convinced that he, too, possessed an intensely personal psychic magnet: that women were not afraid to show Waddell Tiddybumpus their boobs. At least while on the property of Pine Cone Country Club. Boobs of all kinds. Waddell wondered whose boobs he'd get to see was next.

## *Waddell Plays the 18th Hole*

THE 18TH HOLE at Pine Cone Country Club was a par four, and from the Cone Cobb tees it plays 413 yards.

The 18th hole was like a lot of 18th holes. Near the green you have to hit it over a lake. Waddell hit his ball over the lake but into an area of ground under repair.

Knowing the rules of golf fairly well he knew he wasn't required to give himself relief if he didn't want to. Waddell liked the way his ball was sitting up, so he decided to go ahead and chip it onto the green from there and get this thing done.

Waddell chili-dipped it so bad he thought he broke his wrist.

# Waddell Goes into the Men's Grill and Orders a Sandwich

WADDELL WALKED INTO the men's grill still rubbing his wrist. The men's grill was packed with other members of Pine Cone Country Club watching the third round of the Masters on that big TV, just as he'd predicted while he rubbed his stubble. The men's grill smelled like a sweaty cigar cheeseburger Marlboro Lite nacho cheese plate all the way with onions and Texas Pete hot sauce and farts and armpits.

There was mashed popcorn all over the floor.

Waddell plunked down into an empty chair at a table with some other members and started figuring up his scorecard from scratch.

Waddell never kept his score on a scorecard while he played by himself because he thought the mental exercise of trying to remember what you shot on each hole after you came into the men's grill was exciting. The other members at the table didn't turn around to look at him. They were busy watching the third round of the Masters on TV. Waddell pushed a pair of wet socks out of the way.

Hunched over his scorecard, Waddell looked as if he were taking a college entrance exam and was wanting to make a good grade on it.

Without looking, one of the members at the table reached over for his cigar but instead grabbed one of the wet socks and stuck it into his mouth. He looked at Waddell, reared back, and gasped, "*Tiddybumpus!*" as if Waddell had been dead for a while and came back from the dead all of a sudden. Then a member across the men's grill screamed "Kratzert!" and pointed at the TV and the member with the wet sock stuck in his mouth turned toward the TV and then threw the sock at the back of the head of another member at the table in front of him, which hung there on the back of the guy's head for a moment, then slowly slid into the seat behind him.

Six cell phones went off at the same time. Cell phones were not allowed in the men's grill.

Waddell finished figuring up his scorecard.

A waiter had been standing by Waddell's left elbow, unnoticed, for four minutes, and had been continually making the universal, twirling gesture with both of his hands that meant, "Let's go."

Two members had been watching the waiter the whole time and not the Masters on TV and were laughing so hard the veins on their necks and arms were popping out because they had always thought that this Waddell Tiddybumpus old guy was a little whacked out and he smelled bad sometimes and he mumbled. Plus the side of his face was all freshly scratched up, probably from some squirrel attack or something, and there was no way they were going to ask him about it because they knew if they asked Waddell about how he got attacked by a squirrel and the blood all over the front of his shirt then he would probably tell them his life story and they wanted no part of that. They had been members for only two days.

Waddell gave himself a 103 even though he actually shot, allowing for the rules of golf, a score of 121. Waddell had, what he thought, was an endearing habit of rationalizing his way through the process of recording his scores on a scorecard. He drew a circle around his hole in one on the 12th hole. He didn't get all excited about it because he'd had so many holes in one in his life he'd lost count. He was somewhere around sixteen or seventeen he thought, but none of them had been cinematic. Waddell drew another circle around "Cone Cobb" and dated and signed his scorecard. Waddell wrote his member number—69—by his signature.

Then Waddell looked up and seemed surprised there was a waiter standing there right by him. He told the waiter he was thinking about joining Sweet Gum Golf and Country Club next week.

The waiter started to write that down, then stopped. The waiter said, "Oh, my *God*! That's where I *came* from!"

There was something about this waiter that Waddell didn't like. Waddell mumbled, "You could see that Pierre did truly love the mademoiselle."

The waiter looked around the room and then shouted, "Do goddamn w*hat?*"

Nine more cell phones went off.

Then Waddell ordered a green Powerade and a ham sandwich, dry.

## Waddell Gets Home to Lucille and They Get Their Ancient Freak On

WADDELL WALKED INTO his house. Lucille was on the back patio talking on her cell phone and smoking a cigarette.

The dogwood trees in their back yard were awesome this year as opposed to last year.

Waddell waved at her even though her back was turned to him. Then Waddell stomped a foot on the kitchen floor real hard and she turned around and smiled and waved at him with the hand holding the cigarette but kept talking on her cell phone.

Waddell went upstairs and took an especially hot and soapy shower and really scrubbed himself up. He dried off more thoroughly than usual. He got the towel in all the cracks and folds. He rubbed some cologne he'd been using for eleven years onto his neck and into the hair on his chest. His face looked okay. It got scratched by a pine cone while he was enjoying a round of golf. No big deal. It got scratched by pine cones all the time when he was a teenager while he egged passing cars and trucks and people on bicycles while he was hidden in the tops of pine trees. Waddell knew that injured men oozed sex. He had a friend a long time ago who wrecked his motorcycle all the time and boxed at exhibitions at the state fair until he was fifty years old with huge fat guys and a gorilla and a kangaroo one year. Women craved his attention, even bad women. Standing there, nude, Waddell remembered that him and the guy were distant cousins.

Waddell had taken his cell phone out of his golf bag and had brought it home. It was up there with him in the bathroom. He picked it up and hoped it had enough energy left in it and he punched in Lucille's cell number as opposed to just pressing the green button and scrolling around to find her number and then pressing the green button again.

Lucille's message or greeting or whatever it was said she was on the phone and to leave a short message after the beep and that she typically called clients back early the next morning or later that day after her appointments and thanks for calling Re-Max. She said to have a great day.

Waddell waited for the beep, then he left a message after the beep. The message to Lucille said that he'd had a great day on the golf course and it had invigorated him like crazy. He also said that after you finish on the phone why don't you come upstairs because that's where he was. Upstairs in their bedroom leaving her this message, you know, sugar honey, from the bedroom.

Their master was not on the main.

Waddell put on his bathrobe but he didn't tie it.

After Lucille listened to the message she started upstairs and knew that when Waddell got a little obtuse that meant he wanted to cash in some stock and buy something or attempt real hard to make decent love.

She remembered the days when Waddie confidently suggested having some sex as opposed to being obtuse about it. That was before three children and two grandchildren and the grand children's cussing which was wearing the family out trying to figure out where they learned all of the different cuss words and cuss phrases and how to get them to stop it. Lucille knew Waddie was amused at the new phrases their daughter-in-law was using. She'd say to the grandsons in front of everybody, waggling a finger at them and making Waddell squirm, "We'd like for you two boys to make better *choices* or we'll need to re*direct* you—you're certainly not going to act disregulated around here," but neither one of the boys knew what the turd bomb she was talking about.

"And we want you two boys to become *centered*," she'd say, "and *grou*nded."

Waddell told Lucille he was glad his grandsons already had bullshit detectors. That they got that important device from him.

Anyway.

Lucille walked through the bedroom door and a bathrobe dropped to the floor and she got The Total Waddell. It had been two and half years since her last one.

Waddell had written "Go Lucille!" in red lipstick on his chest, which was hairy. He knew that Lucille would figure out how hard it was for him to write Go Lucille! upside down on his hairy chest while looking in the mirror.

This was an extremely arresting sight for Lucille. She stood there without moving or speaking for a long moment. Then Lucille silently mouthed the message. Go—Lu—cell.

Then Waddell said, "Here it is again—for the ages—The Total Waddell." Waddell felt opulent and luxurious for some reason. He smelled great.

A couple in their early seventies—getting it on—looks pretty much like everybody else except there are usually a few more things jiggling around and the amount of time for both people to want to get it over with and move on to the next thing that day is not too short and not too long of an amount of time. Just sort of right there in the middle. And while they are getting it on, a couple in their early seventies definitely do not say the nasty things to each other that younger, unmarried couples do. Kind of.

After Waddell pulled the covers over both of them, Lucille cuddled up against Waddell in what's called the "spoon" position, and then Waddell and Lucille snored each other to sleep under their clicking ceiling fan.

# Acknowledgements

I couldn't write a golf novel, golf novella, or even fill out a scorecard with the eraser without the keen eye of the insistent Mid Ocean champion, Jeff Hendricks, who knows what golf really means to sunburned men in two-tone shoes. I also thank my fine publisher, too, in the form of Ken Coffman and Stacey Benson ... who recently learned quite a bit about the fascinating people who roam the fairways.

## *About the Author*

For many years, Todd Sentell was the director of sales and marketing of one of America's most ootsie-tootsie private golf clubs, a place of ego, prescription drug, greasy cheeseburger, and liquor-addled adult misbehavior. It was a lot of fun for everybody, except for the girl in accounts receivable. An Atlanta native, Todd is also one of Georgia's new and emerging folk and abstract artists.

His comic golf fiction has appeared in *The Golfer*, *Atlanta GolfLife*, and *Orlando GolfLife*. His golf journalism has appeared in *Atlanta* magazine, *Golf Georgia*, *Dossier*, *Golf Illustrated*, the magazine of the Nationwide Championship, and *Fairways & Greens*. He's a two-time award winner from the Magazine Association of the Southeast.

Todd is a highly regarded independent school history, literature, and fine arts teacher. His hilarious and heartwarming online journal of his rookie year of teaching Georgia history to students with learning and behavior disorders, *A Dixie Diary*, is considered the finest teacher journal of its type in American education.

www.ingramcontent.com/pod-product-compliance
Lightning Source LLC
Chambersburg PA
CBHW020537020726
47494CB00006B/1803